Prince of the Blue Castles

By

Timothy Vincent

W & B Publishers

USA

W & B Publishers

For information:
W & B Publishers
9001 Ridge Hill Drive
Kernersville, NC 27284
www.a-argusbooks.com

ISBN: 9781942981268

Cover art work by Patrick Lawrence Smith
Cover photography by Bruce Hardin,
BlueHarvestPhotography.com

A portion of *Prince of the Blue Castles* was first published by *The Bacon Review*, 2013.

Printed in the United States of America

Dedication

To Judy Thomas, educator extraordinaire. As promised.

And to my family, especially my brother, Brian, who saw me through trials both real and imagined during the course of writing this book.

I

Ames set his newspaper aside and turned to look out the kitchen bay window. The morning sun was bright against the glass, but he could still see dew on the lawn. This was his favorite time of day: before the rush, before the silliness, before the barbarism.

He sorted through the mail, separating the bills from the junk. He stopped briefly when he came across the plain white envelope with no return address. It was addressed to the *Suadela Consulting Agency*, attention Wilson Ames. He looked briefly at the short business letter, then carefully put it in his day planner.

He heard his wife moving up in the loft and sighed. He flipped his wrist over and glanced at his watch: 6:45. She was starting early this morning; or more likely, finishing late.

Turning back to the newspaper, he neatly folded it in half and laid it next to his orange juice.

A half hour later, Cynthia Ames wandered into the kitchen, carrying her cigarettes and most of a long, sleepless night. She sat across from Wilson in a wrought iron chair. She hated the chairs, especially in the morning, especially in the winter. She lit a cigarette, turned her head slightly to blow the smoke to the side. She looked briefly across at Wilson, then looked away, her expression a mix of boredom and inertia.

"Morning, dear," said Wilson. He was reading his paper and having his last cup of coffee.

"Hmm." Cynthia looked for an ashtray, frowned as she remembered her husband didn't like her to smoke inside. She stood suddenly and walked to the sink, taking quick draws from the cigarette while she ran the water. She put the tip of the cigarette under the water and then tossed it down the disposal. On the other side of forty, she could pass for ten years younger in the right light. Careful diet, exercise, good genes, and frequent trips to the parlor kept her trim and reasonably wrinkle free. Cosmetics and surgery hid the rest. Men made a point of talking about her eyes. They were green, flecked with gold, and capable. Wilson said it was her eyes that had first attracted him.

"Something to eat?" asked Wilson, looking up from his paper. "I put out some Danish."

She looked to the plate and hid a shudder. "No, thank you."

She walked back to the dining table and sat down on the edge of the chair, crossing her legs again and resting her chin in her right hand. "Something to drink, though." She poured herself a short glass of orange juice, took a small sip and set it down again, stared at the table.

"How was your night??

She looked up quickly. Wilson was behind his paper again. "Oh, a bit long to tell the truth. Edith wanted to see the new club. We ran into some friends there."

"Mmm-hmm."

"Ted, for one," she said, watching the paper carefully. It remained in place. "He wants us to come over tonight for drinks. I said we would."

Wilson pulled down a corner of the paper and grimaced. "Sorry. It looks like I'll be out of town on business. Just got the notice." He hid behind the paper again.

"Well, I suppose I could cancel," she said hesitantly.

"Nonsense," said Wilson.

"I'll ring Edith then and we'll make it a threesome at the club."

"Have fun."

Cynthia stared at the wall of paper between them. She ran a nail across her stenciled eyebrow, covered a sigh. *Wilson Ames*, she thought; *the fastidious, the neat, the naïve Wilson Ames—my husband. A morning person.* How on earth did she get here?

They met first at a party. She assumed the well-groomed, fashionably dressed figure came from money. It was that kind of party, with those kind of people. God, what a mistake that had been. Six years later, she was still sitting in the same tiny kitchenette in the same tiny bungalow just outside the city, carefully rotating her limited wardrobe and jewels for weekend gatherings with Edith and the girls. It was not as if Wilson was stingy with his funds, and Cynthia was aware he sacrificed to keep her in fashion. But there was always that underlying calculation, that careful attention to just how much and how often. *There was money, and then there was money*, she thought. *And if you have to think about what you are spending then you didn't really have money.*

Still, there was something about Wilson that attracted her that night of the party. He was charming for one. A perfect gentleman. But charming only went so far. No, it was something else, a sense of mystery that kept her interested long after she learned he wasn't from money. There was potential in Wilson. Potential for what, she couldn't say.

And somehow that had been enough back then. They were married. She was happy. She waited for the mystery to solve itself.

And the years passed. And here she was, sitting on a hard cold iron chair, fighting a hangover and time and a sense of regret.

Of course, she admitted with a tinge of guilt, there were distractions. Like Ted. She had no delusions that he meant anything more than what he was: a club pro, ten years her younger; an idle, guilty distraction. Ted followed her around for months, playing the happy flirt, making improper but never serious suggestions in the back rooms and small spaces. She did nothing to discourage him. She had come to appreciate the guilty pleasures of forbidden pursuit for its own end. Tonight would see the conclusion of that pursuit, and for a time that would be nice as well. But in the end, she would dump him (or he her; that was happening now more often than she cared to admit). The newness of the thing would wear off, the guilt would outweigh the distraction.

She took a sip of orange juice, made a face. God, she needed a cigarette—or a real drink.

"Where are you off to this time, Wilson?" she asked.

"Dayton, Ohio."

"How droll. Poor thing."

Ames put his paper down and smiled at her. "It's called the Gem City. Birthplace of Aviation. I'll take in the museums. Shouldn't be more than a few days. Maybe I'll take the new golf clubs with me."

The clubs were sitting in the hall closet, a gift from Cynthia. Her interest in golf had faded with the departure of that golf instructor—what was his name? Barry? Barry, she remembered, had not been much of a distraction.

"You do that dear," said Cynthia, standing up and coming over to stand beside him. "I'll manage here. I think I'll catch a little more sleep now." She leaned over and gave him a peck on the cheek, her robe opening slightly to show a bed-tanned breast.

Ames tucked the robe up gently, and met her eyes. He could smell the night before on her; the perfume, the cigarettes, and other intangible remains. "Get your beauty sleep, dear. Not that you need it." He brushed the back of his hand slowly along her cheek, making her smile.

He heard the flick of her lighter as she disappeared up the stairwell. He put his paper down and pulled the mechanical pencil from his day planner, looked out the window to watch a hummingbird in the flower bed.

It shouldn't be long now, he thought, looking to the phone on the wall. To pass the time, he sketched a mountain and seascape along the top fold of the paper. The pencil was a special gift he gave to himself. The lead was soft blue, making dark, heavy lines. He liked to work in blue. He started to draw a castle in the arms of the mountain when the phone rang.

He picked it up before his wife could get it.

"Mr. Ames?" said a voice he didn't recognize.

"Just a moment." Ames waited for the inevitable click as his wife picked up the receiver. He put his hand over the mouth piece and called up the stairs, "I've got it Cynthia. Just business." He listened for the click that meant she was off again.

"Yes," said Ames.

"You received our letter?" said the stranger.

"I did."

"Is it of interest to you?"

"I think we can arrange something."

"Good. Stop by our branch downtown this afternoon. You will be expected."

"I understand."

The stranger hung up. Ames listened just a moment longer to be sure no one else was on the line. He sat back at the table and finished his sketch of the castle, then carefully filed the paper away.

Before leaving the house, Ames confirmed his appointment time with the head of Marketing at Hollings Enterprises. Yes, he could have twenty five precious minutes of the director's time and would Mr. Ames please be sure to arrive promptly? Of course, said Ames, and much appreciation.

He then met a representative from his true client at a local tavern, Jerry's Restaurant and Bar. This client had nothing to do with Hollings. They sat in a booth in the back and ordered drinks.

"We don't think he'll be much of a problem," said the representative, a tall man dressed in a black suit. "But he has a reputation."

"I understand," said Ames, and slid a small piece of paper across the table. On the paper was written in pencil: *Discuss no details. Assume someone is always listening. Use Hollings Enterprises as subject. Write any specifics on paper.*

The tall man read the note, looked around the sparsely populated lounge and raised an eyebrow. "We know the owner," he said.

Ames nodded and took the paper back, folded it carefully and put it in his jacket. "For everyone's protection," he said, "I like to maintain strict confidentiality. On the off chance that this conversation is being recorded, or should you or I have to appear later in a court of law."

"Okay." The tall man sipped his drink. "You have a reputation as well, one the company appreciates."

Ames acknowledged this with a slight nod.

"*Hollings*," continued the representative, choosing his words carefully, "is a new player in our market. We want you to follow up on a deal we offered a while back. They agreed to the terms, took our investment, but now seem to have cold feet. The deadline for…signing has long passed. Our company is still interested in…rescuing the relationship, if possible. We…" The man sighed, then pulled out a notebook and wrote furiously. He tore out the paper when he was finished and handed to Ames who read it, nodded, and put that paper alongside the first.

"I understand."

The tall man considered Ames, noting his small frame and delicate hands. "Are you sure you wouldn't like us to send one of our representatives with you?"

Ames smiled. "Thank you, but I like to work alone."

"Strict confidentiality," said the other.

"Right."

"Anyway," said the tall man, "it shouldn't be a problem."

***

Ames stopped at the Starbuck's in the airport lobby, ordered a tall mocha and took a seat in the back as far from the crowd as possible. He was dressed for the trip in a charcoal gray suit, pastel pure sea-island cotton shirt with French cuffs, black Balmoral Oxford shoes, and a striped red tie held in place with a gold pin. He had seen the barber after breakfast, and his salt and pepper hair now lay carefully coifed in mousse along his head. He took a sip of his mocha, pulled out his planner and pencil, and started to sketch another castle.

A little while later, his flight still some forty minutes to boarding, he needed the restroom. He didn't generally like to use public facilities, especially in airports. The thought of all those strange hands, odors, and other sundry leavings made his stomach curl.

He tried to reduce his exposure by going to a facility out of the general stream of traffic, one that looked recently installed. In this he was partially successful as there was only one other in the room when he walked in. The man was standing at the mirror holding a bloody paper towel to his nose.

Ames would have turned around and walked back out, but he disliked such obvious gestures even more than public facilities. He walked to the back of the room, noting and appreciating the well-scrubbed floors and urinals, the spotless wood dividers with gilt trim, the valiant effort to cover the usual smells and sounds of human waste with pine forest humidifiers and soft jazz. He tried to ignore the incongruent mess standing in front of the mirror.

He finished as quickly as possible and left, glancing only once at the man still standing in front of the mirror with his pile of bloody towels. Their eyes met briefly. The other was clearly embarrassed. Ames was sympathetic, but also deeply resented being put in the position of having to witness his discomfort. He walked by without stopping to wash his hands.

Outside the bathroom he tried to shake the memory, but the image of the blood-soaked paper towels piled on the smooth white marble stayed with him. He pulled out a packet of hygienic wet wipes that he carried in his suit pocket, wiped his hands. He was not particularly xenophobic or squeamish, but the sight of all that unexpected bright red running from the stranger's nose disturbed him.

He retreated again to the coffee shop, ordered another mocha, sat again in the back. He took comfort in the dependable, constructed atmosphere of a well-maintained chain of American commerce. It was not so much the coffee or the brand that he was looking for, but the sense of order and predictability.

He opened his sketch book again, drew a line around a thin tower pointing to a blue half-moon. The ordered, cool lines of the blue castle gradually replaced the afterimage of red vulgarity still rooted in the back of his mind. By the time he finished his coffee, the castle was complete, and they were calling for him to board. He carefully put his mug back on the serving counter to the appreciation of the staff and left, the bloody man in the mirror now a forgotten memory.

***

Cynthia had a point. The Midwest was not known for its glamour, even in a major city like Dayton. And it was raining. Ames checked into his hotel and stared out his tenth floor window overlooking the city. The steady downpour fell like a depressing gray curtain around the skyline, making the hard lines of Dayton a still more somber prospect.

He turned from the view and went over the itinerary in his head. It was a short list: three addresses, including the Grisman Iron Works factory in Huber Heights; the Grisman downtown offices; and Connor Grisman's private residence. He had numbers for all three locations. The downtown offices were the closest, but it was a Sunday. A quick call earlier from a public phone in the airport confirmed they were closed on the weekend.

He carefully laid out his wardrobe and tools for the day's tasks on the room's desk. These included his day planner, mechanical pencil, two cell phones, and three new business cards. He carefully stenciled names and numbers on two of the cards. The third he left blank.

He went down to the hotel lobby and used their public office to look up directions for all three addresses. Then he had the hotel desk call him a taxi. While he waited, he bought an umbrella in the gift shop. He took the taxi to a local rental company, used the company card to rent a black Camry.

The Grisman house was located in a secluded neighborhood, with enormous, well-maintained lawns and tree-lined sidewalks. The driveway was blocked off by a wrought-iron gate. A posted sign informed visitors they should use the call box located on the brick pillar. The pillar was the start (or end) of the high brick wall that enclosed the property.

Ames parked the Camry as close to the gate as possible. The rain was falling hard now, making a cacophony of explosions against his umbrella. He stepped slowly and carefully through the rain soaked pavement and pressed the call box button.

After a minute a female voice answered. "Yes?"

"Mr. Paul to see Mr. Grisman, please." Ames leaned close to the speaker. The rain hammering against his umbrella made it difficult to hear the reply.

"He's not here now."

"I see. When do you expect him back?"

"He's out of town; won't be back for some time. Who did you say you were?"

"Samson Paul. I have an important message for Mr. Grisman from one of his associates."

"Try his office on Monday," said the voice dismissively. "He doesn't do business at home."

"Thank you," said Ames. But the harsh crackle from the box indicated the other was already gone.

***

Standing outside his car and looking down at the Grisman factory from a bend in the road, Ames caught a faint hint of hot iron. The factory grounds were closed off by a high fence topped with barbed wire, a gatehouse standing to the side of the main entrance. The entry gate was a sliding fence, with more barbed wire on top. Behind the fence, rising like some giant rusty jungle gym, was the iron work compound. The parking lot was empty.

A part of Ames reconsidered the wisdom of going forward. He preferred neutral sites and private offices, with prearranged times and dates. Spaces where he could be seen entering and leaving. There was something menacing about the empty parking lot and the shuttered warehouse buildings of the factory. Their hard, industrial silence went against Ames's instinctive aesthetics, made him uneasy. There was no public sphere in which to negotiate space or positions here. Just cold, shuttered boxes reeking of heavy metals and concrete.

He retreated back in the car, shaking out his umbrella and setting it carefully on the back floorboards. He drove slowly down the hill, parked in the designated visitor's section, and walked to the gate.

It was Sunday, and the factory officially closed, but there were two men in the gatehouse just the same. Large men, dressed in black pullovers and windbreakers. They watched Ames as he stepped gingerly through the puddled rain water. One of the men stepped out of the gatehouse, standing just under the small awning out of the rain. He held a hand up to indicate Ames had come far enough.

"Samson Paul to see Mr. Grisman," shouted Ames over another deluge of rain.

"Try his offices on Monday," said the man.

"It is very important that I see Mr. Grisman. Could you tell him this concerns a recent transaction he made with a group out of New York? He will know what that means."

"Are you hard of hearing?" said the man. "I said clear off. Grisman is not here."

Ames nodded, as if this made perfect sense. But he didn't walk away. "Mr. Grisman will want to see me." He shifted his umbrella. "Make the call. If it helps, I'll admit calling him doesn't mean he is inside. That way, you won't be in trouble later."

The man looked Ames up and down, shrugged and went back inside. He talked to the other briefly, then made a call on his cellphone. His partner stared broodily at the rain, ignoring Ames.

The man on the cellphone hung up, spoke briefly to his companion again, and then waved Ames over. Ames walked under the gatehouse awning, carefully folding up his umbrella and laying it outside the door so as not to drip on the floor. He then stepped slowly into the gatehouse.

The brooding man patted him down as the one who made the call watched Ames and the road. Both men needed a shave, and smelled of long inactivity covered with cheap deodorant. The pat down was brusque and quick, a faint blush of red creeping along the heavy man's jawline as he checked Ames's groin area.

"He's clean. Just this." He held up the cell phone, Ames's small day planner, and his mechanical pencil.

The other man, the one who made the call and appeared to be in charge, looked to Ames.

"I need those for my meeting with Mr. Grisman," said Ames.

The man in charge took the cell phone from the first, and waved idly at the rest. The other gave the planner and pencil back to Ames, then went back to brooding over the view. Ames tucked his planner and pencil in his coat pocket.

"And the phone?" asked Ames.

"Follow me," said man in charge, ignoring the question and tucking Ames's cellphone in his pocket.

The fence gate rolled back. Ames grabbed his umbrella and followed the other man across the broad parking lot and into the heart of the works.

***

Ted turned out to be a bit of disappointment. Cynthia sat on the bed in a towel, her wet hair wrapped in another, smoking a cigarette and listening to him sing in the shower. He had wanted to take a shower together, afterward. But by then she was already having second thoughts about the whole thing.

It wasn't that he didn't possess the basic skills or knowledge. She had enjoyed everything on a physical level. No, it was something else, something in his demeanor. It was like he was doing her a favor. He couldn't stop grinning.

She looked down her long, tanned legs. They were still shapely, but now showed the wear and effects of too many years in the sun, too many long nights on high heels. Particularly depressing were her feet. The skin around her ankles tended to bunch and wrinkle regardless of her care or pampering. And what on earth had happened to her toes? Pinched and shiny with calloused knobs where her shoes bit, they were strangers to her. She tucked them under the blanket.

Ted finished up and preened himself in the mirror, obviously for her benefit. He wore only a towel, wrapped precariously low and loose around his hips. He *did* have a good body. No wrinkles or age marks there. But then he was almost half her age, and spent most of his time on the court. He brushed his thick curly black hair with his fingers, glancing at her with that stupid grin. She wondered how often he had to shave his chest and legs. Or did he have it waxed?

He jumped on the bed like a little boy, almost knocking her cigarette from her hand. As he stretched out beside her, he laughed and pulled mischievously at her towel. She swatted his hand away while she put her cigarette out. He laughed again, leaned back against the headboard with his arms crossed behind his head.

"Well, Mrs. Ames, I'd say that was the best lesson we've had yet."

She smiled mechanically, wondering if he came up with that line in the shower.

"Don't call me that," she chided gently. He looked sideways at her, dropping the grin for just a moment. "Mrs.," she explained patting his arm. "It makes me feel old."

The grin was back. "Are you kidding, Cynthia?"

She didn't like her first name on his lips any more than the last. It sounded so possessive. Had he always been this…what was the word? Juvenile?

"You put woman half your age to shame," continued Ted. "Believe me, I know what I'm talking about."

She sighed. There it was again. Even his compliments were a hash of ego and damning faint praise. She suddenly was reminded of Wilson's hand along her cheek that morning. There was nothing possessive or juvenile or egotistic about Wilson. She drew out another cigarette absentmindedly, and wondered if Wilson suspected.

Ted rolled over on his side and watched her idly with his head on the pillows. As if he read her mind, he asked, "Mrs. Wilson Ames…how'd that happen? I mean, I just don't see you with him."

"He can be charming when he wants to be," she answered. She wasn't particularly surprised by the question. Everyone always asked her about Wilson eventually. Edith had been after her about a divorce for years.

"Charming," said Ted, rising up and leaning close with that silly grin. "Charming won't do for something this hot." He laid his left hand on her leg, brushed it up under the towel.

She almost groaned. *Hot*, she thought; *he actually said hot*. Like something out of a bad movie. And to think, she had felt sorry for Wilson and his droll little trip to Dayton. She was the one suffering. She lit her cigarette, blew the smoke coyly in Ted's direction. He made a face and drew back, taking his wandering hand with him.

Wilson, she thought. What was he up to now, alone in dour Dayton? Surely not what she was doing with Ted in NY. The notion made her smile, then gave her pause. But why not? Maybe Wilson's trip wasn't as droll as she thought. Maybe he was doing *exactly* what she was doing. She experienced a surprising pang of jealousy at that thought. It was not out of the realm of possibility. Wilson was charming, and not unattractive. There was something about him. That mystery. Edith thought he might be gay, but Cynthia knew better. Whatever mystery Wilson held, it was not that. He was a thoughtful, eager lover. Very engaged, very much invested in her and their mutual needs.

So why was she so certain Wilson was faithful to her?

Because he was Wilson, she thought.

She chuckled, which Ted interpreted as a sign of play and started to pull at her towel again. She pushed him off reflexively, got up and started to get dressed.

She was thinking of Wilson as she said goodbye.

***

Two more men, also in black windbreakers, sat outside the central offices. They climbed from their folding chairs as Ames and his escort approached. Scattered at their feet were cigarette butts and food wrappers. One of the men hastily tucked a portable PlayStation in his pocket. Ames's escort ignored them as they walked by. The two men stared at Ames.

They passed through a small air conditioned lobby, then along a short hallway with more offices, and finally through a dented, hard metal door that opened onto the vast high-ceilinged enclosure of the main iron works. Just on the other side of the door was a short story balcony with a stairwell of corrugated steps. They climbed down the ringing steps and onto the dark concrete flooring. The floor was full of stains and flash marks, but the concrete was polished smooth, like a still gray pond. Built along the walls of the enclosure were industrial metal-partitioned cubicles. Inside the shadowed cubicles stood fabricated metal projects in various stages of composition. Ames felt like he was walking through some odd, abandoned chthonian museum.

There was little light in the compound and most of the recesses were lost in darkness. The smell of soldering and cold iron pervaded everything, adding to the sense of an industrial wasteland. Their steps echoed softly on the concrete flooring, lost to the darkness and pregnant stillness. The guide weaved them through another labyrinth of corrugated shelving, eventually arriving at the heart of the compound, a large square of heavy machinery enclosed by fencing and littered with warning signs. Another man, standing in front of the housing gate let them in without comment. Ames noted the gun holstered on the man's hip. He also noted a thermos and food wrappers sitting around a chair to the side. They continued walking, arriving eventually at the back.

In the corner of the fencing sat a soot-covered metal desk. Behind the desk, sat Grisman, the man Ames was sent to meet. He was a large man with carrot colored hair, thin on the top and heavy along his jaw and cheek. His beard failed to hide his heavy jowls, or his pasty skin. He was dressed in a button down shirt, open at the collar and revealing tufts of more ginger. Grisman watched Ames and his escort approach, his eyes as hard as the iron structures around him.

"That's far enough," he said, his voice surprisingly high for his size. He looked to Ames's escort.

"He's clean. He brought a phone." The guard put it on the desk and stepped back.

"Anyone else?"

The guard shook his head.

"Call Bill," said Grisman. "Make sure and stay on the line with him until this is over."

They waited while the guide made the call. "Okay," he said, nodding to Grisman.

"Stay on the phone with him," repeated Grisman, watching Ames closely. "Any sign of trouble or activity out there, you tell me. Now, stand over there."

The guard moved behind Ames.

Grisman sat back, his swivel chair squeaking ominously under the shifting weight. He had green eyes. "Sit down," he said, gesturing to a chair across the desk.

Ames looked doubtfully at the stained metal seat. "I'd prefer to stand."

"Sit down," ordered Grisman.

Ames slowly removed a handkerchief from his pocket and laid it out on the chair. He sat down carefully on the handkerchief.

"Doesn't like our accommodations, Stu," said the Grisman with a sneer.

Ames heard the guard grunt behind him.

"If I may?" asked Ames, moving his hand to his coat. Grisman looked to Stu.

"I told you, he's clean."

Grisman frowned, then nodded brusquely to Ames. Ames removed his day planner and pencil, opened up the planner, and took out the three business cards. He picked up the first one and placed it carefully on the desk.

"Mr. Grisman," said Ames, "I'm here representing…"

"I know who you represent," interrupted Grisman, picking up the card. He glanced at it quickly and then tossed it back on the desk.

Ames nodded. "There is a matter of some outstanding debt. Now, the client I represent…"

"Can go fuck himself," finished Grisman casually.

Ames looked to Grisman, assessed the eyes that looked back at his. He did not like to concede even in difficult circumstances, but over time he had learned to read such expressions. This would not end well.

***

Edith insisted on lunch the next day, ostensibly to discuss an upcoming charity event they both sat committee on. But Cynthia knew what she really wanted to talk about, and she almost cancelled. Almost. One didn't say no to Edith.

"So?" asked Edith, her eyes dancing with mischief as she sent the waiter away.

Cynthia feigned exasperation. Her reaction was expected. Edith smiled. Cynthia was tired of the game and wondered why she had agreed to the luncheon. She looked across at her friend; *was she her friend?*

Edith dressed and acted the part of a woman of means. Everything was in place and of the highest standard, from the 600-dollar hairstyle, to the haute couture blouse and slacks, to the simple but breathtakingly expensive natural pearl necklace. But where Cynthia was a carefully packaged and maintained exercise in age-defying sensuality, Edith was a composition of self-assured contentment. Edith came from money, and had married money. She believed the most important thing in life was how one carried oneself in and out of "bad weather"—a luxury she could afford, as bad weather for Edith was being outbid at Sotheby's or an imagined slight in the various enigmatic circles she traveled in.

Cynthia knew she was a special circle of one for Edith. Something occasionally shown off at appropriate parties or events (but never the most exclusive) and a source of vicarious private pleasure for Edith in luncheons such as this.

"Spill darling," teased Edith.

But Cynthia knew that part of the game, part of Edith's fun, required her not to spill, not just yet. "What are you talking about, dear?" she asked.

Edith leaned in, as if to whisper, but her laugh and tones were, if anything, louder. "Why, Ted, of course."

Cynthia tilted her head in wonder, again an expected part of the game. "How *do* you know these things?"

Edith chuckled. "I have my ways. By the way dear, you simply must come with me to see this new act in the Village. He is absolutely delicious, and he would be all over you in an instant." She leaned back in her chair, fingered her necklace with her soft plump fingers, the crimson nails making a sharp contrast to the pearls. "But maybe that's unnecessary now," she continued with a sly smile. "Do we finally have a replacement for the Mysterious One, or is it just another notch on your well-whittled bedpost?"

"Edith!"

"I'm envious, dear!" insisted Edith, reaching out to pat Cynthia's hand. "My own is as whole as the tree it came from."

They laughed, though Cynthia had to work hard to make hers sound genuine. The waiter brought their salads, which spared Cynthia from answering. But when he left, Edith waved her on with her salad fork.

It was suddenly too much. That part of Cynthia which resented everything about social satire, a part she usually kept carefully contained behind a mask of fashionable irony, raised its angry head, if just a little.

"Really, Edith, it's all just a big bore."

Edith raised an eyebrow. "This from the woman married to Mr. Vanilla?"

Cynthia frowned at her salad. "The Mysterious One, Mr. Vanilla; you have such interesting and inconsistent names for my husband." Edith looked across the table, clearly surprised by Cynthia's reaction. Cynthia lifted her head. "I just don't think it's fair to Wilson. Do you?"

Edith feigned insult, nodded vaguely, and tucked into her salad. They ate in awkward silence for a time.

Cynthia sighed and put her fork down. "Sorry, dear. I'm just tired." Then she wiped at her eyes with her napkin. This time Edith looked genuinely shocked by the display of emotion.

"Now, dear," said Edith, reaching out and taking Cynthia's hand. "I...well, please, Cynthia. Don't *cry*." It was as close to an apology as she would ever come.

Cynthia smiled around her tears. "Oh, don't pay any attention to this. I'll be all right."

"Of course you will."

Cynthia dried her eyes, put on a brave smile.

Edith, obviously pleased, returned to her favorite subject. "Darling, maybe it *is* time to leave him."

"Who, Wilson? For Ted?"

"Of course not," said Edith with exaggerated patience. "Anyone can see your worth, and it is far beyond the likes of candy like Ted. No, we need to find you a real man, someone stable...and filthy rich." She laughed at her own joke. "Yes. I have just the man. He'll know what to do."

"Do?" asked Cynthia in confusion. "A man...?"

"Divorce lawyer, silly. It's best to get out there first and strike hard." Edith sipped her drink reflectively. "Though from what you tell me, there's not much to strike at with the mysterious Mr. Ames. What on earth does he do again?"

"He's a special consultant of some kind," said Cynthia.

"And what does that pay, dear?"

"Enough to keep us afloat, apparently."

"But not flying," said Edith. "We need you flying, dear! Don't worry, Edith will take care of everything. And after a respectable time, we'll start the process of finding you a worthy companion. This is just my kind of thing. You'll see. We're going to have great fun."

Cynthia smiled and shook her head. "You're sweet. A dear friend. But I better think about that."

Edith squinted, obviously plotting. "Time is running out, dear," she said with a wicked smile. "Don't think too long."

"Lunch is on me," said Cynthia, feeling her reserves falling fast. She needed to get home. "I've been just a bore."

"Nonsense, dear," said Edith. "Kenneth wouldn't know what to do if I didn't run up an exorbitant monthly bill in the club. Let's him know I still care."

Cynthia managed a soft chuckle.

"You think about what I said, dear," said Edith. "It's just a phone call away."

***

Ames squared his shoulders and chose his words carefully. "Mr. Grisman, are you challenging the debt?"

Grisman smirked. "*Challenging the debt?* Here that, Stu?"

"I hear it," say Stu.

"Shut up," said Grisman, glaring over Ames's shoulder. He turned back to Ames. "What's your role in New York? You some kind of lawyer? You talk like a lawyer."

Ames withdrew his second business card and put it on the desk.

"*Suadela Consulting Agency*," read Grisman, leaning over his desk but not touching the card. "Special Consultant Wilson Ames." He glanced at Stu. "I thought you said the name was Paul something?"

"That was for your protection," explained Ames. "And mine. Wilson Ames is my real name."

"Hmm." Grisman returned to the card. "Specializing in ADR, Mediation, and Private Courier Services." Grisman looked up at Ames. "What the hell is ADR?"

"Alternative dispute resolution."

"So you *are* a lawyer."

"No."

"What kind of name is *Suadela*?"

"She was the Roman goddess of persuasion."

"Christ," said Grisman, leaning back in his chair and putting his big hands behind his head. "New York must be out of their minds to send a lawyer."

"I'm not a lawyer," repeated Ames. "I am, however, a licensed and bonded arbitrator."

Grisman frowned. "Licensed for what? I still don't know what the hell you do."

"I am hired to resolve difficult matters, and to deliver sensitive communications."

"So what's your message?"

"You entered an oral contract with parties listed on the first card," said Ames. "You are now in arrears on payment for half a million dollars with interest. The clients I represent wish their payment, now."

Grisman grimaced. "I'm sure they do. And what happens if I don't pay?"

Ames blinked reflectively but did not answer.

Grisman sat forward with a frown, crossed his heavy arms on the desk. "How did you find me?" he asked.

"It was not that difficult. You're not really hiding out, are you?"

"Sign says closed," pointed out Grisman. "Most people know to come to the office during working hours."

Ames smiled. "Your wife said as much. Excuse me, I assume it was your wife."

There was a long, sudden pause as Grisman looked Ames up and down, his bearing now pregnant with heightened concentration. "You saw my wife?"

"No," said Ames. "I only spoke to her through your box."

Grisman's eyes grew hard. "So, that's the way it is. I expected something like this from New York. You don't look the type, though."

Ames looked momentarily confused, then raised a hand to clarify. "I should be clear. I provide a special service to clients. I do not work for any particular business, including New York, and I am strictly involved on a communications level. I mean no threat—I am no threat—to you or your family. On the contrary, New York has sent me as a gesture of their good will to salvage this relationship."

Grisman smiled sarcastically. "But if I say no, there will be others after you; others who are not involved on a…communications level."

Ames nodded his head slightly. "As you say, Mr. Grisman, there may be others after me. For practical purposes involving everyone's safety, I stay away from such dealings—and discussions."

"Practical purposes being deniability," said Grisman with a smirk.

Ames nodded.

Grisman considered this for a time, then answered. "Well, I tell you what, *Mister* Ames. You wasted a trip." He leaned back, his hand behind his head again. "I don't know what you are talking about."

Ames looked Grisman directly in the eyes. "Mr. Grisman, I have been paid to deliver your reply. Is it your wish for me to state categorically that you deny the debt?"

"What if it is?"

Ames sighed. "I would not recommend doing so, sir."

Grisman shrugged. "I don't give a shit what you recommend. In fact, I'm beginning to wonder if you're not some kind of shakedown artist. Maybe, I should be sending my own message—to you."

"You can call the number on the first card and they will confirm my representative capacity and everything I have said. My phone," Ames looked to the phone on the desk, "is at your service. Any trace of the call will be registered to my business account, which has established a legitimate correspondence with the New York party."

"Christ!" yelled Grisman. "You mean to tell me this visit is on your goddamn itinerary."

"No," said Ames calmly. "That would not be responsible to New York or you. I am paid for my discretion in these matters. Officially, I am representing New York on another matter altogether, one that has transparent authenticity."

Grisman considered this. "But someone will know your phone called from my factory," he said, with a calculating look. "Is that your plan, Mr. Ames: establish you were here, for protection?" He sniffed. "No, I don't think I'll make that call just yet."

Ames blinked once, slowly. "That was not my intention, Mr. Grisman. To be frank, a trace is a very remote possibility, one that would only be warranted if the situation should deteriorate and come to the attention of unwelcome eyes."

"The situation being how I tell New York to go to hell—and what I do with you?" Grisman waited for Ames to respond. "Nothing to say? You're either brave, or a fool. I'm guessing the last one." He looked Ames up and down, suddenly bored. "So you don't think I should tell New York no. Go on: let's hear the rest of the pitch."

"There's no pitch, Mr. Grisman. I'm here to arbitrate, to find a solution for all parties concerned."

"There doesn't sound much in it for me so far."

Ames lifted his head slightly. "Mr. Grisman, over the last few years you have made it very clear that you would like to be a part of a certain elite circle of business. There are rules and conditions to being accepted into that circle. Regardless of your personal feelings toward New York, other members of that circle would have no sympathy or desire to do business with someone who did not pay their debts. You can understand that."

Grisman chewed his lower lip angrily. "I *pay* my debts. I told New York the goddamn Cleveland contract fell through. It wasn't my fault. I was counting on that money to get square."

"New York is aware of your difficulties. I have been authorized to suggest an alternative solution. New York is prepared to clear the debt in exchange for fifty percent of your company."

"Fifty percent! Are you out of your goddamn mind?" Grisman leapt from his chair and circled the desk. Standing, he was even more imposing, a heavy mass of red and white anger. He grabbed the two arms of Ames's chair and leaned in close, his face inches from

Ames's passive expression. "This is my company, asshole. Nobody is going to muscle in. Period."

Ames flinched at the smell of stale coffee and cigarettes spilling from Grisman's mouth. He kept his eyes straight ahead, looking at Grisman's blotched cheeks. "I take it you refuse their offer."

Grisman literally lifted the chair a half-inch off the ground and pushed it away spilling Ames from the seat and sending his day planner flying. He glared at Ames on the floor, his breath coming in shallow, angry eruptions, a twisted hungry smile on his face. *This is a man who enjoys hurting things*, thought Ames, climbing slowly to his feet.

"Put this son of a bitch in the utility cage, Stu," said Grisman, his voice threatening to break like a tightly wound spring.

Ames felt two powerful hands around his arms. He was dragged to the gate like a piece of furniture.

"Wait!" yelled Grisman. "Turn him around."

Ames was spun around again.

"Did you know we have a blast furnace here, *Mister* Ames?" asked Grisman, the hunger in his smile dancing now in his eyes. "Do you know how hot a blast furnace gets? 3600 degrees Fahrenheit is no problem. Any idea what that could do to the human body? Stu here could sweep what's left in a dustbin, and dump it in the trash." He lifted his hands in a gesture of ignorance. "And no one would be the wiser."

"Is that something you are likely to do, Mr. Grisman?" Ames tone was calm, probing, as if they were still discussing terms over the table.

"It wouldn't be the first time, eh Stu?" Grisman watched Ames, the hunger revolving into something uninhibited and determined.

It was an expression Ames had seen a thousand times before, on the playground and in the boardroom. It wasn't just about making a point, or winning, Grisman wanted to break Ames. Something hardwired into his personality lived to dominate others, men like Ames, or anyone they saw as weak.

Knowing this did not make the danger to Ames any less real.   He recognized there was little he could do to deflect Grisman's obsession. His skills were in negotiation and mediation. But these required at least a modicum of middle ground, if not civility. Grisman was in the full frenzy of the predator. Ames's only recourse was time. Time for Grisman the animal to retreat, if only temporarily. Time to create a space for return to reason. To achieve this, Ames needed a distraction.

A gesture then, something to give the lion pause.

With aplomb developed over a lifetime of similar confrontations, Ames stood straighter, feeling Stu's brutal grip tighten. With what movement still remained to him, Ames deliberately brushed the dust from his suit, meeting Grisman's hungry gaze with his own cool detachment. "Then I have my answer," he said.

Grisman's sneer was slow in coming, an expression born of pure malice. He walked deliberately up to Ames and punched him in the stomach. The blow was delivered with the force of frustration and years of heavy work. Ames folded over like a lawn chair, gasping for breath and reeling at the pain.

Grisman leaned over to whisper in Ames ear. "You're just a suit, and a pansy by the look of it." He stood up again, looked down at the struggling Ames. "I'm going to send New York a return message all right, Mr. Suit," he said, the animal still present but now calculating. "You're not going to like it, but they'll get the point. By your own admission, no one else really knows you're here. Besides, you're meat, a suit. Nothing more than meat. It won't matter."

Ames tried to talk, but couldn't find his breath.

"Oh, I know what you're thinking," said Grisman with another sneer. "You want to tell me that someone does know. You want to threaten me with consequences, maybe even the law. It's a little late for that. I don't fear the law. If anybody ever comes around to ask, you came and left, see? I have witnesses. And the authorities, or whoever, are welcome to dig through the dumpster all they want to prove me wrong. Nobody's going to miss another suit. That will be my message to New York." He turned his back to Ames. "Then we'll deal."

Ames was still struggling for breath as Stu dragged him away.

***

Cynthia watched the sun go down outside the kitchen bay window, tapping her nails lightly against the frosted glass table. She didn't like downtime. She liked to be where people were, or at least the illusion of activity. But today was different. Today, she found herself sitting idly in the kitchen wrapped in a strange malaise of indecision. What was she to do? What was she to do about Wilson?

She sighed and tried to enjoy the sun on the glass. Wilson liked the view; he *liked* down time. He could sit for hours in the morning or dusk just watching the view and doing his silly sketches. A part of her was envious of this character trait; another part hated him for it.

Did she ever love him? She smiled ironically. What is love anyway? She certainly had affection for Wilson, and the thought of leaving him—actually *leaving* him—was suddenly more difficult than she imagined. Damn Edith anyway.

But it wasn't Edith. It was her. She had been coming to this crisis for some time. She was just caught off guard by how hard it was now that the moment of decision was actually here. It was one thing to have an occasional romp with the Teds of the world; it was another to actually walk away from Wilson. He was...what was he? Dependable? Calm? Giving? Safe? There were worse things in the world. What had she thought the other morning: fastidious, neat, naïve? She supposed the difference between the two lists would always be a moment to moment degree of distance from and to Wilson. Now absent him, she saw Wilson in a more favorable light. Which one was the real Wilson? Which one was the real Cynthia? Would she come to realize leaving Wilson was a mistake—or staying?

She knew she couldn't go on as things stood.

Or could she?

It wasn't just a matter of age, or boredom—or even guilt. She hesitated over that last notion. She knew something was rotting inside her with every new cuckold of Wilson, but it had never bothered her so much before. Why now? If he knew about the men (and she suspected now he did) he clearly didn't care. And if he didn't know, it was obvious he wasn't about to go looking for trouble. *But guilt?*

She sighed, pulled out a cigarette, and then remembered again Wilson's distaste. She frowned, remembering the first time he tried to tell her. Full of apology, he asked her to consider not smoking at the kitchen table. *Consider*, as if she really had a choice. He looked as if he'd been wrestling with the question all night. She blushed as she recalled her reaction, which was to throw a silent tantrum, pitching the whole pack of cigarettes in the trash and glaring at him from across the table. He had immediately apologized for *his* inconsideration, fetched the cigarettes from the trash (an almost unbelievable act for the hygienically-conscious Wilson) and practically begged her to light up right then and there. She apologized, but he would hear nothing of it. Smoking at the table was her right, he said. It was her home after all; end of discussion.

She had resolved to herself to change *this* behavior at least—for Wilson. She forgot from time to time, but Wilson never complained. Wilson never complained about anything.

She left the cigarette unlit. Who was Wilson Ames? Edith called him the Mysterious One, among other less complimentary things. And for all his simple air, there *was* still that air of mystery around Wilson. It was nothing immediately apparent. One had to know Wilson to know there was more to him. Like everything else, the mystery was a carefully maintained, fastidiously guarded element of her husband. Six years after they first met, she still could not say what made Wilson, well, Wilson.

Maybe she was just projecting this air of mystery, searching for reasons to make Wilson more appealing. Searching for reasons to stay just a little longer. Sitting in the kitchen he loved, trying to figure out what made it so pleasing to Wilson, she thought this last might finally have the ring of truth to it. Wilson wasn't hiding anything. There was no real mystery to Wilson, at least not in a real sense. No, Wilson was just a simple man. A man who was never going to go any further, never make any major contributions or connections. Never question or forsake Cynthia, in any regard. He was Wilson; her Wilson.

The question really then, she thought, *is this: do I want to spend the rest of my life with that*?

***

Stu tied him up by the wrists to the fencing with a utility cord. The binding wasn't overly tight, but Ames's arms were situated above his head, straining his joints and circulation. Finished, Stu inspected his work and gave it a few testing tugs.

"Your boss is not thinking this through," said Ames, wincing as Stu drew the cord tighter.

Stu shrugged. "You don't want to get him angry. You made him angry."

"I assure that was not my intention," said Ames with a touch of irony.

Stu chuckled. "You're either very brave or very stupid, coming here alone. He's been working himself up for some time now, waiting for New York to call. You weren't what he expected. The unexpected tends to make him angry."

Ames sighed. "Your boss seems to be easily angered."

Stu shrugged.

"I saw that picture in your book," said Stu. "Did you draw that?"

"Yes."

"My sister paints. Never saw much use it in myself. Kind of strange, you drawing pictures."

"It helps keep me grounded," said Ames.

"How so?"

"You have to let it out some way. My way is to sketch castles."

Stu scratched his cheek. "You better draw some pictures in your mind then," he said. "You're not going to like what comes next." Then he caught Ames's eyes. "Unless the cavalry is coming?"

"There's no cavalry," said Ames, meeting Stu's eye. "But New York will have its answer one way or the other. Then they'll act. If you think a few factory workers dressed in matching windbreakers are going to stop them, you're deluding yourself as much as your boss."

"It won't be the first time we've been tested that way," said Stu.

"Not this way."

Stu tilted his head, shrugged again. "If I see the opportunity, I'll give him that message." Then he left, closing the gate behind him and locking it.

Ames looked around. The utility closet was another fenced in square, about the size of his office, warning signs mounted to the fencing. The closet doors were guarded with a padlock. He stood as far away from the fencing as he could to protect his suit and relieve some of the pressure on his arms. He didn't think it would be long. Grisman would want to feed his fire while it was still hot.

Poor Cynthia. What would she think? He had no doubt she would land on her feet; she was imminently competent. But she might have a bad spell for a time. Grisman was right: the police would soon drop the matter if there was no trail. Would his wife hire a private investigator? Ames suspected not. Would she marry again? Almost certainly. Was Ted his replacement waiting in the wings? That gave him pause. He certainly hoped not. Cynthia could do better. Competent as she was, Cynthia needed things she didn't fully understand herself. He knew that from the first time he saw her, so long ago, surrounded by preening admirers and hopefuls, looking for all the world as if she belonged to that world. But to Ames, she was mournfully lost. A butterfly in a windstorm. She needed him (or someone like him). He gave her the ground on which to stand, while the rest of her fluttered on in imagined worlds of importance. He was suddenly very worried for her. She would look for similar grounding the second time around, but would she find it? Ted would be a disaster.

He took some comfort in the fact that she wouldn't lack for money. She would be surprised by that fact. It was a tricky business, the will, his money, but Cynthia was set for life. He trusted that she would be sensible and see the gift for what it was and not ask a lot of questions—the offshore accounts were not strictly legal.

The infusion of monthly cash should more than compensate for any hurt feelings about being left in the dark. But would it be enough to keep her away from a mistake like Ted?

He shook the dark thoughts from his mind, and concentrated on his immediate situation. The best thing for Cynthia (and him) was to get home in one piece. He had started something with Stu, on instinct. New York would *not* ignore or forget the loss of Ames. They *would* act eventually. Not for Ames sake, but for their own reasons. Grisman was in over his head. Maybe Stu could get Grisman to see that, to open the doors to reason again.

If Stu relayed the message; if Grisman listened.

When Grisman came, he was smiling again, and carrying Ames's planner. Stu unlocked and opened the gate, but remained outside. Ames tried to read his face, but it was as expressive as a stone. Grisman showed Ames the planner, opened to one of his sketches, a vast castle overlooking a field, all done in blue.

"Stu likes your drawings," said Grisman, still smiling. "Maybe that's why he's taking such a shine to you. Or maybe he's just a pansy like you." Grisman didn't bother to look around at Stu, who remained the embodiment of stone. Grisman tossed the planner casually in the corner. "Nothing in that book of yours but drawings. What kind of planner is that?"

Ames marshaled his resources, every pore of his being open to the nuances of Grisman's body language and facial expressions, every instinct, all his training focused on his intended audience.

"I never keep notes, Mr. Grisman," he said calmly. "For everyone's protection."

"The Prince of Discretion," said Grisman mockingly.

"A quality proven over time, and one I'm sure a man in your position can appreciate."

Grisman lost his sardonic smile. "That's true enough. You can never be too careful." This time he did glance at Stu. Ames watched, waited. *Did Stu say something after all?* Grisman folded his heavy arms across his chest. "So you think the boys from New York will run through my men like shit through a goose."

"I hope it won't come to that," said Ames.

Grisman grunted. "I'm sure you do." He stepped closer to Ames. "Now, I don't want you to get false hope, Mr. Ames. I'm not having a change of heart, no matter what Stu says. I'm just trying to decide if it is worth having Stu work a soldering gun on you for a bit. What do you say, Mr. Ames. Do you have some secrets to spill?"

Ames felt a flush of white-knuckle panic, like a sudden drop in a transatlantic flight. He was going to die. Grisman was going to kill him, as casually as stepping on a bug. He was just considering whether to pull the legs off first. He saw the recognition of this fact reflected in Grisman's hard eyes, and the pleasure this gave the man.

Something long buried in Ames, maybe never to be born but for this moment, reacted to the utter remorselessness of Grisman. He felt an intensity of emotion like nothing he'd ever experienced before: he hated Grisman. He hated his gritty fingernails, his rotten sausage breath, the gleam of drool just in the corner of his worm-like lips. He hated Grisman the bully, the sociopath. He hated the very idea of Grisman and his pathetic little world of crime.

But even as the hate took life, it died again like a still-born spark and another emotion moved to take its place. An emotion more fitting to Ames's core, one he could maintain with ease. When he finally returned Grisman's look, his own expression was filled with disdain.

"There are no secrets, Mr. Grisman," he said flatly.

"We'll see about that," snarled Grisman, apparently frustrated by Ames's reaction. "Stu, get the gun."

Ames sighed. "Mr. Grisman, you are a disappointment."

"Hear that, Stu!" called Grisman after the retreating figure. "Guys about to lose his toes one at a time, and he's disappointed."

"Do you really think your actions won't have repercussions?" asked Ames, his voice calm, his eyes measuring.

"You were here. I got the message. I responded." Grisman shrugged. "I told you: your disappearance is New York's problem, not mine."

"New York is expecting to hear from me tonight, in about…" Ames twisted his head around to look at his watch above his head. "One hour from now. If they don't hear from me they will assume you have declined their offer. They will also know something about your business ethics."

"So maybe I let you make that call," said Grisman assertively. "Here. With me right beside you. Then, I've got all the time in the world." He grunted with excitement. "Maybe I even have you tell them what I want you to tell them."

Ames nodded. "A possibility considered by New York. Which is why I also have to report in person Monday to confirm our arrangement and make my final assessment."

Grisman scoffed. "I'm sure you do. You should have thought of that line earlier."

"Nevertheless," said Ames, "it is the truth. You can confirm it by calling that number on the card I gave you."

"Back to that trick again, huh? No thanks, buddy. New York is going to have to deal directly with me. That's my answer to both of you."

"As you will," said Ames slowly. "Either way, they will know something about you."

"I'll take that chance. They'll come around when they see the color of my money."

"Yes, they will want the money," said Ames. "But they will never deal with you as an equal after this. That precious circle you want so much to be a part of will be closed off to you forever."

"Over a messenger?" sneered Grisman.

"I told you my services are very valued in that circle, Mr. Grisman. Discretion combined with genuine neutrality is a rare commodity anywhere. It is very prized in that particular community. After today, no matter what our personal outcome, you will know that."

"You're just trying to save your skin."

"No. I'm just doing my job."

Stu returned then, a heavy soldering gun in his hand and an extension cord over his shoulder. He plugged the cord in a nearby hanging socket and then put the other end in the bottom of the gun. He handed the gun to Grisman who was watching Ames carefully.

"Take his shoe and sock off," said Grisman.

Stu grabbed Ames right leg, lifted it up until he had the foot in both hands. Ames had to hop on one foot for balance, his wrists and arms straining painfully against the cords. Stu pulled the shoe off without undoing the lacing. Then he did the same for the sock.

"It takes just a few minutes to warm up," said Grisman waving the gun. "Any particular toe you feel attached to?"

"It is not too late, Mr. Grisman," said Ames, leaning back against the fence as Stu held his foot in the air. He felt the sweat pour down the side of his face, knowing this undermined his words. "Let me go. I will call New York and tell them you are willing to deal. I promise you, I will forget all this in my report. As I said, my reputation for discretion is beyond reproach. If I tell you I won't mention it, you can be assured I will not."

But Grisman was looking at the now glowing tip of the solder gun. A small, malicious smile slowly crossed his face. "They always beg when they finally see the gun, eh Stu."

"He's not begging," said Stu.

Grisman lost his smile, gave Stu an angry look. He turned to Ames, studied him. "No, you're right. He's not begging. You're a cold fish, Mr. Ames." He stepped close. "Hold him."

Ames saw Stu swallow a sigh, then brace himself along Ames's leg. His hands were like a vice around his foot.

"Hold it tight now," said Grisman with quiet heat. He too grabbed the foot, holding it around the arch. His powerful hands squeezed the foot until Ames thought it would break. "I think we'll start with the little one. Now don't go passing out on me, Mr. Ames."

"What question am I supposed to be answering, Mr. Grisman?" asked Ames, trying to keep the tremor from his voice.

"What?" asked Grisman, momentarily confused.

"You said you wanted some secrets," continued Ames. "Secrets about what?"

"What are you talking about?"

"I know nothing about New York than what I have already told you," continued Ames. His foot, held by the two strangers, felt oddly disconnected from him. By contrast, he felt a dangerous tightening along his hamstring. "I have no wish to have any of my toes damaged, so if cessation of your actions is dependent on my cooperation then I would greatly appreciate if you pick a topic I can cooperate with."

"Jesus Christ," said Grisman. "You sure do sound like a lawyer. Forget the secrets. This is just for being a pain in my ass." Then he brought the gun down on Ames's little toe and opened the door of pain.

***

A fire of undirected determination was building in Cynthia, fueled by a whirlwind of conflicted emotions and possible directions. Only one thing remained clear: she would not spend another day wrestling with herself over Wilson. Something one way or another must be done. It was time. She could not continue to live her life this way.

She almost picked up the phone to call him then and there. But no, that was not fair to Wilson. *Sweet, gentle Wilson.* You didn't leave a man like Wilson over the phone or by note. He deserved better. She would wait and confront him, here, across the goddamn kitchen table. She'd make a full confession. Ted, the rest of it. Yes, and then at last she might see some answer to the mystery that was Wilson Ames—if there was a mystery. For all Wilson's careful demeanor, he'd surely react to the real truth! He practically crumbled just to hear she was unhappy.

Poor sweet, gentle, unassuming Wilson. It might actually break him. She felt miserable just thinking about it.

***

His first thought was of Cynthia, a desperate need to find her, help her—against what, he couldn't say. His next was of the unbearable pain in his foot. It was as if his toe were on fire, a constant, unbearable burn that peeled his skin like dry paper and singed exposed bone. He groaned, unable to open his eyes to look at what Grisman had made of his toe.

"Who's Cynthia?"

It was a familiar voice, but not Grisman. Ames opened his eyes, saw Stu squatting beside him. Ames was on the ground now, one hand still bound to the fence. Grisman was nowhere to be seen.

"You called out to Cynthia," continued Stu.

"My wife," gasped Ames. He still could not look down at his foot, dreading what he would find.

"Passing out was the smartest thing you've done yet," said Stu, standing up. He carefully put the soldering gun on the ground out of reach of Ames. "He only enjoys it when he gets a reaction."

Ames finally looked, his need to know more compelling than his fear. The toe was an ugly red and black nub of charred skin and blood—but it was still whole.

"Where is he?" asked Ames.

"Calling that number, I guess." Stu folded his arms across his chest. "I think you got to him after all. I didn't understand at first, but you actually played him, didn't you? You knew when to push his buttons and when to pull back. He's not used to...subtlety. He's about as subtle as a fist in the face."

"I wasn't so smart," said Ames, looking at his toe and taking a long, trembling breath against the pain. It came to him suddenly that he had told Stu his wife's name. That was a mistake. He needed to concentrate. He could not afford any more mistakes.

"That's nothing," said Stu. "He meant to do a lot worse." He chewed his lip thoughtfully, leaned against the fencing. "Tell me, how you knew we used to work for the factory?"

"You have the look, but not the depth."

"Come again?"

"You look to be tough. I suspect you have done some things I could not. But the men who will come after me are professional. Cold professionals. You don't have that yet."

Stu considered Ames. "He might make a deal."

Ames shrugged, grimaced again as the movement exacerbated the pain, then carefully shifted to a more comfortable position.

"But it won't matter, will it?" continued Stu. "You're going to tell them about this if he lets you go— or, like you said, they're going to know something happened to you if he doesn't."

Ames looked to the floor, trying to will his way through the pain and concentrate on the next step.

"They're going to come no matter what now, aren't they?" sighed Stu. "After this." He looked to Ames's toe. "You tried to warn him. He's not smart like you, though."

Ames looked to Stu. "You're name is Stewart, right?"

"Everybody calls me Stu."

"Well, Stewart, if you have the chance, I'd find another employer, and soon."

Stu frowned. "Not likely."

They heard the steps before they saw Grisman returning. He looked thoughtful, almost puzzled as he stepped through the gate. He folded his beefy arms across his chest and glared down at Ames.

"Well, you spoke true enough about the call. They're waiting to hear from you."

Ames looked to his watch, which was on his free wrist. He must have been out for forty minutes. He looked up to Grisman. "I can still make that call."

"But now you've got something more to say," said Grisman bitterly, glancing at Ames's ruined toe.

Ames took a big breath. "Yes."

"What about your promise?"

"I promised I would forget everything up until the point you went too far."

Grisman sneered. "Doesn't matter. Tell them what you want." He turned to Stu. "Call in a few more boys. Make sure they know what they're doing, and see they have the firearms to do it with. It's your ass if they don't."

Stu nodded, looked once to Ames. "And him?"

"Leave him to me."

Stu nodded to Ames briefly when Grisman's back was turned, and left. Grisman waited until his steps had died away, and then bent over Ames. He pulled out the cell phone Ames had given him.

"They said they would deal, but only if they talked to you." He looked Ames in the eye. "If I let you go, will you play square?"

"In my pocket is another business card. Take it out." Grisman carefully did this, looked the card over.

"It's blank," he said.

"Give me a pen."

Grisman patted his shirt pocket, looked around, saw the tossed planner and mechanical blue pencil. He went over, picked the pencil up and brought it back. He handed it carefully to Ames.

"Now the card." Grisman gave him this as well.

Ames held the card in his shackled hand and carefully wrote on it with the blue pencil with the other one. When he was finished, he took the card in his free hand and handed the pencil and card to Grisman.

Grisman took them, read the card. "What's this?"

"My private business number. With that you can contact me and arrange for my personal representation in your future business negotiations, including the one that will be coming once I've reported to New York."

Grisman blinked in slow comprehension, surprise, and finally suspicion. "Why would you do that?"

"Because a damaged toe will not mean that much to New York or my other clients. My death would, but not that. If offering you my services expedites a deal, then I'll do that. I'll see you get the best deal with New York. I get to walk out of here. New York resolves a problem with the least amount of trouble. Everyone gets something they want or need. That's how this business works."

"This is for real?" asked Grisman.

"It is."

"New York will never buy it," said Grisman, looking again at Ames's toe.

"They will."

Grisman rolled his tongue around his cheek. "You're right about their trust in you. Which makes me think you're right about the rest of it. I want in, Ames. But I can't afford to have them turn me out in six months, and that's what fifty percent of my business means."

"How much money can you get your hands on right now?"

"About a quarter million. But that represents my rainy day fund."

Ames stared at Grisman. "Mr. Grisman, this is that rainy day. If I can get them to take two hundred and twenty five thousand, and twenty-five percent interest in your business, would that be acceptable to you?"

Grisman grunted, countered. "The quarter alone, with interest, and I promise to have the rest by this time next year. But the business stays mine!"

Ames bit back a new wave of pain, answered calmly. "No. They will not accept that."

"Then fuck them!" said Grisman, standing up again. "And fuck you!"

Ames carefully moved his damaged foot out of Grisman's path, grimacing as he did so.

"Mr. Grisman," he said, channeling his pain into authority.

Grisman spun around angrily, the dancing hunger momentarily back in his eyes. He glanced to the soldering gun, then back to Ames. Ames waited it out, watched the hate grow colder with expectation. "What?" asked Grisman, his curiosity getting the better of his anger.

"Twenty five percent is manageable," continued Ames in a calm, professional tone. "You will still have controlling interest." *For now*, thought Ames, *but in a year you'll be nothing more than a figurehead—if you're around at all.* Grisman was right about that. "This is the price you pay for missing the deadline," he continued. Then he dropped the carrot: "And entry into the circle."

Grisman wrestled with this for a time and then threw his hands up. "All right! Twenty five percent and the quarter. But I get in! You make that happen, you get to walk out of here."

"Agreed. Now, will you free me so I can sit down in a chair?"

Grisman handed him the phone instead. "Make your call from there. Put it on speaker. After that, we'll see." He looked away.

"You understand whatever agreement I manage over the phone will have to be confirmed by me in person tomorrow in New York?"

Grisman's fat lips twitched with frustration, but he nodded, still staring off in the distance.

Ames dialed the number.

Stu found a first aid kit somewhere, and saw to Ames's toe. He pronounced Ames fit to travel when he finished, and stepped back into to the shadows. Grisman looked at Ames with an odd, somewhat distracted expression.

It's a look of disassociation, thought Ames; *an act of self-condoned revision, dismissal, and forwardness.* He knew then that what happened between them, for Grisman, was a thing to be forgotten, or if recalled, seen only in the most positive, casual terms of merely business, something to be moved on from, now and forever. It was a familiar reaction to Ames. He was well-versed in the ways of denial.

"You didn't tell New York about that," said Grisman, glancing at Ames's toe and giving him a knowing look.

"It wasn't important to the negotiation."

"Will you tell them later?"

Ames looked at Grisman. He was not out of the factory yet, but he didn't think Grisman was likely to stop him now. There was too much on the table for him. He could answer him honestly, without fear. He did so knowing the other would misinterpret it anyway.

"Mr. Grisman, what good would it do?"

Grisman grinned. "You're all right, Ames. I can see why they use you. I'll remember this." He held up the card gratefully. "No hard feelings?" He held out his hand.

"May I have my pencil and planner back, sir?"

Grisman took back his hand slowly, his grin flickering on and off. "Sure. Stu."

Stu handed Ames the pencil and planner and Ames put them in his suit pocket. He met Stu's eye briefly, saw the flicker of a frown on his face.

He sees it, thought Ames. He didn't have to tell New York what happened over the phone. They would see for themselves when he stopped by the office.

Ames left Grisman, Stu, and the factory without another word. He limped his way to his car, thinking of Cynthia.

***

He stopped by the Hollings office for his appointment, to complete the cover. The people at Hollings were sympathetic about his injury and listened politely to his pitch. They promised to contact Ames's client soon with an answer. And that was that. The meeting was on record.

Back in New York his real client, Haines, wanted to know what Ames thought of Grisman. Haines was one of Ames's longest acquaintances. They met in his office, Ames sitting across the desk from the other man, his bandaged foot propped on the plush carpet. They were of the same age, but a world apart in position and power. Haines was well-versed in Ames's rules. Neither man mentioned Grisman by name.

"Hollings sent over the contract today, along with the upfront fee," said Haines. "Thank you. Everyone is pleased with the outcome."

"Happy to help." But Ames did not look happy.

"You have some concerns about the...Hollings partnership?" It was Grisman, of course, that Haines was speaking of.

Ames nodded. "My assessment of the situation is this: Hollings represents a high-risk investment. They are very aggressive, but lack the portfolio and experience to manage at the next level."

"Do you see them as potential competitors to our market?"

"They would very much like to be a major part of your market. In fact, I would say they would like to own your market."

"Serious competition, then?"

"The most serious. But more importantly, they represent an unknown quality; very volatile, one that might create collateral damage to your organization."

"And you would recommend aggressive action on our part to cut-off this potential competition?"

"The most aggressive."

A pause. "This assessment is your professional opinion? Not one colored by personal experience or bias?" Haines looked to the bandaged toe.

"I only offer objective, professional opinions in these matters. My personal opinions are never voiced or take part in my assessment. This is a quality I believe you have come to appreciate over time."

"I have. Thank you, Wilson. The secretary has your fee outside."

That fee was for is "work" with Hollings, again for the record. Ames knew the real money would be sent to his private account in the Caymans.

***

Sitting in a taxi on the way home, he thought about the whole affair as he sketched a blue castle in the clouds. He hadn't lied to Grisman, or Haines. He never lied, if he could help it. It wasn't necessary, and often led to trouble. His assessment *had* been objective, accurate. But just the same, Ames took a certain pleasure in knowing that his words had started an unpleasant chain of events for Grisman and Grisman Industries.

Then he remembered, for what he hoped was the last time, the hunger in Grisman's eyes as he held the soldering gun to his toe. This was followed by a similarly unpleasant memory of their goodbye. Grisman had been all smiles, believing that the likes of Ames could never really hurt him or have any real significance in his life.

He blinked away the images, and turned back to the sketch. It showed a square top structure of rough stones sitting along a hill, clouds playing around the crenellations like so many daydreams. He added a touch of shadow to the top, a hint of evening to come. Finished, he studied the image for a time, then put it away.

Now it was just a matter of coming home to his other life. The hospital had said he would keep his toe. They had given him some wonderful pain killers, cautioning him to take more care in his hobbies in the future.

And so it was over. An unpleasant scar and a memory, one recorded and then forgotten in a blue castle sketch. Time, again, to return to normalcy.

***

"Darling! Whatever happened to your toe?"

"I stubbed it on chair, sweetheart. Nothing to worry about."

Cynthia joined him at the kitchen table, her plans momentarily derailed by the sight of Wilson's heavily bandaged toe at the end of his extended foot. "It looks serious."

She fumbled at her cigarette purse, trying to put the distraction into place. But her prepared speech collapsed under the weight of this new and unexpected sight of a fragile Wilson. The stained bandage was so out of place, so unlike his normal, put-together self. It was almost a shock to see it there; like finding a finding a piece of rot on an otherwise whole fruit.

"How was your trip?" she asked mechanically.

"Boring. You were right to miss it."

"Wilson…." she hesitated. "We need to talk."

"Of course, dear. Can I trouble you for a drink, first?"

She welcomed the distraction and practically jumped for the bottle in the cabinet.

Her eyes, Ames thought, as he watched her make the drinks at the sink. Just now they reminded him of something, something recent and unpleasant. He recalled then where he had seen that expression before. Grisman. When he let Ames walk out of the factory, Grisman had worn an echo of that expression, a certain distracted determination. It disturbed him on many levels to see it on Cynthia, and he suddenly wondered what this great talk was about.

And with that thought, Ames understood his world was about to take another turn, one that threatened to upset his carefully maintained sense of well-being and order as much as Grisman's mindless hunger. He didn't want to hear what Cynthia so clearly wanted to say. He wanted to find his pencil and paper, to draw another escape until the matter went away on its own. But watching Cynthia fidget with the drinks, he knew that was not possible. He must act, and act now.

Instinct, or a sense of synchronicity, led him to again seek distraction, as he did with Grisman; to force retreat, and open the door of doubt. *Delay and distract*, he thought. *And pray god it's not too late.*

"There was one thing," he said as she turned around, and before she could speak again. "Quite strange."

She brought the drinks to the table, set his in front of him. "Yes?" she asked, but it was clear she wasn't listening.

He watched her sip her drink, her mind a thousand miles away. He wondered briefly if he had driven her to this point. He thought again of her standing in that long-ago room of admirers, smiling at everyone, seemingly in control and in her element. He thought he had grounded her with his trusting, unquestioning nature, and thus freed her. But perhaps he only rendered her flightless for a time, touching the butterfly's wing with the crippling oil of his self. Perhaps she needed more than just constant assurance, and a willingness to look the other way. Perhaps she had enough.

The thought of losing her was almost too much to bear. But equally troubling was holding her against her will. For a moment he hesitated, unsure if he could, or even should proceed. That he could talk her into staying, at least for a time, he was reasonably certain. But for how long, and what would that mean? He had never used his manipulative abilities on Cynthia, not in any serious sense. Theirs's was a mutual, albeit complicated understanding of accepted roles and expectations. Part of that understanding included never speaking of those role, part of it was a willingness of Ames to look the other way. For which, in return, he had Cynthia—in all the ways that mattered to him.

Now, something had changed. Identifying that change was critical.

He did not think she knew of his own double-life. There were no signs of reproach or hurt in her demeanor. This wasn't about him. Not that way, at least.

But that didn't mean it wasn't about deception. No one knew better than Ames what it meant to carry a secret. Had Cynthia finally had enough of her own? It would explain the blind determination in her face, the self-recrimination.

Dare he risk the truth? It might serve. It might shock her into reassessing, provide a new foundation from which to build their relationship, one of shared secrets, complete trust. But it would come at a terrible price and risk, for him and her. She would be exposed, in more ways than one. His world was dangerous.

He looked across the table. To keep her he would risk almost anything, even that. If it were truly necessary; if it would be enough. He shuddered at the implications if it were not. *But only, only*, he thought, *if there was no other way.* He looked down at the drink in his hands, saw again the hard, angry eyes of Grisman looking back at his. *Perhaps, not even then.*

He knew there might come a day that he might have to decide, though. This might be that day. He hoped not. He had other options to try first. He knew his wife. She was not a creature of calculation and commitment. She was the butterfly in all things, including her own mind.

Distraction, he thought; *then, a carrot*. A small coin on the table. A test of her resolve. A reminder of what was at stake. A willing concession. It would skate dangerously close to troubled territory. It would be a mix of conflicting drives, like all difficult arbitration. But it couldn't be blatant manipulation. Never that. Not with Cynthia. He had to show without exposing, offer without demanding—and in the end, let her make her decision.

God, he thought, *let it be enough*.

Cynthia realized that neither of them had spoken for some time. Was she to blame? Had her distraction upset Wilson? She searched desperately for the train of conversation, recalled his last words. "What happened, Wilson? What was so strange?" *Had he said strange?*

"Yes. It was very disturbing, actually."

Cynthia fetched a cigarette and tapped it on the table, looked back to Wilson to continue. She was growing impatient again. She wanted to get this done and over with.

"I stopped in the airport bathroom," he continued slowly. "There was a man there, bleeding from his nose. Bloody paper towels were everywhere. I almost walked out, it was so disturbing."

Cynthia stared at Wilson, her face twisted in mild shock. She had no basis from which to understand his story, or more importantly, how it fit in her plans for confrontation. Yet Wilson sat there, watching her expectantly, as if waiting for her to respond in kind. She looked to the kitchen sink, dumbfounded.

"I've disturbed you, darling," said Wilson, and suddenly he reached out a hand to cover her own. "I'm so sorry. Forget I said anything. On to more happy thoughts. How was your dinner with Edith and Ted?"

"Ted?" started Cynthia, again suffering a non sequitur. "We…. Wilson, there is something I *have* to tell you."

"Yes dear," said Wilson, squeezing her hand. "By the way, though the trip was miserably boring it was successful. There's a little extra in the account, just for you. Why don't you buy something nice and we can take in dinner and a show this weekend. Would you like that?"

"A show?" She looked in confusion down to the well-manicured hand holding hers, looked up to see Wilson smiling at her. Safe, naïve, dependable Wilson.

"You could ask Ted and the others to come if you like."

A sudden image of Ted sitting next to Wilson almost sent her reeling. "No dear, not Ted," she said. "He turned out to be a bit of a fool."

"Poor darling. Then maybe just you and me. Of course," Wilson smiled shyly, "I'm afraid you must think me even more a bore."

She looked to Wilson, her mouth half open, trying to make sense of his words, searching for some segue to her leaving, the image of Ted sitting beside Wilson still in her mind.

Boring, she thought. *No, not boring. Never boring.* She looked down to the hand still holding hers, noticed again the smooth skin, the well-trimmed nails. Yet it was not an effeminate hand. There was a warm, inner strength to the hand in hers, like a piece of ivory.

Wilson smiled softly at her. *Safe, naïve, Wilson, who smiles so sweetly, but so…what? Carefully?* Like his appearance, the smile was oddly enigmatic, a suggestion of something more, but nothing one could put a finger on.

No. Not boring.

And Cynthia realized as she held his hand that the safe, dependable mystery of Wilson was, on some level, hers and hers alone. She may never solve it, or understand its fundamental nature, but it acted for her. Wilson gave her that, and more. Much more.

Was she really prepared to walk away from that? Wilson gave her stability. And yes, let's be honest, an illicit freedom. One that would never be questioned, one that was not being questioned even now in his kind, trusting expression and silly stories of bloody noses in bathrooms. How typical of Wilson to be so unaware. He even brought up Ted.

Her heart fluttered with a growing and unexpected sense of relief. What was Edith's meddling, really? Vaguely disguised jealousy? No, she realized with sudden assurance, she did not want to give up just yet on Wilson, the mystery, or the constancy.

At least, not today.

She squeezed his hand. "Dinner and show with you would be wonderful, Wilson," she said, smiling.

He tilted his head in pleasure.

"Only," she continued, acting on another sudden impulse, "can I take a rain check? Edith wants me to see this new lounge act in the Village, and she simply won't go without me. I could still use that new dress though. If the offer still stands."

"Of course, dear." He patted her hand, let it go, and carefully climbed from the table.

"Where are you going?" she asked.

"Just want to do a little work," he said, picking up his sketch book.

It did her heart good to see how happy she'd made him.

II

Reuben ran a nicotine-stained thumbnail across his hairline, tried to cover a yawn. He waved apologetically to the man across his desk and looked for something amid the clutter of papers and files, spotting the empty coffee cup in the trash can almost in the same instant. He looked wistfully to the hall and the coffee machine, and then back to the man across the desk. The little man was wearing the same patient but determined expression he had ten minutes ago when he first sat down.

Reuben made a point of looking to his watch. It was five after seven, an hour after his shift officially ended. More to the point, it was exactly thirty minutes since his wife called to see when he would be home. He looked to the man again. Prim, well-dressed, a flower pinned in his pocket; not the type usually seen in homicide after hours, on a Friday night. Unless they were being processed, or someone at the front desk thought they were being funny.

"How can I help you?" He snuck a peak at the post-it by his phone, "Mr. Ames."

"Actually, sir, it is more what I can do for you."

Reuben sighed; one of those. He leaned back in his chair, took a longer look at Mr. Wilson Ames. Even sitting, Ames looked small, neat. His salt and pepper hair was trimmed close, his features ordinary, forgettable. If he had to guess he would say bank teller, maybe funeral director. He didn't look bat-crazy. But then, they rarely did. He should call his wife. Fifteen minutes, he decided, that's it.

"Always appreciate a helping hand," said Reuben, wondering what form that help would take: "*Detective, my neighbor is Osama.*" (It didn't seem to matter he was dead; it only deepened the intrigue for the conspirators)..."*Was Homicide aware that aliens had infested the IRS?*"... "*I know who killed JFK, and Elvis.*"

"This is rather awkward," said Ames. "It doesn't involve a homicide."

"Unfortunate," said Rueben. "Homicide's my specialty. That's why it says Homicide Division on the door. I even have a badge to prove it."

Ames smiled. "I take your meaning. You'll forgive me if I am direct?"

"On the contrary, it would be most appreciated, Mr. Ames."

"One of the men in your division has been seeing my wife."

Reuben raised a lazy eyebrow, but Ames had his attention now. "Seeing?"

"I think you know my meaning, detective. I suspect you even know the man I am speaking of."

"This is none of my business, Mr. Ames," said Reuben, summoning as much dismissive authority as he could muster. "If you have a complaint about one of the detectives you should direct it to the Department's Human Resources division. That's their expertise."

"I hope that will not be necessary. Such an action might result in the man's suspension, or worse. I have no desire for that. It would only compound the problem in my opinion."

Reuben scratched his hairline again. "I don't see how I can help."

"I am here," said Ames quietly. "To prevent any further...escalation. As you might guess, knowledge of this situation has caused me great distress."

Reuben looked Ames up and down as if searching for signs of distress, finding none.

"I would hate," continued Ames, "to have this unfortunate circumstance escalate. Imagine if I should come home to find my wife and this man alone together."

Reuben stared at Ames, sucked his teeth. "I imagine you think I'm now a witness for your defense," he said. "If things should…escalate."

Ames brushed some non-existent dust from his trousers, crossed his knees. "That was not my intention, detective. Though, what you say may be true."

"Don't be too clever, Mr. Ames. We have some pretty clever folks here, too."

"No doubt. But you misunderstand my frankness. You see, I really am here to prevent a crime."

"Let me suggest you be very careful with your next words, Mr. Ames. Threatening an officer of the law, regardless of circumstances, is a serious offense."

"The crime I speak of is not mine, detective, or one of passion. Though I suppose that is always a possibility in such circumstances. No, what I'm speaking about is an escalation to blackmail, by the man who has made me a cuckold."

"Come again?"

"The detective in question, your partner to be specific, is trying to blackmail my wife."

Reuben frowned, picked up a pen top, looked it over, and started cleaning his ear with it. "With what? You just said you already know about the affair."

Ames sighed. "Sadly, that is of no help in this circumstance. You see, I don't want my wife to know of my awareness."   Ames looked to his immaculately manicured hands, as if searching for a way to explain. "It is not the first time she strayed. We have what you might call an unspoken agreement. The key, by the way, is that it remain unspoken. My wife apparently ended the affair, or tried to, a week ago. Unfortunately, your partner is behaving quite boorishly and is trying to force her to continue anyway."

"Then this is not about money?"

"No, not yet. Though I suspect it is only a matter of time."

"It all sounds very personal, Mr. Ames. And again, and for the record, not my business."

"Consider yourself covered," said Ames, with a small frown.

Reuben pulled the pen top out of his ear and tossed it on the desk. "These are some very serious allegations, Mr. Ames. Do you have proof?"

"Acquiring such proof would be just as damaging as directly confronting your partner."

"Let me get this straight," said Reuben, hunching over his desk and drawing closer to Ames. "Are you saying you don't know for sure they are having an affair?"

"A husband knows, detective."

"Mr. Ames…."

"I know, detective," insisted Ames. For a moment the carefully put together façade of charm dropped and Reuben saw a hint of something else, something surprisingly worldly. "And," added Ames quietly "so do you."

Reuben sighed. He had no doubt Ames knew what he was talking about. It was not the first time his partner Manning had run afoul with a husband. The man seemed fixated with married women. What's worse, they seemed fatally attracted to him.

Under normal circumstances, Reuben would send Ames packing and give Manning a heads up. But these weren't normal circumstances. For one thing, the blackmail aspect was ugly. What the hell was Manning thinking? Had the fool fallen for the woman?

But another thing was Ames. Reuben wondered why the man seemed so familiar. Or was it the name? He didn't really worry that Ames would actually do anything. Manning could handle himself, and passion and violence were not the first words that leapt to mind when looking at Ames. No, it was something else.

What was it about that name…Wilson Ames?

He made a point of picking up the topless pen, opened his notebook. He scribbled some nonsense down for effect, then said, "Mr. Ames, this all sounds dangerously premeditative on your part."

For a moment there was just the hint of something distant, something removed and calculating in the well-groomed man across the desk. Then it was gone again, and the tidy banker-like persona was back in place.

"If I wanted to kill your partner, Detective Reuben, I wouldn't be here. I'd just…discover them, and that would be that."

Reuben's mouth twitched. He put the pen down. "What do you expect me to do?"

"Talk some sense into the man before things get to a point where everyone loses."

"What makes you think he'll listen to me?"

"He will," said Ames confidently. "He's your partner."

Reuben looked forlornly to the coffee machine. "Let me call my wife."

The interview with Reuben had been a mixed affair, at best. Ames suspected he would have to take additional steps, which was not ideal. Not ideal, at all. To make matters worse, work called the next day. He didn't really want to deal with all that entailed right now. But he couldn't ignore this particular call. He cancelled his private lunch and afternoon plans, then called Cynthia to tell her he might be late for dinner.

He took a cab from his house, asking to be dropped off at major shopping center near his destination. As the cab pulled away, he sat back in the heavily scented seat and retreated in his overcoat like a worried turtle. He wasn't just worried, he was angry. It was an unfamiliar emotion for Ames. Frustration, disdain, even disgust, yes; these were old acquaintances. But anger was something different. Ames didn't approve of anger. It represented a loss of control, a concession to chaos. It was bad for business.

But he was angry now—white-hot, behind the eyes, catch in your throat angry. Angry at his wife. Angry at the timing. Angry at that fool, Manning. Angry at the seeming inevitability of it all.

In the six months since his unfortunate meeting with Grisman, and the still more troubling near disaster with Cynthia, things appeared to revert to normal. Ames's toe had healed, leaving a shiny scar and a permanently missing piece of toenail. Work had continued as usual. And most importantly, his relationship with Cynthia had returned to its former form. Including, unfortunately, her indulgences.

But it was a false spring. Her latest fling, Manning, was a disaster, on every front. Cynthia actually looked lost, almost debilitated in her hopelessness. More than once Ames thought she would actually confess everything—a possibility almost as frightening to Ames as losing Cynthia altogether. Their carefully constructed and maintained distance and dependence was hanging by a thread again. But clearly things could not go on as they were either. Damn Manning!

And now this, a call—summons, really—from work. Not completely unexpected, but unwanted just the same. He sighed into his scarf, reached up a gloved hand and pulled the soft wool down below his chin. He turned to look out the window. The dirty gray of winter infested the city; it was a fitting complement to his mood.

No, he thought, *that wouldn't do*. He needed to concentrate; the meeting was important. He pushed his marital issues aside and tried to focus.

He had a very good idea why he was being called in. That knowledge contributed to his anger as well, though in this case it had nothing to do with Manning. He ran a gloved finger distractedly down the window, drawing a condensation bead. He had expected resistance to his retirement. He had worked diligently over the years to establish the possibility, but knew the actuality would be difficult. Still, he'd hoped (maybe naively) that the rules would see him through. Those rules included his independence, a consultant for hire but never for keeps. He had always been very clear about that. He established the rules, and lived by them, all so that when he reached this point in life he could stop, walk away, no strings attached.

He sighed. He had been naïve. To some of Ames's private line of clientele, strings—complicated and perilous though they may be—were a constant, a given, a necessity. Strings that bound and pulled and directed, like the cords of animation tied to the puppet. It went with the work, and it was understood that those strings were for life. Even for Ames.

Feeling frustrated, he pulled off his gloves, took out his mechanical pencil and pocket notebook. He flipped to the page of his latest sketch, a crumbling castle on a crest overlooking the ocean. Unlike his previous sketches, the castle (little more than a broken foundation suggested by a few lines and some shadow) was not the subject. Instead, a panorama of beach and sky and sea and sun, all in fine blue lines, drew the eye. It was not his best work, but he had spent an inordinate amount of time on it. He had started it the day before he gave his first tentative retirement notices. He considered the sketch in the poor light of the cab window, braced himself against the door seat, and carefully shaded in the deeper ends of the ocean.

So theirs was not what you'd call a traditional marriage, his thoughts jumping back to his personal problems. He touched up a wave near the shore. *Yet it remains a functional one. And satisfying for both parties.* Ames was as certain of that as a man could be in his position. Cynthia was free to leave any time. He suspected she had considered it seriously around the time of Grisman. But she stayed. He knew she stayed in part because he made it easy to.

Why shouldn't she have her secrets? I have mine.

He considered the sketch again. *Maybe a lonely tower along the page line? No. Enough for now.* He closed the notebook, put the pencil back in his jacket pocket. The traffic was heavy with holiday shoppers, but they eventually neared his destination. He put the notebook in his jacket as well, and spent the rest of the trip staring out the snow flecked window.

Haines stood with his back to the office door, looking out the window at the snow falling outside. Handsome, fit, his thick hair and close beard touched with just a hint of gray, he continued to stare indifferently as the door opened and Ames entered.

He turned and smiled briefly, waved Ames to the chair across from his desk. Dressed in a charcoal blazer, white dress shirt open at the collar, and tailored slacks, Haines looked like a model for a business casual outfitter. But then he could afford to dress as he pleased, even in the dead of winter, even on a Monday.

"Make yourself comfortable, Wilson," he said, taking his own seat behind the enormous black marble desk.

Ames took off his overcoat and scarf, folded them over his arm. He sat slowly in the chair, crossed his legs, and put the scarf and coat neatly in his lap. He touched his tie knot, sat straight, and looked straight ahead.

Haines watched him with amused interest. "We've known each other a long time," he said.

"Thirty years."

"You've done very well by yourself. I knew you would, even back then."

Ames didn't answer. He brushed a piece of dust from his overcoat.

Haines watched the gesture with an almost paternal tolerance, remembering days passed.

They had met at school. Haines was in his element, an elite among the elite, his family rumored to have tenuous ties to something or someone important. No one was quite sure what, which, or why. Ames was mysterious as well, in that no one knew or cared who he was.

But Haines took an interest in the quiet young man who seemed so removed from the day to day college experience. There was something about Ames that intrigued him, something vaguely familiar. He made it a special point to know Ames, as much as anyone could know Ames, sitting next to him in class, inviting him to discuss lessons over coffee or a beer. What little he garnered out of these short exchanges only wet his appetite. There was a mystery to Ames he wanted to solve. He kept in touch after school, saw to it that Ames was invited to certain private gatherings, even introduced him to Cynthia, Ames's eventual wife. And over time, Haines began to understand what made Ames so special. He also saw an opportunity.

Like everything about Ames, it involved a paradox. People didn't appear to take Ames seriously, they hardly noticed him, but they *talked* to him. Somehow, despite his passive nature (or maybe because of it?) people responded to Ames. He projected the perfect sounding board: a passive listener, an impartial respondent, the soul of discretion.

These qualities had a profound though very subtle effect on those around Ames. Haines had seen it play out many times over the years. People didn't just talk to Ames, they confided in him, often in their first meeting. They couldn't remember his name or what he looked like five minutes later, but they would open up their most personal problems or fears to him while he stood there, practically forgotten.

But—it wasn't all one way. Haines saw how Ames subtly used his gifts to get what he wanted, when he wanted something. Most of the time, this was simply to deflect attention from himself. Ames appeared to thrive on his obscurity. But on rare occasions, like his pursuit of Cynthia, he could subtly shift events, words, even perspectives to suit his needs, all while maintaining his ambiguity. In this, he was remarkably successful; Haines knew he was not immune to the effect himself.

It was a quality that Haines had envied, and wanted, all those years ago.

It was Haines that first proposed, very carefully, very tentatively, the opportunity he saw for Ames. Ames responded, but not in the way Haines anticipated. In some ways, it was more than Haines envisioned, better. In some ways, less. The fact remained, however, the role Ames cut out for himself—his independence—had become a critical element to Haines and the others. Everyone, including Ames, had prospered.

But now that prosperity was threatening to end.

"So," said Haines, leaning back. "Now you want to retire."

"It's time."

"Is it?" Haines studied Ames carefully. "You know, when I first heard the news I thought, well why not? Wilson, of all people, might actually be able to get away with it. For a time."

"For a time?"

Haines smiled slowly. "People in our line of work don't retire, Wilson—at least not above ground."

Ames pursed his lips, as if considering this for the first time. "But I'm not in your line of work," he said. "Whatever that line might be."

Haines chuckled. "You know perfectly well what my line of work is."

"I must correct you there. I've been very careful to never really *know* anything about any of my clients."

Haines stared at Ames, his patronizing smile fixed firmly in place.

"I have been very careful," continued Ames, "for just this purpose, just this conversation. Having never exposed myself to direct knowledge of my clients' work, I have no direct knowledge to be indiscreet about. They are safe. I'm safe. I can retire."

Haines dismissed this with another chuckle. "The famous Wilson Ames's rules of engagement: no specifics; everything done in euphemism; never even a hint of illegal matters to be brought up while you're in the room. Wilson the adjudicator. Wilson the currier and messenger. Wilson the discreet. An invaluable service for all those organizations or people who can't afford indiscretion or documentation of any kind."

"I believe I have held up my end of the terms."

"Oh, no doubt."

Haines tapped a tanned, well-manicured finger on the desk. "Yet, we have a problem, Wilson, just the same."

"My retirement…"

"Forget about your retirement. That's not going to happen, and that's not what I'm talking about."

Ames paused, shifted slightly forward in his seat, assumed an expression of concern. "I have no idea what you are talking about, Geoffrey."

Haines dropped all pretense of pleasantness, measured Ames with a decidedly colder expression. "You were seen downtown yesterday, Wilson. Talking to people. People decidedly outside the rules—our rules, if not yours."

"I assure you," said Ames, sitting back again, "it has nothing to do with business. It is personal."

"A personal problem?"

"Yes. I will handle it."

"So," said Haines slowly. "You admit there is a problem."

"A personal problem," repeated Ames.

"A problem that involves the police," said Haines, putting his hands on the table top, "is never personal."

"I'm handling it."

Haines frowned. "Why didn't you come to me for help?"

"That," said Ames simply, "would be indiscreet."

"Not nearly as indiscreet as sitting in a homicide office."

Ames took a moment before answering. He looked to the desk then back to Haines, spoke quietly, thoughtfully. "I can see how you would think it a mistake not to tell you," he admitted. "But you must remember I am an independent contractor, and an essential element to my success is that I answer to no one in particular. If I called on you over this personal matter the others would feel—quite rightly I would argue—that you had a greater hold over my services. I would I lose my status as a truly neutral party."

Haines shook his head. "Wilson, you don't seem to understand. You of all people don't sit in a homicide detective's office. You don't come within a block of them."

"Again, consider," responded Ames calmly, "What could I tell them? That was the point of all the rules, the indirection, the distance. I have nothing to tell anyone because I know nothing."

Haines looked to him in amused wonder. "You really believe that, don't you? You think that your little rules mean that much?" He leaned back, crossed his hands. "Wilson, the only thing that protected you all this time is what you might say."

Ames frowned. "The rules…"

Haines scoffed. "Forget your rules! We all assumed you have reams of damaging material locked away in a lawyer's office, just waiting to be opened and distributed in the event of any trouble."

"I have taken no such measures."

Haines looked incredulously at Ames. "On the off chance that's the truth, I wouldn't advertise the fact."

"My discretion…"

"Isn't worth the effort you put to it; not in this case." Haines waved a hand in the air. "Oh, don't get me wrong, many of us appreciate your rules. We're a generation built on compromise, Wilson, and your rules are a refreshing change, a point of stability if nothing else. But no one takes it as seriously as you. No one expects it to be without compromise as well." Haines leaned against his desk, arms crossed. "And now you've gone to the police."

"I told you, it's personal."

"And I told you, that doesn't matter."

"What do you want, Geoffrey?" asked Ames.

Though his demeanor remained relatively calm, it was clear to Haines Ames was struggling inside. "I can only tell you so many times you have nothing to worry about. Be reasonable."

Haines took his time answering, enjoying the site of a ruffled Ames. "That's right, Wilson," he said. "You can only tell us so many times—and you won't even get *that* chance with some of our mutual acquaintances." He threw his hands up. "Jesus! I'm trying to help you, Wilson. That's why I brought you here. We do go back. I know you and..." He stopped suddenly, reconsidered what he was about to say, then started again more softly. "I don't think you really understand how dangerous this is, Wilson. First this idiotic attempt to retire and now the police...." He sighed. "Forget whatever past we might share. If that means nothing to you, so be it. Some of us, myself primarily, value your services too much to simply throw them away because you're being naive." He leaned forward, willing Ames to listen, to understand. "If—and it's a big if—if we can reach an understanding today I think I can convince the others to hold off." He paused. "And I'm going to ignore your precious rules for just a moment to make sure you understand what I'm talking about. You won't live to see next week, Wilson, if we don't clean this mess up today, now."

The two men stared at each other for a time, Ames expression distant and inscrutable; Haines hard and insistent. The moment dragged on. Ames reflexively raised a hand to his jacket where his notebook and pencil rested, but dropped it a moment later. He licked his lips, blinked once, looked down to his hands folded across the coat on his lap.

"You want me to do a job," he said, looking up, his face and tone resuming that familiar, open profes-sionalism.

Not for the first time since they met, Haines wondered what cold internal resources Wilson Ames tapped to achieve such disengagement. He seemed at times little more than a suit and a voice, a catalyst to bridging difficult, often emotionally-charged conflicts simply by being there in all his detachment.

Haines started to answer, some of the hard lines retreating from his expression and tone as he tried to match Ames's detachment. "Yes, I want you to do a job. But I also want you to tell me what drove you to police—and let me help."

Ames's smile was apologetic, but equally determined. "I'm afraid that's not possible, Geoffrey. I will handle my personal business alone. As I said, it has to be that way, whatever the consequences."

Haines measured the other's resolve for a time, his tongue running reflectively along the back of his bottom teeth. Finally, he raised his hands as if to concede the point. "So be it, Wilson. But you *will* do this job—and drop the retirement nonsense."

Ames seemed to consider this, then nodded once. "Yes. I'll do the job."

Haines was relieved. For a moment, he thought Ames's obstinacy would put them both in an untenable position. He was not bluffing when he said Wilson's life was at stake. News of the "retirement" had sent troubling shockwaves through his group. More than one had asked the ultimate question. At least now he had something to work with.

"For what it is worth," he said by way of conciliation, "I'll speak on your behalf to others. It may be enough that you're still willing to work."

Ames tilted his head in gratitude. "I appreciate that. And please, let anyone who has questions know that I am always available to discuss the matter, discretionary rules still applying of course."

Haines smirked. "Of course. Now about that job." He saw just the faintest flicker of irritation cross Ames's face and realized that the dream of retirement would not so easily be abandoned. But the irritation passed in the same instant, replaced again by the professional expectation.

"Yes. When would you need me?"

"Now."

"Where?"

"Scottsdale. Shouldn't take more than a day."

"What kind of job?"

"Courier. A private message. Nothing outside your rules."

"What's the message and to who?"

Haines wrote briefly on a piece of stationary, handed it to Ames.

Ames read the names, gave the paper back to Haines.

"I'll leave tomorrow morning."

Haines shook his head. "You'll leave tonight. There's a direct flight. I've arranged everything."

Ames started to speak, but changed his mind, nodded in acquiescence.

"And no more talk about retirement, Wilson," said Haines. "That's a dead issue."

***

He didn't remember saying goodbye, or checking out, or leaving the building. He found himself walking on the city sidewalk, cold and shaken to his core. *How did this happen? Because you let it happen, fool.* He had deviated from the most fundamental of all his rules—he had imposed his will. He had mixed his worlds. He should never have gone to confront Reuben, especially at the police station. He'd grown careless, distracted by the dual pressures of Manning and his retirement.

And now he was paying for it. He was losing, or had lost, the most essential element of his other existence:

anonymity. If, answered his darker perhaps wiser self, that ever really existed. He heard again Haines brittle dismissal: "*You think your little rules mean that much....*"

The cold wind made his eyes water, bringing him back to his surroundings. He was standing in the middle of the sidewalk. How long had he been standing there? He pulled his coat around him as if he were pulling his mind to order, oriented himself. He considered his options. Home was impossible. If he saw Cynthia now, fresh from his defeat.... But he needed a place to sit, to reassess, to make plans. The museum, he thought. It was just a block away. He started walking purposely against the wind.

When he entered the heated lobby, he immediately took the stairs to the top floor, found a small, familiar bench across from an early Rembrandt. He had the place to himself. No one stopped at the realists anymore, or if they did it was not for long. If he was sitting across from a Chagall or a Dali he might as well be in Times Square. He let the still, pregnant air of marble, art, and lighting work its way into his reeling, bruised psyche.

How did this happen, he asked again? It was always going to end this way, answered that darker self. He could curse Manning, despair of Cynthia, and question Haines. He could look for a thousand rationalizations, a score of people to blame. But the truth was he had been lying to himself. He had made a deal with the devil and the terms where always going to end badly.

He felt the hard casing of his notebook and pencil in his jacket pocket, a presence usually so reassuring. He looked around the carefully contained other-world of the museum, feeling but not responding to its cold-warm remove. It was no good. Haines had awakened him to the truth: his world was not crumbling because of others or some outside force. It crumbled because it had to. He had built his house on sand. He had created a fantasy of choice, a lie to help him sleep at night. Good lord, he actually thought he could retire! The look on Haines's face…. His stomach churned just thinking of it.

It occurred to him then he was suffering more for his so-called autonomy than his wife's repeated infidelity and her latest, disastrous discretion. He almost laughed aloud for the irony, but remembered where he was and stifled it with his scarf.

Cynthia! She would certainly leave him now. She would have to. She would sense the change in Ames, the loss of confidence, of self. There was no room in Cynthia's world for a half-Ames, a broken Ames, a simple, everyday Ames. And that was what he was now: a piece of the cog. He didn't even have the benefit of being an important cog. He was a rented tool used by the likes of Haines; used and apparently easily discarded or replaced.

It had all been for nothing.

Discarded…replaced. *The retirement was a dead issue.*

A small chill that had nothing to do with the cold confines of the museum ran down his back. He replayed his conversation with Haines over in his mind, this time forcing himself to see the issues and responses objectively, from multiple interpretations. His trip to the police; his refusal to tell Haines the personal issue; the threat Ames represented to Haines and the others. He had told Haines there was no threat because of the rules, that he didn't have a stash of damning evidence somewhere, and Haines had almost laughed in disbelief.

Or was it relief? What would he do, he asked, if he was Haines? The words rolled over and over again in the mind…*A dead issue.*

What was he walking into in Arizona? Was this next job really his last?

Dead issue.

Should he run? He had the money and the means to disappear for a time. But not forever. He was not so naïve or ignorant of the resources of those he worked with to imagine he could simply assume a new life. And then there was Cynthia. There would be no running without her—and she would never run.

He heard the sound of steps behind him, the small whining voice of a child, the urgent, concerned whispers of adults. Out of the corner of his eye, he saw a couple walking with their little girl between them. As they drew close to his bench, the girl, she couldn't have been more than four, suddenly vomited on the floor. The father grabbed her quickly, but there was little he could do. He held the little girl like a doll, trying to keep the sick off her clothes. He met Ames's eyes, looked away, embarrassed. The mother was already wiping the spittle off the girl's face, half-scolding, half-consoling her with heated whispers. The little girl started to cry.

Ames stood, removed his handkerchief, and walked over. He handed it to the woman, who smiled gratefully. He looked down at the mess on the floor, leaned over and whispered to the little girl, "I know exactly how you feel."

***

The heat of Arizona hit him like a gentle, sweaty slap to the face. The contrast in temperature shoved against Ames's disillusionment, knocking it off balance. For a moment, he stood under the crystal blue sky and wondered where he was. Then slowly, like a man rising from a long but troubled sleep, he moved.

He made his way through the airport to the local hotel. He noticed the man in the linen suit, who had been on the same flight, standing behind him at the registration desk. They would both suffer for their fashion choices outside the safe environs of air conditioning modernity.

They shared that, thought Ames. *Maybe they shared other things, as well.*

Ames used his real name to check in and made a point of asking directions to the Mahrin Building, going over it twice just to be sure the front desk clerk would remember. He had an early morning appointment with the division manager of NU-Techs the next day and he didn't want to be late, he explained to the patient clerk. The meeting had been arranged last night by Haines people. Ames was ostensibly there to propose a telecommunications venture between NU-Techs and a division of Haines's enterprise. It was a legitimate meeting. Ames would make a pitch in the morning, though Haines didn't expect Ames to really close a deal. This was just preliminary, a feeler.

His real assignment was later, in the same building in a private room off the lobby. There he would sit with Alderman Charring—and deliver the message. An afternoon at most, Haines had insisted. He'd book the return trip for the next day.

Haines, thought Ames, *his acquaintance of long standing. The man who introduced him to his wife. The man who had made all the arrangements.*

Finished, Ames turned suddenly and nodded apologetically for the delay to the man in the linen suit. The other smiled in return, not meeting his eyes, and then stepped quickly forward to confirm his own registration.

Ames saw the man again the next morning, standing in the lobby, dressed in more climate appropriate clothes. He was reading a paper, but his eyes were unfocused. Ames walked by him without acknowledgment, and to his waiting taxi. He half expected the man to follow him out a moment later, but the revolving door remained still. He sat back in the taxi, closed his eyes and considered all the possible ordinary explanations. It didn't help.

***

Alderman Charring was a third generation local politician in a fast shrinking world of influence. He had made a political living serving the public good, or at least what those in real power considered good-enough for the public. And the Charrings had been a part of it all, taking their share, smoothing the waters, and marking their territory as the public face behind the private power. And times had been good. There was a Charring Bank, a Charring Hotel, a plaque in the Scottsdale Museum bearing the legend, Charring. There were three Charrings attending local private schools (a nephew and two nieces) and a whole crop's worth of Charring gravestones in the cemetery.

Times, indeed, had been good. But lately, Bertrand "Bernie" Charring wondered if it was all coming to an end. He had barely held his position the last election, and that only by a bit of creative voting box irregularity. The box was probably even now sitting in Pepper's van somewhere in the desert, a waiting time bomb that threatened to keep Bernie up late at nights. Worse still, by winning he had gone against the wishes of those same private powers who put him there in the first place. And that *did* keep Charring up at night, and jumpy most of the day.

It had seemed so right when he made that call to Pepper, faced with the realization that he was about to lose his first election. Now…now he was beginning to wonder if that was such a good idea after all.

He would explain, he reasoned to himself; *they owed him. What could they do about it anyway?*

Charring met the man from New York with a fixed smile. He shook his hand warmly, almost gratefully, and pulled one of the small wooden chairs around the card table so they could sit close together. The small back room was dank and poorly lit, but it was secure. The two men sat in stark contrast. The thin, well-groomed man in the black suit sat quietly, his posture perfect, his attention fixed on Charring. Charring, on the other hand, sprawled in his chair, his meaty hands propped idly across his belly like a small tent. His posture suggested a man working off Sunday dinner on porch swing, his big brown eyes flickering only occasionally to the man across from him.

"Well, sir," said Charring, rolling one cow eye at the man across from him. "What can I do for you?"

"I assume you know why I am here?" said the small man quietly.

The cow eye blinked once thoughtfully. He looks like an accountant, thought Charring, or some other kind of bean counter.

"The election," said Charring.

The man across nodded. "A surprise victory, if I'm not mistaken?"

"And I hope," rumbled Charring, "a pleasant one."

The other man didn't answer right away.

Charring squirmed, rolled his large buttocks back on the chair and lifted the front legs precariously off the floor. "I suppose some people would rather I lost?" he asked with a wry smile, refusing to acknowledge the implication.

Still the man from New York said nothing, his expression fixed and unreadable. Charring swallowed around a suddenly dry throat, looked down at his fat hands for inspiration, found none.

"Anyway," said Charring with a forced shrug. "I won."

"An election," repeated the small man carefully, "as I understand it, you were not expected to win."

Charring tried one more time to bluff his way through, knowing it was only a matter of time. "Polls and prognosticators can be—and often are—wrong." He chuckled. "Thank God."

The small man turned his head as if considering this answer carefully.

Now we'll see, thought Charring.

"The people I represent today are very grateful for all your efforts in the past," said the other. "For the good people of Arizona, of course."

Charring nodded, the two big brown eyes becoming a tight pool of concentration. The little man talked funny. He seemed even more reluctant to talk about the issue than Charring.

"They wonder now, if you would like to take on a larger, more prominent role?"

"Come again?"

"The Senatorial race is approaching."

"I was just re-elected Alderman." Charring was struggling to make sense of what just happened. Had the man really just asked him to run for Senate? "I'd have to resign."

"Yes," agreed the small man, conceding the point. "We think it will be overlooked."

Charring blinked around his confusion, still trying to get a hand on the situation. He'd expected anger, threats, and a punishment of some kind—but not this. "Not an easy thing to do, jump from Alderman to Senator."

"You will have the full support of our mutual acquaintances."

Charring sat forward again, rubbed a big hand along his chin. *Full support.* "I don't know, friend," he said slowly, looking to his hands, "I think the good people of Arizona will not look kindly on my sudden interest in the Senatorial position, seeing as how I'll be leaving them in the lurch to get a new Alderman." He gave the other an up-from-under look. "And then there's the incumbent

Senator, which is in my own party, and who has had a lock on the position for some time."

The small man met his eyes. "As you said, polls and prognosticators are often wrong. And you will have the full support of your friends. The incumbent will not enjoy that support this time."

Jesus, thought Charring; *they've got the Senator, too*. He always suspected as much, but never had proof.

"And as to your replacement for the Alderman position," continued the other. "That won't be hard to find, will it? It was a very close race."

Getting, thought Charring, *the man they wanted in the first place*. "And if I say no?"

The other hesitated, his expression growing more serious, but without signs of anger or threat. "I go back and tell them you're not interested."

"And that's that," said Charring.

"As far as I'm concerned, that will the end of it."

But not the end for me, eh, thought Charring. "Can I think about it?" he asked.

The serious expression took on a shade of regret. "I fly back tomorrow. I will give them an answer one way or another. If you haven't made up your mind by the time I leave this room then it is the same as a no—as far as they're concerned."

What little backbone Charring had left picked that moment to make a stand. "You might remind your bosses about horses and changing in the middle of streams and such," he said bitterly.

"They are aware of the adage," said the other agreeably. "And they are not my bosses. I am a consultant of sorts, sent here to access the situation."

What did that mean, thought Charring? *Access? Access and do what?* He looked to the small man for signs of violence. He knew looks could be deceiving in that way. *And he's a cold fish, this one. He sits there like he could be a million miles away.* He chewed his lip, watching the man across from him pick at pieces of invisible dust.

It doesn't matter, he thought. *They'll send the other type eventually, if I say no. Not tomorrow or next week, perhaps, but someday soon. A faulty brake line...a mysterious aliment...a burglary gone horribly wrong.*

"All right," he said with a sigh. "I'll do it. It will play hell with the process, but if that's what they want...." He shrugged, unable to finish the thought, tasting the bile of defeat in the back of his throat. Better than the alternative.

The small man nodded, suddenly distracted. "They'll be happy to hear that. Someone will contact you shortly to help with the transition."

There was a pause. Charring looked to the other man, wondering what was off. He'd given the answer they wanted, so why didn't the guy look happier? He felt a moment of panic. Was it all a game? Was the answer irrelevant and the man just playing with him?

"Well," said Charring hopefully, "I guess that settles the matter." He stared at the small man, demanding some kind of closure.

The other frowned, clearly distracted by his own thoughts. He looked around as if searching for something. "I'm sorry," he said to Charring. He stood suddenly, almost stumbling, an act so out of character with the calm exterior that Charring felt another round of panic. But the man just stood there as if waiting for Charring to say or do something.

Lost for something to say or do, but finding himself wanting to help the other man despite the circumstances, Charring fell back on mindless banter. "Jesus, friend. You look like the one that got the bad news."

The other's expression alternated between confusion and expectation and finally settled on something in between. He blinked slowly, staring at Charring, but not seeing him. "Do you think it strange that I'm here delivering this message?"

Charring snorted. "Isn't that your job?"

"Yes," said the other slowly. "I mean, don't you find it strange that they should send me here *now*, when clearly they could just...." He trailed off, looked down at Charring apologetically.

Christ, thought Charring, *did he just imply it would be easier to kill me?* He frowned in anger. "Is this some kind of joke?"

The other blinked once, a small blush creeping across his cheeks. He seemed to come to himself, standing straighter. His passive inscrutability fell about him again like a second skin.

"I'm sorry," he said again.

Charring could only glare at him. Clearly something was off.

The small man nodded once to Charring. "Good luck, Alderman." He turned to leave.

"Just a minute!" Charring stood, his face a blotchy mix of anger and fear.

The other stopped but did not turn around. Charring saw the tension in the well-tailored back, wondered frantically at its cause. "This is settled now, right?" he asked. "I'm going to do what they asked."

"I'll let them know," said the other quietly, and walked out.

Charring fell back in his chair, suddenly unsure of anything.

Ames walked out of the Mahrin building feeling the contrast of cold sweat along his back in the heat of the afternoon sun. He looked around the nearly empty street, half expecting to see the man in the linen suit waiting in the shadows of the alley or a running sedan. But there was no man, no car. He hailed a taxi and went back to the hotel.

The hotel lobby was quiet. He went to his room, hesitated outside the door, and finally walked in. There was no one there. No one sitting in the dark with a gun.

His return flight was scheduled for tomorrow morning. Haines had scheduled it that way. Ames loosened his tie and sat at the desk. He sat for five minutes without moving, listening to the struggling ac unit, waiting and wondering. Finally, he pulled out his notebook and pencil.

He considered the sketch of the castle by the sea. Slowly he tore it from the notebook. There were no ashtrays or matches in the room. He carefully ripped the paper into tiny pieces, and put them in the waste basket.

He considered the now blank notebook.

Ten minutes later, he was still staring at the blank page. He was still waiting. Waiting for a soft knock or click at the door; waiting for man in a linen suit or someone like him.

Should he call Cynthia? The thought went through him like a shot of adrenaline and he saw the pencil in his hand start to shake. He had never been this keyed up before. To hear her voice, perhaps for the last time. He put the pencil down and reached for the phone. He started to dial an outside number and then stopped. He put the phone back slowly in its cradle. Why worry her?

He had known danger before, but always before he had the backing of men like Haines. Now one them, perhaps even Haines, was the danger. He *should* call Cynthia.

But he didn't pick up the phone again.

The rules, he thought bitterly. He thought they'd be enough. Maybe though, it was all compromise, as Haines said. The thought disturbed Ames on a fundamental level. Was that his reality? Deluded compromise?

He picked up his pencil and sketched a long line down the middle of the page, then another. He made a blue shadow at the base of both. Slowly over time, a broken line here, a shadow there, the castle emerged. It stood remote, crumbled near the top, but solid in the foundation. He pressed the tip of the pencil near the blank edge and considered what context to put around the castle. *What context,* he thought sadly, *or what compromise?*

The pencil sat for a long moment on the paper as Ames looked away. In the end, he left the castle alone, the context unanswered, or answered with the whole of all possible contexts. He closed the notebook and put everything away in his suit pocket. He got undressed, made sure the door latch was off, and then crawled into bed.

He didn't remember falling asleep.

***

He woke, stared for a time at the ceiling. It didn't mean anything.

He got up, showered, clipped his nails, and dressed in a fresh shirt and his best suit. He chose a red tie for the day. It seemed somehow appropriate.

He asked the receptionist to call a taxi, giving himself plenty of time for the airport, or whatever. He made sure his ticket was in his pocket next to the notebook and pencil. At the last minute, just before he left the room, he took the notebook out and signed the picture: *For Cynthia...Love.*

There was no one waiting in the hallway, or on the elevator.

He was in the lobby though, dressed in the linen suit again, no paper this time. He watched Ames the whole time as he made his way across the lobby and checked out at the reception desk.

Ames turned from the desk and walked across the lobby to his waiting taxi. The man followed.

Ames stopped with his hand on the door, turned to the man. "I'm heading to the airport. If you're heading that way we can share the cab."

A small smile touched the other's lips. "Thank you, no. I'm not heading that way. Have a safe trip." He hailed another taxi. Ames felt something deep in his core release, his hand on the door shook slightly with relief.

As the other taxi pulled up the two men considered each other.

"For what it's worth," said Ames, "he agreed to resign."

The other stared at Ames. Then, "It doesn't matter."

Ames climbed into the taxi and out of the heat.

***

No one met him at the airport. He had told Cynthia he'd take a cab home.

He found her in their bed. It was three in the afternoon. He took his shoes off and walked quietly across the carpet, but she sensed him just the same. She woke slowly, her auburn hair plastered against her cheek, sleep in the corner of her blue eyes. She reached a hand out and he took it in his own, leaned over kissed her on the forehead. She pulled him into bed with her. He held her in his arms.

"You're home," she said sleepily.

"I'm home."

She looks better, he thought. There was an emerging sense of guilty pleasure about her, but that was not unusual. *The crisis has passed. Had Reuben persuaded Manning to end it after all?*

"I missed you," she said, running a hand up and down his chest. It was a nervous hand, a desperate hand, a hand that didn't know its own mind.

He kissed the top of her head. She smelled of too much sleep and cigarette.

"I want to get away for a time, Wilson. Can we go somewhere? Can we afford it?"

"I think so."

"Will work let you?"

"Yes," he said, staring up into the ceiling, wondering if it were true. "Anywhere you'd like to go."

***

The next day, a short web search of Scottsdale's news and events told him of the unexpected death of popular Alderman Bernie Charring. Charring apparently suffered a heart attack in his office in a rare moment alone. Friends and insiders cited the stress of a very close campaign. He was survived by his wife and two children. A special run-off election would be held and Charring's recent opponent was expected to carry the field comfortably.

He read about Manning in the paper. The detective was found dead in his car outside a crack house. He had been there for more than twenty four hours, slumped down in between the seat, shot once in the head. Toxicology reports were being conducted. No suspects as yet, but the police rounded up the crack house for questioning. Manning's presence in that neighborhood was a mystery as he was a homicide detective and had no current connections to the area. More details would be forthcoming.

Ames thought about Cynthia. He debated leaving the paper out for her to see, then changed his mind and put in the garbage pail outside, carefully burying it under other trash.

He spent the rest of the day making traveling plans with Cynthia. She was leaning toward Paris, but finally decided on Venice after talking briefly with the travel agent. Three weeks. She looked to Ames with a question. He smiled yes. When did they want to leave? As soon as possible she said over the phone, again with another question to Ames, who again agreed. Passports in order? She looked with panic to her husband. He nodded reassuringly. He always kept them up-to-date. She beamed at him gratefully. They could leave on Friday, two days from now. No, they couldn't make it sooner. She confirmed the reservations and then hung the phone up quickly, as if denying herself the opportunity to change her mind.

"I haven't a thing to wear, she said abruptly.

"We'll buy some things over there," he suggested.

She closed her eyes halfway in pleasure. "I need a cigarette." She flew out of the room.

Two days, thought Ames, sitting at his desk, staring at the space where his wife had just been.

He let Cynthia do the packing. She had of course gone shopping anyway. Her purchases were reckless and without regard to cost. Only as she was putting everything in their new luggage did she stop and look at Ames in horror.

"Lord, what have I done, Wilson? We can't afford this." She threw a shimmering turquois Louis Vuitton down on the bed.

"Actually, we can," he said reassuringly. "I just finished a big project, which paid very well." If he were to tell her how much they were really worth, it would lead to other dangerous confessions. That was against the rules. *Haines would call it a compromise*, he thought bitterly.

"Well that's good," she said blankly, sitting down on the edge of the bed, her energy ebbing again as fast as it flowed.

He watched her closely for a moment. The extended stress over Manning had played havoc with her looks, making dark shadows under her eyes and drawing out her high cheeks bones. She had lost weight in her shoulders as well, making her look older, sickly. The sudden relief was there too, of course, a frantic glimmer in the eyes, but it was tinged with something else: the vague sense of guilt. *Where did that came from*, he wondered, thinking of the paper in the trash.

"Darling," he said, drawing her blank expression to him. "I want you to let go. Spoil yourself. We can absolutely afford it. I promise. You deserved to be spoiled."

She winced around a smile. "I don't know about that," she whispered, then brushed a sudden tear from her face with a frown. "God, I'm a mess, Wilson. You'd be better off going without me."

"No," he said, "I wouldn't." And she wallowed at the certainty in his voice, nodded gratefully.

"Now get yourself together," he said casually. "I'm going to run to the bank for some traveler's checks. Won't be long."

She picked up the Vuitton and smoothed it out, a small, secret smile on her face.

***

They met in the same office. Ames sat in the same chair. Haines sat behind his desk. Haines was dressed as usual, but Ames was noticeably more casual this time, dressed only in a sweater and jeans under his heavy coat.

Haines looked Ames up and down. "I don't think I've ever seen you untucked before, Wilson."

"I'm going on vacation," he answered.

"I think that's a good idea," said Haines without hesitation.

Ames watched him in turn for a moment. Haines looked as if he didn't have a care in the world. As if all the drama about Ames's retirement or the Alderman had never happened.

"The Alderman," he started.

Haines waved him off. "Sorry about that. Looks like it was a wasted trip."

There was a short silence.

"But it wasn't a wasted trip, was it, Geoffrey?" Ames was careful to keep his tone neutral, but he watched Haines carefully. "For me, or the other one. You know the one I mean. The fellow who paid a visit to the Alderman after my meeting."

Haines shrugged, turned slightly to look out the window, his expression softening a bit with a distracted smile. Ames looked to the window as well. It was snowing again. Clean, soft, magical snow. *Snow*, he thought; *I should put the new castle in snow.*

"You'd be happy to know," continued Ames in the same even tones, "my problem has gone away as well. The personal problem."

"Has it? Good."

"Yes," said Ames, "but you knew that, too."

Again Haines did not reply. He was still looking out the window, still smiling.

"Manning, my problem, is dead," said Ames. "Manning was a police officer." He paused. "I wondered for a time why Reuben, his partner, wasn't sitting on my doorstep yesterday. That's who I went to see at the station the other day, Reuben."

Again he waited. Again Haines refused to engage.

"But why should he?" continued Ames. "He knew I had an alibi, didn't he? I was in Scottsdale at the time Manning was taking a bullet to the head."

Finally, Haines responded. His tone was light, but Ames saw the slight rise in his shoulders. "Careful, Wilson. You're getting dangerously close to breaking your precious rules."

Ames looked down. "You don't like my rules, Geoffrey. You like compromise."

"I don't *like* compromise. I just accept it."

Ames nodded at this. "Was it you? Or Reuben?"

Haines turned to stare at Ames, all trace of humor gone now. "Does it matter?"

"This time, yes."

A puzzled frown creased Haines's forehead. "This time?"

"I need to know it was not..." Ames swallowed around the name. He was going to say Cynthia. Stranger things had happened. She'd been desperate. It *was* a possibility. One he wanted to eliminate. "The situation was such," he started again, and faltered again. He took a deep breath. "I told you it was personal."

"I've never seen you this way before, Wilson. You're practically human."

"Please, Geoffrey."

Haines frowned. "I don't think I want to answer you, Wilson. You're going to work for us for a long time yet, and you were right—those rules of yours are important."

Ames licked his lips. "I don't need to know the details. I just need to know it was not...her."

Comprehension slowly dawned across Haines's face. "Ah, I understand now. No, you can rest easy on that count. It was not her."

For a moment, Ames retreated in relief. He looked up to find Haines watching him curiously.

"*I* took care of your personal problem," said Haines. "I told you, I take care of my friends, Wilson."

Ames looked to the snow outside the window again, then back to Haines. "But we're not friends, are we Geoffrey?"

Haines turned his head slightly as if hurt, then sighed. "Regardless, the situation had to be taken care of."

"I told you I would handle it," said Ames.

"Yes you did."

"You agreed to leave it with me."

Haines frowned. "Let it go. I didn't do it just for you, Wilson."

Ames nodded slowly. "Business."

"If you like. What else matters?"

Ames looked to the snow again. "Cynthia is your friend. You take care of your friends. You just said that."

"Ah," said Haines, raising his eyebrows in chagrin. "I did, didn't I?"

Ames blinked slowly. "You introduced us. I never asked you how you knew her."

"Cynthia was—is—a friend," said Haines. "A very good friend." There was just the hint of hesitancy in his words. He seemed to regret the turn the conversation was taking. "Just a friend," he added a moment later with a tight smile.

Now, thought Ames; *she is just a friend now.* He looked to his lap, then back to Haines. "I see." The two men considered each other.

It was Haines who finally broke the silence, shaking his head and offering another empty smile. "I truly envy your reasoned detachment, Wilson. It is a gift."

But while Ames appeared calm, behind his composure he was reeling.

Good friends, he thought. *They were good friends.* The possible implications of that statement were only now just starting to make themselves clear, including one he had never imagined. *I assumed it was Reuben, or someone else in the police station that told Haines about Manning...*

But what if it was Cynthia?

Was it possible? Were his two worlds more intimately linked than he imagined? The thought that Cynthia might actually speak to Haines about Manning, ask for and receive his help...He felt the bile rise in the back of his throat, swallowed it down again with an effort of will, conscious that Haines was watching.

"You were right, Geoffrey," he said, looking Haines in the eye. "It was naïve of me to think I could retire."

Haines studied Ames, his expression as measured and confident as his eyes. "I'm glad you see that now."

There was another long silence.

"And you were right about the other thing, as well," said Ames finally, reflexively brushing the lint from his knee.

"The other thing?"

"About the records. The lawyer that waits to send them should something happen to me. One can never be too careful. There are rules, but there are compromises as well."

The smile fell from Haines's face. "I can never tell what you are thinking, Wilson." He chewed his upper lip. "It's what makes you so valuable...and frustrating."

"I suppose so."

"So we understand each other?" asked Haines, his voice tight with suppressed anger. "It's back to business as usual."

"After my vacation, of course."

"Of course. I'll be sure to let everyone know that you're back in form. That all is settled again in our little corner of the world."

For a moment both men listened to the soft patter of snow falling against the window. Suddenly Haines leaned back in his chair, his smile once more in place, the confidence returned. "I can't tell you how happy I am you came by, Wilson," he said.

Ames stood, dismissed.

Before the door closed behind him, he heard Haines call out, "And give my best to Cynthia."

Not snow, thought Ames, standing outside the door and thinking of the castle sketch. *Snow is clean. There is no compromise to snow.*

III

They had found something again. Somewhere in Venice. Or maybe it was before, when they left—had to leave? It didn't matter. His mind for once was undivided, at rest in his world extant, needing no additional grounding, no carefully constructed curtains of self-preservation to hide behind.

He was not so naïve as to think it would last. Cynthia's fidelity was an afterthought to their marriage, a tentative condition neither expected in great lengths of time. It was not a necessity to maintaining the relationship. But this was different. There seemed a renewed determination—appreciation?—on her part. He was determined to enjoy what he had now, without compromise or hesitation.

They reached out to him via the answering service. It was late in the fourth week of their vacation. He called the private number from his cell phone. He was needed, in China of all places. He didn't speak the language, he reminded them. Not necessary, they said. The head negotiator, Michaels, would handle the negotiations. He was relatively new, but competent. They wanted Ames in the room, just to be sure. He had to be there in three days; could he manage it?

His first instinct was to say no, not wanting to risk his precious renewal with Cynthia. But he asked for a day to think about it.

The timing was not bad. Though still enamored with everything Venice, still apparently content, Cynthia was showing signs of restlessness, a need to return to familiar grounds. It was time to leave. He mentioned going home to her that night. She looked relieved. Then he told her about the job opportunity. He didn't tell her the specifics, of course, just that he would have to go to China first.

"I'm not sitting in the house by myself," she said. "But take the job. I'll stay with Connie for a few days. She's always begging me to come out there." Connie was her sister and lived in Oregon. "Call me when you get back and I'll join you then."

He called the contact the next morning. He was interested, but there were concerns.

How much time would this involve, he asked?

A day, two at the most, they insisted.

And what, exactly, was he to do?

His role was important but not active. A second set of eyes on the final terms of the deal. He would attend as a hired consultant, sit in on the proceedings, but not participate. The real meeting would take place later, at dinner. They wanted him to make sure they got what they came for.

Nowhere in all this conversation was the actual product or anyone's real name used. Everything was done in euphemisms and innuendo. Even the details of the client's expectations were discussed only in terms of a number and a condition. But both parties understood what was expected of them by the time the call was over. It was one of the reasons they wanted Ames. He was experience, he knew the rules. He was a known quality.

In the end he said yes. To return to the fold, to reestablish himself. To know again. In truth, the thought of picking up his old routine was not, altogether, an unhappy one. Looking back at it now, he saw that his attempt to retire was a mistake. Haines had corrected him of that mistake. It was as simple as that.

They took separate flights on the same day, enjoying the taxi ride to the airport like guilty lovers in the last stolen moments of a getaway. *Was this how it was for her with the others*, he thought? *Did they hold hands like school children, defying the world briefly before returning to the day to day, to the sanctioned and familiar, to the routine?*

He saw her off. His flight was an hour later.

When she was gone, he took a seat near his gate and pulled out his notebook and blue pencil.

He started a castle and seascape, one of his favorite subjects. This time he penciled a soft line a few yards off the beach and, slightly higher, a ridge of sand and grass built by the endless habit of tides. In the weedy grass, he started the tower, a singular, thin and rectangular structure, with a proud crown of parapets and one lonely grille covered window near the top. It was that small window that attracted his attention, and he spent some time imaging what was behind its shadowed frame. He used the edge of his pencil to suggest vague shapes and figures, an exercise in miniature impressionism, a sketch within a sketch.

He heard them call his flight to board, and put the sketch away.

***

Michaels met Ames at the airport and gave him a lift to the hotel in his private car. They sat in the back and chatted on the way. It was as close to a secure site as they would manage. It was certain the rooms were bugged.

"I understand I have you to thank for the number," said Michaels wryly.

Ames winced slightly. "Sorry about that."

"Why did you have to make it so damn high?"

Ames didn't bother apologizing again and merely smiled sympathetically.

"Okay," said Michaels, pushing on. "It is what it is. Now, as I understand it, your role is two-fold. You'll be a face for us in the front end meeting. They'll know who you are by the time of the meeting, but they'll wonder why you are in the room at this late stage. They'll raise a fuss—they can be very particular about numbers, seating, and such—but I don't see them saying no. Likely, they'll just throw another body in the mix on their end to balance things out again. They'll have more on their end of the table, by the way. That's balanced for them."

Ames listened politely, nodding his head and smiling encouragingly. He liked Michaels. The younger man was dressed formally in a gray pinstriped suit and sky blue tie, nothing out of place or too flashy. He looked tired, and probably was. He'd been in meetings with protocol secretaries for about a week now. He was a tall man, and despite his age, bald on top and inclining to fat. He tended to keep his double chin down, as if to hide it. *Or maybe*, thought Ames with a smile, *it was to emphasize his impressive dome*. The waxed pate did have a certain gravitas about it, like a boulder on a ledge threatening to run downhill.

"It's in the second meeting," continued Michaels, "the private dinner, that we may need you most. Our client is very particular about this deal. He's had some trouble in the past with this group. He wants to make sure that we get exactly what we order and that the other side understands that. No watering down the tea or other money-in-pocket schemes."

"I understand," said Ames. "Those were my instructions as well. Hopefully, it won't come to that."

Michaels lowered his chin, making a series of deep furrows in his forehead. *Yes*, thought Ames, *it was a most impressive and effective look.* He looked forward to seeing it at work in the meetings ahead.

"It will most certainly come to that," continued Michaels. "The important thing is we have to make it clear this time we won't stand for it. I'll need you to keep me on that page. They'll try to wear me down with yet another long and hopelessly detailed examination of the specifics today. They may try to slip something in at that time, but I doubt it. They know we'll be watching for it. The real aim will be to wear me down."

He rubbed his eyes. They were the rheumy red of the drinker—or someone who hadn't slept well for several nights.

"This is supposed to be the final meeting," said Michaels. "We sign today. But the contract means nothing. It will be later, during the celebration dinner, that's when they'll try to finagle a point. Probably about the one thing we can't compromise on: the number and quality. It must be 500." He looked to Ames expectantly.

Ames nodded. The boulder grew more lines. Michaels grunted his understanding.

"500 every time, then," he said. "And it must pass mustard. I can negotiate price, but I can't compromise on those two points."

"Correct," said Ames.

Michaels sighed and turned to the window, the clean pate now growing cloudy with worry.

The public meeting took place in a business suite in the Crown Royal. The room was modern and so common that it might well have been in New York, or London.

Except it wasn't. A tall, reed thin hostess in a red and white uniform managed two similarly dressed girls. All the help had long silky black hair, tied in neat loose knots along their slender necks and shoulders. They were neither present nor invisible. Like a living extension of the room's purpose, they were just there. They anticipated needs or responded to a pointed cup or a nod with quiet alacrity, their faces carefully absent of expression.

There was only one break in this carefully maintained demeanor. One of the younger girls actually smiled at Ames's clumsy thank you in Chinese. It was one of his favorite aspects of China: the way their faces transformed with their smiles. It never failed to charm him. He suspected the girl knew that on some level, but it didn't change his pleasure.

Monogramed writing pads and pens were provided to each member, along with exquisitely styled tea cups and a bottle of water. The two groups sat on opposite sides of an immense rectangular table of polished wood. The chairs were comfortable, the room warm and private. Ames sat at the end of Michaels's group, where he was politely ignored by both parties.

The first meeting was the predicted endless series of one paper, one point, one contention at a time. Sometimes it was simply a matter of clarification and agreement. But other times, it broke down into surprising heated arguments over the most trivial matters. Ames suspected these were negotiation tactics. He watched Michaels carefully over the first few until he was certain Michaels understood their purpose as well and could handle them.

The number came up more than once. Michael and his team were polite but firm: non-negotiable. The expressions across the table never changed, they would nod their understanding, move on, and then come back to it again as if it were a new subject. Nothing was non-negotiable, they seem to say, without ever making the point too blunt. It was just a matter of time and the proper approach. They tried numerous.

After the third attempt, and successful counter by Michaels, Ames ignored these as well. Instead, he turned his focus on the body language of the men, and one woman (the official translator,) across the table.

The most intriguing figure was Michaels's opposite, Mr. Ling. He rarely spoke, though it was obvious the others deferred to him. Ames would guess him to be in his late fifties. If his hair was dyed, it didn't show, but his face carried the years, sagging a bit in the smooth cheeks and under the eyes. Ling was clearly a man used to power. It emanated from him, in ways both subtle and evident. He made his intentions clear with a slight tension in his eyes or a barely lifted finger, and once, the start of a smile. Ames was fascinated by the man, sensing in him something both familiar and strange.

There was no time set aside for breaks during the discussion. If someone wanted to get up, they simply turned to another member and handed over the floor. But the talk never stopped. Ames, of course, could stretch or relieve himself any time he wanted, as could the other two members of their party. They were unessential, subordinates. But he felt for Michaels. The other side pinned him down with polite insistence of his attention, regardless of which person led the discussion. It was another tactic: a gentle, spoken war of attrition, one detail at a time.

Some four hours later, they finally broke for a lunch. As nothing had been signed yet, each group retired to a different room to assess and reload while they ate. Michaels spent most of that time going over things with the other members of the team, and eating. Before they returned to the meeting room, he pulled Ames aside.

"It's going all right," he said. He looked to Ames, who nodded his agreement.

"But then," he continued with a wry smile, "we've only discussed the number a dozen times. Another dozen to go." He laughed nervously at this own joke.

"Anyway, on the plus side I've managed to keep us under budget. We've got some room to maneuver there."

He sounded tired to Ames, despite his optimism. He was ducking his chin almost constantly now. "I don't want to go through another day of this," he continued. "I wish I could contact our client. I know I could sign right now if we could just drop the number a little, say 450...." He looked to Ames hopefully.

"That you can't do," said Ames.

"I know, I know." Michaels stared at the carpet, then back at Ames. He reached out and squeezed Ames's arm. "Sorry. I'm tired."

"You're doing fine," said Ames. "Just a little while longer." But he was thinking of Michaels's opposite as he said it. The silent Mr. Ling showed no signs of wear.

"I've just got a bad feeling I can't shake," confessed Michaels, dropping to a whisper. "We're holding our own, but somehow that doesn't seem enough."

Ames considered this for a moment. He hesitated, choosing his words carefully. "Maybe you're right."

Michaels stared in apprehension at Ames. He seemed to collapse without falling, the intimidating brow becoming nothing more than the premature balding of a young, overworked, out of shape and outclassed man. "You think I'll lose it, don't you?"

Ames held Michaels eyes for a moment, measuring the man.

"Yes," he answered finally. "In the next session, or at dinner, they'll simply state the number is not possible and there'll be no one at the table to challenge it. You are the lead, the only one they'll take seriously. And you'll be too tired to say no. They'll suggest another number, the number they want. Quality control won't be mentioned, as they will insist it's a given. But it's not, as we both know. They'll get their number. The quality control will be off the table."

"I won't allow it," said Michaels.

Ames shook his head. "You will. You've already lost. You said as much yourself."

Michaels started to respond. Ames gently waved him down. "Hear me out. The number they suggest will be close to your number. They may even say they'll do their best to make your number anyway. They'll be *reasonable*. Lots of polite, understanding eye contact. You'll be flattered, grateful for even that much. Anyone would be. But it won't be our number, and they'll have made their point—they're not held to a number, or to the quality control. Best case scenario, you push negotiations off to another round. They'll be happy to oblige as it is a concession to their way of thinking anyway. And it is. Eventually, they'll wear you down, and then you will wear the client down. Because that's just the way it is. Either way, today or next week, they'll win."

"What am I doing wrong?"

"Nothing," answered Ames truthfully. "No one could do anything different in your position. In fact, you're doing quite well. It's just how things are here. They have all the time in the world, even if they don't. All of this is just talk, even if it isn't. To them, everything has been decided. They're just waiting for us to catch on."

Michaels continued to look upset for a half minute, then sighed. "I've heard about you." Defeat invested his face and tone. "Can you do it?"

"No," said Ames quietly. "At least, not like this. I'm not there, at the table. Not really. I don't have the necessary time in, or the relationship. I'm too far down the line to impact his behavior."

"His?"

"Ling's."

Michaels nodded. He stared hopelessly at Ames. "So, I'm the one on the hook. I'm the one who's going to blow this."

Ames coughed slightly. He held Michaels eyes, made sure that he was listening. "That idea, of calling the client, it's a good one. I should make the call though. With your phone," he added apologetically.

Michaels looked puzzled, but after a moment handed Ames his phone.

"You know…" said Michaels, looking up and around the room, touched his ear, and then back to the phone.

"Mm hm," said Ames with a nod.

Michaels started to move away.

"Stay here," said Ames.

Ames dialed the overseas number. When he was connected he spoke in a slightly muffled tone. He knew it would be still picked up, but he had to make a show of care or the game would be over before it started.

"It's me," he said.

Pause.

"Not very well." He raised a conciliatory hand to Michaels through another pause.

"The number," said Ames.

Longer pause.

"You have a counter bid?" asked Ames.

Another pause, then: "I understand. Raise again."

Short pause.

"Right." Ames hung up and handed the phone back to Michaels.

Michaels face went from slightly put out, to confused. "Well?" he asked.

"Double the number again," said Ames. "We need a thousand. And no concessions on the quality checks. They will be run by our inspectors every time. Payment will only be on those orders that meet the standard. Failure to deliver any order on time and in the right quantity will result in a penalty, to be paid in the next shipment."

Michaels stared at Ames as if he were insane.

"Or we walk away," finished Ames.

If a boulder could collapse on itself, thought Ames, *Michaels is the very image of it.*

Ames gave him a moment to recover, then said in a much closer whisper, "Now, here's what to expect...."

If the potential partners overheard the lunch conversations, they weren't giving anything away in their expressions. Ames watched Ling carefully. Was there just the slightest sign of irritation in his bearing?

"Mr. Ling wants to address the quantity issue." This from the translator at the end of the table. She shuffled through some paper, chose one and put it carefully in front of her.

Ames glanced at Michaels, then back to Ling. Michaels, skirting the delicate line between interruption and response, took up the point as if it were a question.

"I'm glad you brought that up," he said.

The girl, still holding the paper, looked to Mr. Ling for direction. Ling ignored her, taking instead a pointed interest in a spot on the table just left of his hand.

Michaels pressed on. He was stepping all over the indirect sensibility that he'd so carefully cultivated over the last four hours. Ames, watching the other side, could see that they did not approve of the shift.

"The original number won't do," said Michaels. "We are going to need a 1,000 per. Quality checks on each shipment. Payment only upon approval by our team. Failure results in a penalty and/or instant suspension of the partnership."

There was a short, pregnant silence. Reactions across the way varied from embarrassment (for Michaels) to muted anger. Ames was particularly fascinated with Ling's response. For the first time, he actually looked animated, his eyes lifting from the spot on the table and watching Michaels with whimsical interest.

No surprise, though, thought Ames. *No one on the other side is acting surprised.*

"That is impossible," said one of the subordinates. "We suggest 250."

Michaels shook his head. "It must be 1000," he said, as assured as the other. But he looked at Ling as he said it.

"Perhaps, given the sudden shift in proposal," said another junior a little closer to Ling, "we should reschedule another meeting." The others started to pull out their smart phones to demonstrate their willingness to help in this matter.

Michaels, still looking at Ling, said, "Unfortunately, I cannot commit to another meeting. You'll remember we originally intended the deal to be signed last week." He glanced to the junior who suggested another meeting. "We feel it is in the best interest of all parties to resolve this issue today."

This caused a furry of silent, intense eye contact among the other side of the table. Before they could respond however, Michaels leaned forward, his expression and tone calm, friendly, but decidedly final. "We've been very patient, and appreciate your patience as well. We are agreed in principle and detail as to all the issues but this one. There is no reason for another meeting as this is our firm position. If you should choose to decline," he paused slightly, "we understand. Either way, I would personally like to thank you for your time, and hope that we may someday do business in the future. I should also add, my employer sends along his sincerest appreciation and highest respect, regardless of your decision today."

He opened his hands, as if to show he had nothing to hide. "If you need a little time to talk it over, we can wait outside."

"Obviously," tried another junior, "we cannot answer that question without research. What you are asking for completely changes our production requirements. Another day, perhaps two…"

Michaels shook his head regretfully. "I'm afraid this offer ends the moment we leave this office today."

The looks he received from this pronouncement were as clear as any from that side of the table all day. It was as if Michaels had insulted Mr. Ling personally, and some of his team looked ready to strike out in anger.

But Ames, focusing again on Ling, noticed the eyes were even brighter.

"Why the sudden change?" asked Ling, instantly silencing his side of the table.

Michaels bowed his head slightly, acknowledging the honor of being addressed directly. "We anticipated resolving this last week. We are now behind schedule."

"That does not answer Mr. Ling's question," said the man just to his right.

It all had the air of high drama on the other side of the table, but Ames suspected it was rehearsed. He had no doubt they overheard his earlier call to the client. They knew Michaels was going to ask for a higher number. Ames had anticipated this response and prepared Michaels for it. Of course, there was still the very real danger that it wouldn't work. It depended how much Ling wanted this contract, and how much he knew about Ames's client. *And*, thought Ames, *how much Ling would put up with*. He could just stand up and walk away now and that would be that.

When Michaels finally spoke, it was almost, but not quite an apology. "Things have changed."

Ling's eyes crinkled up in mirth. "Perhaps there is another bid?" he asked.

"We were to have exclusive bidding rights," chirped the right-hand man angrily. "That was understood."

Michaels never looked away from Ling. "And it was our understanding that we would resolve this last week."

Ling smiled. "It seems we both are victims of misunderstanding."

Michaels nodded.

"A moment," said Ling. He stood, and his group stood with him. They walked to the far corner of the room. Michaels's group did the same in the opposite corner.

"I hope you know what you are doing," he whispered to Ames.

Ames was watching Ling, who was standing looking out the window while his group conversed.

"They'll come back with a counter proposal…" he said.

"I was pretty damn clear," began Michaels.

"There's always a counter," said Ames, turning to Michaels. "You can go higher on the money if they insist. Use your judgment. They *will* insist on a lower number, regardless. If it is around the original 500 you'll take it— but only if they sign today and agree to the quality checks."

Michaels looked to Ames, a question on his lips. Ames silenced it with a slight shake of his head.

A moment later, Ling was sitting down again, his team falling in behind him like shuffled cards. It was the right-hand man who spoke. Ames noted that Ling had not said a word to anyone in the group during the discussion. But it was clear they spoke with his approval. How he managed that was a skill Ames would pay a great deal to learn. Maybe they had anticipated the ploy and had already worked out their response. The huddle had been just more show.

"We can go 400," said the right-hand man, sounding as if he would have to take food from his own children's mouth to manage even this.

"600," said Michaels, surprising Ames and everyone else at the table. "And the quality control measures are in. And we sign today, now."

The right-hand man looked down at his hands on the table. It was clearly Mr. Ling's call.

"500," said Ling simply.

Michaels smiled. "Five hundred. I'll have the paperwork drafted immediately."

The two men stood and shook hands. Suddenly the tension in the room was gone. Smiles were all around. Peace had broken out.

Later, at dinner, the paperwork examined in detail and signed, there were many toasts and at least the illusion of goodwill. The fare was colorful and extensive. One course after another found its way onto the giant glass lazy-susan. The guests took small portions from the serving dishes with their chopsticks or the provided spoons, and sent the revolving glass around again. Baijiu, Chinese rice wine, was poured for everyone in small shot glasses. In addition, there was beer or wine, or if preferred, juice or soda.

Michaels sat in the place of honor beside Ling. The two talked quietly through the dinner. From time to time an individual stood up and walked around the table to another, their shot glass held up like a gift with one hand underneath the bottom and the other around the glass. After the toast, each showed the other the empty glass. All of Ling's team made their way around the table at some point in the evening, toasting each member of the western group, usually Michaels first. Most of the westerners did the same.

Ames found himself sitting beside the right-hand man. They toasted one another frequently. Ames preferred red wine and used this glass after the first formal group toast. He had tried the baijiu his first trip to China. It was surprisingly sweet…and strong. He avoided it when he could.

The attempt came late in the night, after everyone was relaxed and feeling their cups—and it came from the right-hand man. Clearly, the Chinese had reassessed Ames's role.

"Surely, Mr. Ames," he said, after yet another toast and a brief aside about Chinese cuisine, "today was a productive, although, trying day. It is always interesting when different cultures work together."

It was the first time anyone had mentioned the meeting in anything but glowing, congratulatory terms. Ames wondered if the other was referencing the Ancient Chinese proverb (curse?) of living in interesting times. He noticed both Ling and Michaels stopped their own conversation, ostensibly to better concentrate on the sweet rice desert.

"I'm happy it worked out for everyone," said Ames.

"Indeed. Though, you have made a challenge for us. This number…" The right-hand man trailed off with a slight shake of his head.

There was a sudden drop in volume all around the table, though no one was crude enough to stop altogether.

Ames took a sip of wine. "I'm sure you will manage. The world is collectively impressed with Chinese industry and determination."

The right-hand man smiled proudly. They toasted again.

"But," said the other, when their glasses were down, "we also rely on our new partners' understanding, should matters unforeseen occur."

"Let us hope," said Ames, "for everyone's sake, that does not occur. I do not worry on this account, however. I know a man of Mr. Ling's quality will take preventive measures to insure all the terms are met."

"Indeed," said the right-hand man, slightly less enthusiastic. "Mr. Ling is a man of great quality."

"As is my client," said Ames, raising his glass again. "To quality." The right-hand man raised his in kind, his smile perfunctory.

"It always amazes me," continued Ames a moment later, looking distractedly to the table. "People of quality…"

"Yes?" prompted the other.

Ames blushed slightly. "I do not mean to presume." The other encouraged him, though it was obvious he wanted to return to the subject of the number.

"It's just I've noticed over the years how quality often finds quality." Ames looked admiringly in Ling's direction. Ling had dropped all pretense of ignoring the conversation and was watching him closely. The table grew very quiet.

"It was one of the reasons my client approached this offer in the first place—Mr. Ling's reputation."

Ames lifted his glass in the direction of the host. Ling nodded graciously and returned the toast. Both men polished off their glasses. Then Ling turned once again to Michaels and asked him how he found the soup. Conversations all around the table started up again.

The right-hand man smiled at Ames and excused himself, turning to his companion on the other side.

And that, thought Ames, was that.

On the way back to the airport, Michaels stared out the window at the dirty gray air. He told Ames he slept fourteen hours.

"Well, you did it," he said after a time.

"You did it," corrected Ames. "I was just there to see you through."

Michaels pulled a face. "Right." He looked out the window. "Thank God for that other bid. I just wish you'd told me about it earlier, it might have saved me the beginnings of another ulcer."

"There was no other bid," said Ames, looking to his hands. He sensed more than saw Michaels's reaction, the way he processed the news, how quickly he regained his composure. It is a measure of his quality, thought Ames.

"How did you know Ling wouldn't just walk out?" asked Michaels eventually, his voice small and a little tight.

"I didn't," admitted Ames.

"The client…" said Michaels.

"Knew the risk. Besides, the bid was not the point. That was just a face-saving act for Ling—if he needed one." Thinking on it now, Ames realized he didn't.

"Still," said Michaels, "that was a big chance. I've seen it go the other way. You're lucky Ling didn't close up shop and wish us luck."

Ames flicked a piece of lint off his knee.

Michaels shook his head, then smiled, obviously too pleased with the results to care about this detail. "Five hundred," he said, looking out the window. He said it again, as if tasting the number and finding it surprisingly sweet. "And on paper." He shook his head again.

Ames looked to him, hesitated, and then, for reasons he couldn't define, he let Michaels in on everything. "That paper means nothing. Our clients, on both sides of the table, do not do business—the real business—that gets recorded on pieces of paper."

Michaels turned to him in surprise. "Then Ling has no intention of making the number?"

"Probably not."

"And our client knows this? Doesn't care?"

"Yes, he knows. He cares, but not enough to break the deal."

"But…all that insistence on the number." Michaels closed his mouth in a hard line, the familiar furrows in his forehead deep and angry. "What the hell?"

"The client knows the situation," explained Ames. "And he knows because of our work—your work—he'll get his number. Most of it, most of the time. And when he doesn't get the number, because things do happen, you can bet Ling will make it good." Ames paused in thought. "Eventually," he added with a smile.

Michaels looked confused, hurt, angry, but mostly frustrated.

Ames regretted telling him now. Not that he didn't understand Michaels's frustration. Being left out of the loop on such a critical point could be crippling to a negotiator. But if Michaels had known the truth about the bid, he might have given the fact away.

"You're going to need a thicker skin if you want to continue this line of work," said Ames gently. "And not just with people across the table. Often your clients and colleagues can be just as fickle and deceptive. Particularly your clients and colleagues."

Michaels swallowed his first response. When he spoke it was controlled, even. *Yes*, thought Ames, *he could be very good at this.*

"All right," said Michaels eventually. "Tell me all of it. If you can."

"I asked the client to pick what was more important," said Ames. "The number, the quality, or the deal itself. He could pick one. That would be our bottom line. Everything else was in play, but not that. Then I explained, to get what we wanted we had to be prepared to walk away. That meant selling it straight. Ling would know if it was a bluff."

"And the client thought it safest if I didn't know," said Michaels slowly. "I had to be honestly frustrated, confused by the shift in terms."

"And Ling would know the difference," said Ames. "I apologize for leaving you out. It was my call. At the time, you were an unknown."

Michaels chewed around a frown. "Would you tell me now? I mean, with what you know of me now, would you tell me?"

Ames sighed. "Probably not. It's not that I think you couldn't pull it off. It's just a safer play to leave the speaker out of it."

There was another long pause, Michaels looking again out the window. "I can see that," he said finally, turning back. "But don't be surprised if I pull it on you someday, if the situation is reversed."

"I would expect you to. If it helps the client."

Michaels grunted. He shifted in his seat, the boulder of skin creasing with new questions. "But if it wasn't the number, what was it?"

"It was the quality," explained Ames. "That was the client's choice. You can be certain that the quality will be there, even if the number isn't. No diluting the tea, as you put it."

Michaels's eyes grew tight. "That little conversation with your dinner guest. All that talk about quality."

Ames nodded. "Yes, that was the real close. In the end, our client wanted quality insurance above everything else. I stated the obligations and repercussions in clear terms Ling would value: his reputation."

"Clear terms?" snorted Michaels.

Ames smiled. "Well, when in China…."

***

Two days later, sitting in his kitchen, Ames was surprised by how easy, how comfortable it had been to slip back into the work, the life. Old habits and expectations returned without effort or regret. The sketch he had finished on the flight home was sitting in his files. The only documentation he ever kept of his work. He would remember Ling and Michaels and the dinner when he looked at the tower on the beach. He would remember them all, fondly.

Feeling good, he decided to call Cynthia. He checked the clock on the wall. The time difference was about right.

She took the call by the pool, the sounds of children playing in the background.

"Oh, thank god you called, Wilson."

"How are you dear?"

"Wonderful. And hopelessly bored. Why must nieces and nephews be so damn childish and uninteresting? I suppose it is all point of view."

"I'm sure you're right."

"So, you're home now?"

"I am."

"Miss me?"

"Of course."

"Good. I'm coming home to make you miserable again."

"Can't wait. When will you arrive?"

"Oh, I suppose I can't just up and leave. My sister would never forgive me. Let's see. It's Friday, right?"

"Yes," he answered.

"Then expect me Monday sometime. That should be about right."

"Lovely. Should I meet you at the airport?"

"Don't bother. I'll catch a cab."

There was a short silence.

"Venice was lovely, wasn't it?" She sounded almost intimate despite the distraction cries in the background.

"It was."

"We'll go back again, won't we, Wilson?"

"If you like."

Another pause.

"Tah."

"Goodbye, dear."

He went to bed, a warm glow filling his being like a good scotch.

Standing in front of the bathroom mirror the next morning, razor in hand, he paused. Had he heard a knock at the door? He looked down, listening. He saw Cynthia's hair dryer. She had left it on the sink counter again. He pushed it back from the edge. The remaining cream along his cheek started to run.

No, he decided. A false echo. He made two careful strokes along the bottom of his chin to finish up, and rinsed the blade.

Wiping the tiny daps off behind his ear he heard the knock again, this time followed by the ringing of the bell. He quickly checked his face in the mirror, smoothed his salt and pepper hair back with his hands, and stepped to the bedroom. He pulled a thin, blue V-neck sweater from a hanger, climbed into a pair of linen pants and raced down the steps to the front door barefoot.

He opened the door, blinking in the morning sun. A man in a hat and heavy overcoat stood framed in the doorway. The sun was directly behind him so it was difficult to make out his face at first, particularly as the hat was pulled low.

Not many men wore hats today, thought Ames distractedly.

"Hello, asshole," said the man. "Remember me." He took a step forward, becoming clearer. The face that looked up from under the hat was vaguely familiar. The man tilted his head back slightly, as if giving Ames a chance to recall.

Ames studied the hawkish nose, lightly freckled by sun and age, the hard gray eyes sitting in a bed of fatty wrinkles, the lifeless, curly gray hair poking from under the hat and around the ears.

Then it came to him. Barber.

Barber. The girl. Joel Anderson. The rules.

Hello, asshole.

He felt a trickle of overlooked water run down his neck, tracing a cold path down his spine.

Barber grinned, seeing the recognition in Ames's face. He glanced briefly over Ames's shoulder, then back.

Ames didn't turn, willed himself not to turn.

"That's right, asshole," said Barber. "You're too smart for that old trick."

But a moment later, a moment too late, Ames heard the soft press of a foot in the carpet, saw a shadow out of the corner of his eye. Something wrapped itself around his neck, choking off his breath, pulling him back from the door.

Barber stepped through quickly, closing the door behind him. The man dragging Ames by the throat stopped, but didn't release his hold.

"I told you he'd be too smart to look back," laughed Barber.

Ames raised a hand to the arm around his throat, felt it tighten in response.

"Now, now," said Barber. "You can just relax, Asshole." He stepped around Ames and his unseen assailant, walked to the living room, and pulled the curtains shut. "In here."

Ames was forced-marched into the living room. The man holding him smelled faintly of talcum powder and mint, his coat sleeve rough and scratchy. Ames heard

Barber walking through the house, sounds of doors being locked and more curtains being drawn.

After a time, Barber returned, dragging a chair from the kitchen with him. He sat and took his hat off. There was a bald spot on the top of his crown that had not been there twenty odd years ago, and the curly brown hair that remained had faded with time to a rusty gray. Barber rubbed the bald spot, watching Ames and the man that held him.

"I told you," he said, speaking to Ames's captor. "No trouble from Mr. Ames. It's against his nature." He laughed, a brutal spit of derision, and pulled a gun from his pocket. He laid the barrel casually against his knee, pointed in Ames direction.

"Get it," he said to the man holding Ames.

The choke hold was released. Ames, rubbing his sore neck, glanced in the direction of the retreating figure. He saw another hat, another overcoat similar to Barber's. Then the coat and hat were out the door.

Ames turned back to Barber, who was watching him with casual hatred. The knee without the gun bounced up and down like a spring, reminding Ames again of the past. A moment later, he heard the front door open, followed by a soft footstep and an odd crinkle. He turned. The other man was back, carrying a folded sheet of plastic, a black silk bag, and a roll of duct tape. Ames turned back to Barber, who was rocking in his chair now.

"Right here," said Barber, pointing with the gun to the white carpet. He stood suddenly, lifted the chair by the armrests, and carried it with him to the edge of the room.

The other man spread the plastic out and put it over the carpet. Barber then brought the chair back and put in in the middle of the tarp.

"Wouldn't want to get your nice floor messy," he said, winking at Ames. "Must have run you some coin." He nodded to the chair. "Sit," he ordered.

Ames stepped slowly to the chair, the cold plastic sticking to the bottom of his bare feet. He sat, feeling another cold bead run down the back of his neck.

Barber nodded and the other man stepped to the chair. He was still wearing his hat and coat. The coat hung awkwardly on the thin, almost emaciated frame. The man put Ames's right arm over the support, ripped a length of tape, and wrapped it around Ames's wrist and the chair. He did this five more times, then did the same with the left arm and both ankles.

As he worked, their eyes met briefly. There was no heat in those eyes, only apathy, and the occasional amused curiosity at some sign of pain or discomfort. Ames had seen the look before, mostly on hulking men standing in the shadows of a room or sitting in the back seat of a car. Eyes that stared at everything and nothing, quiet and still—until they weren't. But this one was different. For one, he had none of the carefully developed physical menace. His face looked ravaged by fever, almost anemic. Too, he lacked the professionalism of the others. As he worked he lost some of his abstraction, became animated. He trembled at the flicker of pain across Ames's face. *This was not a job for Barber's companion*, thought Ames, *it was an obsession*. When he was finished, he stepped back, glanced at Barber, then back to Ames, his eyes hungry and distant.

Barber took the black silk bag, handing the other the gun. Stepping in front of Ames, he lifted the bag and held it just over Ames's head.

Leaning close, he whispered, "Nothing to say, smart ass?"

The smell of coffee and the fetid remains of Barber's breakfast spewed past the yellowed teeth, spraying Ames with bits of egg, toast, and spittle. Reflexively, Ames pulled back.

Barber laughed. "What did I tell you, Al?" he asked, turning slightly to the other man. Al didn't answer but continued to watch Ames with lethargic hunger. Barber turned back again to Ames. "You've got no idea how long I've been wanting to do this, asshole." Then he pulled the bag roughly over Ames's head.

Ames heard the sound of more tape being ripped from the spool. A moment later, someone pulled the bag tight, drawing the rough fabric down on his nose and mouth and making it difficult to breath. He heard the rip of more tape, then panicked as the tape was wrapped around the bottom end of the bag, sealing it under his chin. He struggled for breath now. The fabric filled his mouth and nose, his lungs were screaming for air. He lurched in the chair, raging against impending, inevitable asphyxiation.

It was the muffled sound of Barber's laughter that saved him. This wasn't the end, he told himself. They didn't want to kill. Not yet, not like this. He forced himself to relax, to take gentle, slow breaths and release them in similar fashion. There was room in the bag; the fabric was porous enough. He had simply panicked. After a time he was able to breath almost normally. It was never quite enough or comfortable, but he wasn't going to suffocate.

Barber stopped laughing.

There followed a long silence. Ames tried to remain still, but every sense of his body was tight with expectation. He sensed someone standing close to the chair, smelled again the bitter-stale aroma of coffee and bad breath.

"This is not going to end well for you," said Barber close to his ear.

Then nothing.

When the blow finally came—a moment, an eternity later—it fell like a sledge hammer, all the more frightening because he couldn't see it coming, would never be able to see anything coming under the bag. He felt his nose and cheek explode in pain. Shock carried him through the first moment, then the center of his face opened up like a nerve, a heavy throb of ever increasing agony. It was if someone were grinding a cold metal boot against his nose, pushing it deeper and deeper into the recess of his brain.

Before he could recover, he was hit again. His head snapped to the right, then rolled back like a child's spring toy. He felt something hot gush from his nose and over his lip, tasted his own blood. His ears were ringing. The bag started to clot, sticking to his nose and mouth, and now he really couldn't breathe. He bent over as far as his binding would let him, his stomach roiling. He shook his head from side to side in a desperate attempt to draw more air. A different sense of darkness, one that had nothing to do with the absence of light, engulfed him.

He made one last unsuccessful attempt to breathe, but only swallowed more of the bloody bag. His body arched savagely against the chair, his last thoughts before the darkness: *Barber. The Girl. Joel Anderson...the Rules.*

***

It was in the early, heady days of discovery and new direction.

It was just after he left the firm.

It was just before he met Barber, and made the Rules.

Haines had called him to his office downtown, for a chat. Ames was happy to attend. He wanted to talk to Haines, too. He was curious about a woman he met at Haines's party the night before.

Haines, even back then, looked every bit the man-of-means he was and would continue to be in all the years

Ames would know him. He was missing the tight beard, but already wearing the Gucci tailored suits, high end shirts, and expensive loafers of a man who didn't have to worry about money. Ames didn't carry the same glamour and prestige, though he too dressed in a suit. His hair was neatly trimmed, and in those days more pepper than salt in color. He was in some ways a softer, quieter version of Haines.

That day, Haines offered Ames a job. It was an offer that would change Ames's life.

The meeting started innocently enough. A friend, explained Haines, had need of someone with Ames's skills: a negotiator, an arbitrator. Ames would be compensated, of course. Was he interested?

Ames mulled the idea over. He had represented Haines, as a favor, in similar capacities, mostly conference meetings or confidential messaging service. Once, he brokered a deal between Haines and a competitor. Haines had been pleased by Ames's work. Ames suspected there was much more to the proceedings than what he saw, but he was comfortable playing a smaller, uninformed role. He knew, vaguely, that Haines might not always deal in the established, that is, legal, arenas. Haines had been very good about not putting Ames in the difficult position between choosing to participate in a crime or walking away.

Well, he thought, sitting across from Haines, *there was the luggage. That was borderline.*

Whenever Haines sent Ames on a trip, he would insist that Ames stay at a hotel of his choosing. Ames was to go out for a few hours, sometime before he went to the airport, and leave his luggage on the bed. Haines made it clear he was not to come back early.

Ames had no idea if he actually carried anything. He was never stopped at the airport—one of his selling points, according to Haines, his natural state of inconspicuousness. They never really talked about the arrangement with the hotel, beyond that first request. It was a condition that Ames insisted on and that Haines agreed to. Ames simply continued the practice as if it was his own idea.

But this was something different. This wasn't Haines, a known acquaintance, sending him on an errand. This was a genuine client, a stranger in fact. It wasn't clear yet that he was being asked, or would be asked, to do something illegal—the latter was as troubling a possibility to Ames as the actual act of breaking the law; he simply did not want to know on any level, before or after. But the possibility was suddenly very real that he would hear something he didn't want to hear.

He looked to Haines, slightly put off that he should put him in this position.

So far, there had been nothing ostensibly unlawful about his activities for Haines. At least, not that Ames was aware of.

But would the third party agree to such conditions? Would he play by the rules?

He asked Haines to tell him more…carefully.

Haines chuckled, knowing what Ames meant.

A man named Barber, he explained, had a problem. One of his hirelings, his head of security in fact, had run out, and apparently taken Barber's girl with him. Joel Anderson, the hireling, was now down in his ranch house in West Virginia. The girl wasn't.

"The thing is," said Haines, pausing to give Ames a knowing-look. "Barber is relatively new in my…circle. He wants to be a player, and he has the means, but we're not sure if he's…trustworthy. He's smart enough to know we don't like unnecessary publicity, though, and he's asked for our advice." Haines paused. "Joel Anderson *is* a known, and respected in our group. He's done work for me, as a matter of fact. I would like to…" Haines glanced at Ames, "keep Joel in the business. If possible."

"But Barber has other plans?" offered Ames.

"Perhaps. He's keeping his cards close to the chest." Haines frowned. "And as others are watching, and interested, I can't afford to be on the outside looking in on this one."

"Barber, these others, they know of your fondness for Anderson?"

Haines sighed. "I wouldn't call it fondness. Let's just say, appreciation. But yes, that's one of the complications. I would hate to see a man of his talents wasted. But I can't go stepping on Barber's toes either, not if he's going to be a player, which looks a possibility."

"What do you want me to do?"

"What *I* want you to do is talk Joel down from the ledge. Get him to come back. To me, if he likes. I want to hear his side of the story. With Barber involved, I'm sure there is another side. Tell him I guarantee his safe…." Haines stopped, smiled an apology. "I guarantee his continued employment while we sort this out." Haines lifted his hands in the air. "What Barber wants you to do is another matter. I don't think he cares one way or the other about Anderson's continued…employment. I think he just wants to cover his ass."

"And the girl?"

"The girl…" Haines looked thoughtfully to the edge of his desk, apparently a little surprised by the question. "The girl is not an issue. For me, at least. I think Barber would be interested in where she is, though. Might score you some points there."

"Do I have to meet Barber?"

Haines grimaced. "Now we're getting to the complicated part. What do you think?"

Ames guessed what the complication might be. "Is he paying the bill, or you?"

Haines nodded slowly. "Exactly. He is."

"Then, it is only fair I see him." Ames caught Haines's eye. "Report to him, as well?"

Haines didn't answer right away. "I'm of mixed mind on this, Wilson. I like having you to myself. But I also recognize that your talents are bigger than what I'm using you for now. You are going to be in demand. In fact, a few of my colleagues have already mentioned as much. You going to see Barber—that will change things, for both of us."

He sighed, bounced his fingertips off each other, and considered Ames. "So, we've come to a crossroads in our little relationship. Either I make you officially mine, thus eliminating some of your value as a true neutral, or I have to let you go. There are things to consider on both sides. I'm starting to draw some attention now, so there's that. If you work for me—officially—you'll draw some of that attention as well." He gave Ames a curious stare. "On the other hand, I can make you a very rich man."

He leaned back, opened his hands. "So there it is. We've been dancing around this for some time, Wilson. Do you want to be in this life, or not?"

The question hung in the air. Ames was not sure how to answer it, or even if he should. He looked to the floor. It occurred to him that there was another possibility.

He had been thinking about this very situation, ever since that first blind flight with who-knew-what in his luggage, if anything. He had been surprised at how calm he'd been on the airplane, even through the security check. He knew there was a possibility that something illegal was in his luggage, something that could put him away for a long time. He knew, too, that his claim to ignorance was thin at best. Ignorance was no excuse for the law.

But all through the flight he had sat calmly, doodling a castle on the edge of his planner calendar, without, apparently, a care in the world. As he looked at the sketch while waiting to debark, he wondered why he chose that particular subject, why he cared so much for the way the lines in the castle tower worked, why he wanted to add a bit of shadow near the base. Why this, and not his problematic luggage, was the focus of his attention.

He thought about the castle all the way through check out. And later, when he laid the bag out on his hotel bed, unopened of course, and called an answering machine service. He thought about that shadowed base as he told the service he would be out for a few hours, but if anyone needed to get in touch with him, here was the room number he could be reached at. Then he gave a time that he would be back. He finished the sketch in a coffee shop. When he returned to his room at the scheduled time, his luggage was sitting on the bed just as he left it.

And that was that.

When he eventually received his "consultancy fee" from Haines, a surprisingly large figure, he began to think of bigger possibilities. But even then he was thinking about the sketch.

And now, as he considered expanding his role with the likes of Haines, of taking on new risks and possibilities, he thought about his next subject, the next castle.

He looked up from the floor. "I'll see Barber."

Haines cocked his head in surprise. "Great. I'll arrange the meeting. Before that, I'll have one of my men give you an orientation. You are now, officially, on my payroll. Frankly, I'm surprised, Wilson. I'd never imagined you'd want this kind of..."

"No," interrupted Ames. "No. I don't want to join your organization."

The smile fell from Haines's face. "I don't understand."

"I want the work, but I want to be an independent operator."

"You want to be a boss? In the business?" Haines looked at him incredulously.

"No. Not a boss. Not even in the business."

Haines shook his head in confusion. "I really don't understand."

"I'll be a gun for hire. Sorry, bad choice of words. A specialist. A consultant who works…" he searched for a word, "difficult situations."

Haines raised his head in understanding. "Ah, I see. No, Wilson. I'm afraid it is you that doesn't understand. This business doesn't have consultants. We don't use them. Goes against the whole principle, you see? It is too dangerous. For everyone." He looked meaningfully at Ames. "Too, on your own, you'll have no one to support you if things get nasty. And it always, eventually, gets nasty."

"Hear me out," said Ames, softly. And then he proceeded to explain the role he visualized in more detail.

When he was done, Haines only stared. Then he shook his head. "I don't know, Wilson." He frowned, looking down at his desk, shook his head again. "You know, to even have a chance at this you'll have to walk away from me. You can't be mine, or no one will trust you. You really will be out on your own."

"I know."

"You also understand that this…role…is not exactly innocent. You will be working with a certain criminal element."

"Please don't say that again," said Ames flatly. "I'm sure we are not talking about the same thing."

Haines snorted, looked at Ames as if he were insulted. "I know we play our little game of denial with your luggage, but…"

"What game?" insisted Ames, his face a mask of naiveté. "I *know* that I alert you to times you can reach me, and when I will be out. But that's just for communication purposes. Right?"

Haines blinked around an incredulous smile. "Wilson, you can't pretend…"

"I'm not pretending anything, Geoff. I'm not assuming anything either. This is how it will have to be— if it is going to work. You have to trust that I know nothing of your business specifics. You have to trust that if asked, I have deniability. That's how I can work for you, for the others. I can be a neutral, because I will be genuinely discrete. I will be safe, because I will know nothing. I'll deal in abstracts."

Haines was shaking his head again. "We don't always deal in abstraction. Not in this line of work. Sometimes you have to deliver the message at the end of a gun."

"I'll assume that was a metaphor."

Haines laughed. "How long can you keep that up, Wilson? You'll go crazy trying to ignore what's going on, what you're seeing. And eventually, the authorities will pull you in—if you work with my crowd, that's inevitable. What will you say to them? '*I didn't know*.'" He paused again. "But that's not the only danger. One of my colleagues might nervous about the little man with all that inside knowledge, and decide to clean up a loose end."

"I can do this, Geoff. Trust me."

Haines stared at him, took a deep breath. "I think it's a mistake." He chewed his lip. "But I can see you're determined to try. I think we're both being a bit naïve."

Both men stared in opposite directions, each lost in his own thought. When Haines finally spoke, his voice had lost some of its casual tone. "Okay. I'll give Barber your number. I can put a word of recommendation in, as well. That's all right, isn't it? Or is that against your rules?"

Rules, thought Ames. *Is that what I'm doing, making rules?*

"A recommendation would be most appreciated," he said. "I don't mind people knowing you value my services. But don't give him my home number, or name. For now. I'll call you a little later with a number. I'm going to set up a legitimate consultancy operation."

"You've been thinking about this for some time, haven't you?"

Ames shrugged. Then, after the slightest hesitation, "Geoff, I'd like to stop the luggage trips, too."

Haines eyes narrowed.

"I've got to be legitimately neutral," insisted Ames. "I can't take the risk that someone thinks you own me."

He watched Haines take this in, saw the change in his expression and bearing. Gone now was the friendly, playboy banter of their college days where they met. For the briefest of moments Ames caught a glimpse of Haines and his underworld ethos.

"Okay, Wilson," said this other Haines, one Ames hardly recognized, one that he had long suspected existed, but hoped never to really see. "Just remember, you asked for this."

Ames nodded, a slight tremor running down his back.

"Call soon with that number," said Haines. He stood up, then stopped and sat back down. "I just remembered, you had something you wanted to ask me?"

For the first and practically only time since the two men met, Ames blushed. "That girl from the other night," he said. "Cynthia."

A slow grin crossed Haines's face. "Yes?"

"I wonder if you know how I can reach her."

"As a matter of fact, I do." Haines reached for his rolodex. He found a number, wrote it down on a piece of paper and handed the paper to Ames. His eyes were full; with irony or mirth, Ames couldn't say.

"She asked about you, you know," said Haines, grinning, some of the old charm creeping back in his voice. "Wanted to know who my polished friend was. I never really noticed before, but you do clean up well, Wilson."

Ames ignored that, put the number in his pocket.

"I've known Cynthia for some time now," continued Haines, the smile growing larger. "She's a bit high-maintenance, Wilson. And expensive." Ames frowned, the question on his face. Haines waved it off. "Oh, no. Nothing like that. She's not professional. Just old-fashioned expensive."

"Thanks for the warning."

Haines chuckled. "I don't know what's more foolish: Barber, or Cynthia. Good luck man."

Ames created the *Suadela Consulting Agency*, set up his own answering service, and left his new work number with Haines. The next day, Barber called and left a message. Ames returned his call, and they arranged a meeting. After the call, Ames went for a drive, his mind racing, his nerves dancing. He was excited, and conflicted.

He stopped in a mall, walked through the consumer circus. He had no real plans or intentions, and little awareness for what he passed. Then a craft shop caught his eye. He walked in and looked through the art supplies, but didn't see anything he liked. He walked on until he came to a high-end stationary store. He bought a silver case notebook with blank, cream white pages, something that could fit in his pocket. He also bought two mechanical pencils. He discovered he had choices as to the color of lead. After a few moments of reflection and experimentation, he chose a dark blue. He didn't let the clerk bag the items, but put them in his coat pocket.

He found a coffee shop, ordered a tall mocha, and sat at a corner table. He opened the notebook and sketched a blue castle in an open field, with one lonely cloud to mark the skyline. He drew each line carefully, as straight and true as he could manage by hand. When he was finished, he looked at his work. There was something off. The castle looked too…what was the word? Modern? Flat? Bare? He couldn't say. He would come back to it later. He closed the notebook, put it in his jacket pocket again, along with the pencils, and finished his coffee. He was oddly calm again.

He walked to a public pay phone and called the number Haines had given him. Cynthia picked up on the second ring. Yes, she remembered him from the party. Yes, Haines had told her he might call. Friday night? Could they make it Saturday? She had plans Friday. Saturday it was.

He drove home, his mind still racing, his nerves dancing again. But this time, he wasn't conflicted.

He met Barber in a work trailer near a construction site. It was Barber's idea. At first, Barber wanted to meet at a restaurant, but Ames said that wasn't convenient. In truth, he was worried about being overheard, but he didn't tell Barber that. Barber got a little short, and insisted they meet on his terms, not Ames's. Ames, surprised at the reaction, agreed to a different time and place to get Barber off the phone as quickly as possible. Thus, the work trailer.

It was typical of construction site office space everywhere: narrow, cluttered, and smelling of moldy carpet and sour sweat. Barber was waiting behind an old steel desk, his legs stretched out across the top. He was dressed in a mustard yellow short-sleeve shirt, with argyle socks poking from his cuffed brown trousers. Another man, in a black t-shirt two sizes too small and smelling of onions, stood just behind and to the left of him.

Ames was dressed in a herringbone suit, purchased new for his inaugural session. He wore an ash colored tie with a pearl stick pin, white oxford shirt, black belt, and freshly polished shoes. He took in the smoke stained walls and threadbare carpet, the pile of rags along the metal cabinets, the overflowing tin ashtrays that seem to infest open spaces like some kind of fungus or mushroom, and regretted his choice of wardrobe. He tried to stand as small and still as possible, as if in this way the grime would overlook him.

Barber set his legs down, his right knee bouncing in fidgets as he sat up and crossed his thin arms on the desk. The loose brown curls on his head looked out of place. *Hair more fitting for a child or woman*, thought Ames. He got another whiff of onions when the man in the small shirt quietly belched.

Barber reached in his shirt pocket for a pack of cigarettes, the box crushed and nearly empty. He lit one, looked as if he were thinking about offering one to Ames, and then put it back in his pocket.

"So here's what I want," he said. "Anderson's holed up in his cabin. Refuses to come out."

Ames took a seat in the rickety chair across from the desk. Barber looked surprised, then said, "Oh, yeah. Take a seat. Anyway, I need to know where that girl is.

You tell that son-of-a-bitch he don't tell me, I'm gonna have Pete here…"

"Just a minute," said Ames, raising a hand slowly. "I want to set some ground rules first about why I am here, and what I can do."

Another look of surprise, this one mixed with anger, crossed Barber's face. Again, he checked himself. "What are you talking about?"

"I know our mutual acquaintance spoke with you…" started Ames.

"Haines," interrupted Barber around his cigarette.

"This is one of the things I want to make perfectly clear," said Ames calmly. "No names. I'm here as a consultant, for a *business*," Ames let the word hang hard in the air, "arbitration. I am a totally neutral party. I will represent your position, and listen to the other party's…"

"My *position*? Other party? What the hell are you talking about?"

"Sir, if you will allow me just a moment to explain."

Barber looked around to the man in the corner, nodded at Ames. "You hear this shit? What the hell did Haines send me?"

"A professional," said Ames. "One who will be able to represent you with no risk, for anyone. I will be able to do this because I will only be acting as a neutral arbitrator. I will not know the details of your business, or you personally. I am here to negotiate, as I understand it, a conflict of interest between party one," Ames nodded to Barber, "and another party. As I understand it," he repeated carefully, "the second party has currently taken an unauthorized leave of absence. I am tasked with bringing that party to the table, to resolve this issue."

Barber seemed to consider this, one eye closed up against the smoke from his cigarette, a wry twist to his mouth. "Okay…Mr. Professional." He winked at the big man beside him. "But you left one thing out. I want the girl back. That's most important."

Ames nodded. "I will do my best to facilitate any communication in that regard."

Barber frowned, stabbed his cigarette out in a tin ashtray, upsetting the ash already in there. "You sure Haines sent you?"

Ames stifled a frown. "To be more exact, he recommended me. I'm here by your request."

Barber's eyes narrowed to two suspicious lines. "But you report back to Haines."

"I don't work for Haines, if that's what you mean. I am a consultant."

"So you keep saying." Barber lit another cigarette, his knee bouncing again like a piston as he considered Ames. He blew the smoke in Ames's face. "I want the girl," he said bluntly. "And I want Anderson." He waved off Ames's reaction to the name with a snarl. "Get it straight, Mr. Wilson Ames. Yeah, I know *your* name, too. That's what I want. And if I don't get it, there'll be hell to pay."

Ames decided there was nothing more to be said. If anything, too much was out in the open. He stood up, offered his hand, which Barber ignored. He left.

He took a taxi back home, made a drink and sat in his living room in the dark. He was disappointed. Disappointed in the meeting. Disappointed in himself. Everything went wrong. Where had he lost control?

I never had it, he thought. *Barber didn't see me as something to value, respect, or fear. He didn't see me at all.*

Haines was right. This wouldn't work. He was just a tool. He'd be lucky if Barber didn't kill hill him and this Anderson both. What was to stop him? Haines? No. That bridge, if not burned, was closed. Ames had seen to that.

He took a sip of his drink, searching for a silver lining to the cloud, or at least a way out. The best he could come up with was a straw's chance of getting out altogether. He plotted the possible directions and responses for a time, going over contingencies, risks, counter-proposals, until he finally had a general plan. It might work.

But he would be walking away, once and for all. That left a bitter taste in his mouth. All that possibility, thrown away.

Cynthia, he had thought, still searching for silver linings. He had that, at least, to look forward to. That was a possibility of a different nature. If he survived.

He finished the drink, rattled what was left of the cubes, stood and carried the glass to the kitchen sink. He checked to make sure his doors were locked, then climbed upstairs for a shower and bed.

Tomorrow, he thought, staring up through the dark at the ceiling. *I'll fly to Anderson's home tomorrow, manage the situation in the shortest, practical way possible, and hopefully come home in one piece—and quit what I never should have started. Then, if I'm lucky, I'll be forgotten. Then I find a real job. One with a pension, and coffee breaks, and the slow, inevitable race to the bottom. But one that comes with a good chance of seeing tomorrow.*

Anderson was holed up, as advertised. His ranch house was up against the edge of a mountain shelf, the back overlooking a valley. There was literally nothing around the front but rocks and grass and brush for miles in all directions. He would see anything coming up the one dirt road to the house long before it got there. The back was a straight drop down for a hundred feet. There was nothing coming from that direction either, unless you were a goat.

Ames drove up the dirt road in a rented car. Anderson didn't have a listing for a phone of any kind, so he couldn't call ahead. The road ended at a heavy gate. The gate was in a fence encircled the last two hundred yards to the house. There was a call box on a post next to the gate.

Ames pressed the call button, getting a burst of static, but no answer. He pressed it again, held it down, and said, "My name is Wilson Ames, Mr. Anderson. Mr. Haines sent me. Can I come up? I'm alone."

There was a long pause, then the gate made a clicking noise and opened up. Ames drove through.

The ranch house was one story, with a full length porch and awning across the front. There was a swing on the far end of the porch, and a small barbeque grill just off to the side of the house. All the windows were boarded up. The front door was obviously new. It looked like something that belonged in a bank.

Ames parked just in front of the porch, his window down, both hands on the wheel. He climbed slowly from the car. Somewhere inside the house dogs were barking. Big dogs. The air was chilly, despite the season, but Ames decided to leave his suit jacket in the car anyway. He was careful to hold his notepad and pencils up so they could be seen clearly in his hand for what they were. All his movements were slow and deliberate.

He closed the door, and walked to the front door, his tie blowing in a mountain breeze. He stopped just in front of the door, the dogs growing more frantic. A heavy voice, partially muffled by the closed door, silenced them. Then the door opened a fraction.

"Turn around," said a man from the shadows.

Ames turned slowly around.

"Give me your wallet."

Ames blinked in surprise, then handed his wallet to the large, freckled hand that came out of the shadows.

One of the dogs started up again, but the voice told it to be quiet. Ames saw one, two, three different snouts poking in and out of the open space between the frame and door.

There was a moment while the man presumably went through the wallet.

"Now, what you're carrying."

Ames handed him the notepad, which had the mechanical pencils clipped in front.

Another pause. Then, "Empty your pockets. Turn them out. All of them."

Ames did this, putting his money clip on the porch.

"Get back now!" snarled the voice inside.

For a brief, startled moment, Ames thought the man was speaking to him. Then he heard the click of heavy nails retreating against a wood floor and a snort of canine disproval.

The door swung open and Joel Anderson stood back and to the side, holding back the biggest dog Ames had ever seen.

"It's all right," said Anderson, his voice, like sandpaper run over a grainy board. "Baron won't hurt you. Unless I tell him to."

Baron, the dog straining under Anderson's tight grip, didn't look to Ames as if it understood the terms.

"Come on in now, Mr. Ames," said Anderson, looking past Ames's shoulder, but still keeping to the shadows.

Ames stepped through the door, and Baron managed to put a quick, wet nose against his crotch before Anderson shut the door and pushed him aside.

"Baron! Down!" he barked at the dog. The dog retreated half a step, its big brown and black eyes staring at Ames. Two more dogs, only slightly smaller than Baron, were standing off to the right, watching Ames with much the same anticipation.

Ames turned back to his host, such as he was. Anderson was a big, tall man, with short-cropped, carrot colored hair and a full, almost colorless moustache. He was heavy in the neck, jowl and belly, though it was the kind of heavy natural to some big men. Ames suspected Anderson was hard to fit for clothes. His hands were freckled, the freckles almost pink against the skin. The fingers were scarred with time and use, the knuckles swollen and slightly red, like an old boxer's. He wore a thin, button down, long sleeve shirt, the cuffs unbuttoned and hanging open around two massive wrists. His jeans were cuffed at the bottom over a pair of hiking boots.

Ames turned a little more and saw a number of closed circuit screens by the door, each showing different parts of the land around them, including two views of the gate and one even further down the road.

"Let's go in back," said Anderson. The big man nodded for him to follow, then led Ames through the hall. "Something to drink?" asked Anderson as they walked. "I'm afraid all I have is whiskey and water."

"No. Thank you."

The back room had more screens, with more angles of the property and house. There were speakers, too, from which could be heard an orchestra of insect life and the occasional airplane. Baron followed them in the room and squatted by Anderson, who took a seat in a worn but comfortable looking armchair. The other dogs remained in the foyer near the door. Anderson waved Ames to another, smaller chair across from him.

The room was long and narrow, running most of the length of the house, and made of heavy pine. In addition to the closed circuit screens, speakers, and furniture, there was a mattress on the floor, and a worktable. On the table was a small gas stove heating something in an aluminum pot. Close to Anderson, on a slightly smaller coffee table, were two automatics, a rifle, and stacks of ammunition.

There was also a box under the table with what looked like small black pineapples. A shotgun was leaning against the other side of Anderson's chair in easy reach.

The room smelled of dog, man, pine, and canned food. But it was surprisingly tolerable for all the closed space, time invested, and natural element. Ames saw a tightly lidded trash can in the corner, and a candle by the stove. Everything, including the surveillance equipment and wires, was neatly arranged. The hardwood floor looked to be recently swept and mopped. There was no dust on Ames's chair, or anywhere else he looked.

"I'd offer you some stew," said Anderson. "But it's poor fair. Just can goods here. Haven't had a guest in a while. Sorry."

Ames smiled. "That's quite all right. I ate before I got here."

Baron took this moment to sprawl out on his belly, looking occasionally to Anderson, his tongue rolling out to one side of his panting mouth. He sounded like a giant bellow.

"I know you," said Anderson, reaching down to rub the dog's ear between his fingers.

Ames could not have been more surprised.

"Well, I heard about you," said Anderson, making a gesture with his hand. "I make it my business to know as much as I can about these things. Someone mentioned a new boy working for Haines. Not muscle, not a suit. A carrier or lawyer of some kind, quiet, but smart. You were on the radar, but just barely. Lot of mystery around you. I looked you up." His moustache dipped on one end while he chewed his lip for a time. "Not much to find. A very normal, very uninteresting life. No scandals. No hidden pockets of money—least not that I could find. No background to speak of at all. I followed you for a time just to be sure." He chuckled at Ames's surprise. "I'm very good at that kind of thing, Mr. Ames. Anyway, I didn't see anything different from what I already knew. To be honest, you don't seem the type for this business."

"I'm not in the business, really," explained Ames. Then, maybe because of the presence of so much surveillance, or maybe because he was determined to give his consultancy one last chance, he insisted, "I'm *not* in the business. I'd appreciate if you'd keep that in mind while we talk. I don't want to know any specifics. For your safety, as much as mine."

Anderson looked at him, grunted. He had a strong face, with clear cheek bones and deep eye cavities. His eyebrows, like his moustache, were nearly colorless, but the ridges of brow were round and heavy. It was difficult to see the color of his eyes, but Ames thought they might be green.

"So, Haines sent you here," said Anderson. He frowned as Ames hesitated. "Or was it someone else?" His hand dropped over the armrest, closer to the shotgun.

Ames tried to remain calm, and send calmness across the room. Baron lifted his head slightly. "I'm technically here on Barber's account."

The big hand rested now on the barrel of the gun. Baron growled lightly.

Ames took a deep breath, let it out quickly. "It's difficult to explain."

"Try me."

Ames noticed that Anderson kept one eye and ear on the screens and speakers while they talked.

"I assure you," said Ames. "I'm alone."

"Uh-huh."

"I know you have no reason to trust me." Ames shifted in his seat, trying to remember his plan. "I do know Haines. He said to tell you he'll vouch for your continued employment." He let that hang in the air for a moment. "You can report directly to him."

"And Barber?"

Ames looked to the shadowed irises. They *were* green, and they were hanging fire now. He shook his head.

The gesture was made without conscious deliberation. Instinct, perhaps. Instinct and the man across from him. A man that could control a monster like Baron with only his voice. A man who holed up against the likes of Barbers for reasons Ames did not know, but suspected he would agree with. A man who ate beef stew out of can, and looked like a cousin to a Yeti. A man who kept a clean house and offered him a drink. A man who looked like he already knew the answer to the question anyway.

And so much for my plan to stay uninvolved, he thought.

Originally he planned to leave Barber out of the matter altogether, focus on Haines's offer of safety and get Anderson to meet with him. At that point, he hoped to hand the matter over to Haines and remove himself from the equation. Let Haines deal with Barber directly.

But now he knew that would never fly. Anderson would know there was more to it than that. Ames knew that as sure as he knew his own strengths and weaknesses. Anderson would never agree to go to Haines without dealing with the matter of Barber first.

Ames broke what would later become one his most firm rules. Because the rule had yet to be made. Because it as early days. Because it was Anderson—and Anderson already knew the answer.

"Barber, I do not trust."

Anderson nodded once, a sharp downward thrust of his heavy jowl. "That's a good start." He climbed to his feet. "I'll get those drinks now. Then we'll talk."

It went something like this, explained Anderson. He had been in the Army, had a little trouble, was discharged, and then kicked around in the hot spots for a time with the mercenaries. Eventually, he came back state-side. There he found his skill sets were most appreciated with a certain group that liked to operate off official books. He hooked on with one of these and soon made a reputation for himself in the private security business.

Things happened. Things, said Anderson, which were out of his control. His employer went away—for tax evasion. Anderson found a new employer. That didn't work out either. This time the cause was a little more permanent. His employer took his own life. Anderson began to see this line of work was a bit unstable. He started hiring himself out to projects instead of individuals. Bigger payoffs and less investment. Build the nest egg, and retire.

Barber was to be one of those projects. It was a simple affair. Barber needed someone to train his security staff. Right up Anderson's alley. He didn't particularly care for Barber, but he didn't see why that shouldn't let him take his money.

"And then I met Beth," said Anderson.

They were sitting in their chairs, sipping Anderson's whiskey and water. Baron was on the floor next to Anderson, his eyes closed and his head on his paws.

"You see her kind all the time around these men," said Anderson. "Beautiful but broken. As empty as a pocket, and willing to find anyone, anywhere to make them feel like they finally arrived, they won. Men like Barber learn to spot them early on. They throw the money at them, the power. The lucky ones run away. The others fall like bricks. They last for a time. Then the new model moves in and they're in the way. Then they take another kind of fall. They don't bounce back very well. They haven't had the training for it. Some don't bounce back at all." Anderson took a long drink and looked away.

"Beth was no different than any of the rest," he continued. "But for one thing." He looked to Ames, hesitated. "Even now it is hard to say." He blushed. "Believe it or not, she cared for me." He gave Ames a quick up-down glance. "Well, at least that's what she said. God knows why. Not for my looks, I'm sure." He looked again to Ames, shrugged.

"It happens," said Ames.

"I guess it does. We started talking one day, made each other laugh, found we liked it and kept finding reasons to do it again." He finished his drink. "I'm not going to say much more about that." He made another drink, offered more to Ames, who shook it off.

"Anyway, Barber found out." He looked at the floor, his eyes holding fire. "I'm damn good at my job, and you can bet your ass I was careful about this. I was biding my time until I could figure a way out, and I was close, but….."

He shook his head. "Beth, well she wasn't built to lie, or even carry a secret. I tried to warn her, tried to get her to find reasons to not see him, to stay away until I could arrange things." He shrugged. "Anyway, he found out. Barber. He lit into her good when he got her alone. I think he had similar plans or worse for me. But I had taken steps to know if something like that was up. I do that with all my work. Always have a cover-your-ass plan, Mr. Ames. Always be ready for the floor to fall out from under." He took another long sip. "I got Beth out of there. Right under his nose. I should have put a bullet in his head, but I wanted to make sure Beth was all right first." He looked to Ames. "And she is. And will continue to be, because I hid her where he'll never find her. She's going to have a new life now. I saw to it she has the means."

"How did you leave it with her?"

For a moment, Ames thought he crossed a line. Anderson glared at him, and Baron lifted his head.

But then, "I told her the only way this works is we go our separate ways and never try to see each other again."

"You don't think she'll try to find you anyway?"

The big man shrugged, tried to smile. "I said she liked me. I didn't say she fell in love. I'll be that long, lost, last good friend. She'll move on. Probably already has."

Ames looked to his drink. "What now? What do you want me to tell Haines?"

Anderson chewed his moustache. "I'm through with that life. I'm out."

"And Barber?"

"He can come by any time he likes."

Ames hesitated. "He strikes me as the kind of person who will stop at nothing to get what he wants."

Anderson laughed. "I hope he tries." He looked to the guns and the cameras, reached down and rubbed Baron's head playfully.

Ames finished his drink, looked for a place to put it down.

"I'll take it," said Anderson, standing up. He put the glass down on the work table next to the bottle and the guns.

"Well, I guess I should be on my way," said Ames.

"What will you tell Barber?"

Ames looked to the floor as if thinking about his answer. "I will tell him," he said, carefully, "that the employee wishes to remain retired."

Anderson chuckled. "And the girl?"

"The girl is a personal matter between Barber and her. I don't know anything about the girl." Ames shrugged. "Which is true."

"Barber is not going to be happy."

"No. Probably not."

"He has a tendency to shoot the messenger. I've seen him do it."

Ames looked to the floor again. "That would be very unfortunate."

Anderson lifted the heavy ridges in surprise, then dropped them again as if guessing a secret. "Haines," he said flatly.

Ames ignored this. It was too complicated to explain, and of little importance to Anderson anyway.

Anderson stuck out one of his massive hands. "Good luck to you, Mr. Ames."

Ames shook the hand. "And to you, too, Mr. Anderson."

When he returned, he went straight home. He had five messages on his new answering service demanding he call immediately. All from Barber. All increasingly hostile. He erased them. He took a long shower and went to bed.

The next day he called Haines and arranged for a meeting for later that afternoon.

"Well, Wilson," said Haines, "I've been getting calls from our mutual acquaintance. He's waiting for your report."

"I wanted to talk to you first."

Haines gave him an appraising look. "Go ahead."

"Anderson won't come in."

"I know."

Ames blinked in surprise.

"Joel Anderson was killed last night," explained Haines. "About the time you were catching your flight home. They found his body at the bottom of that big drop. Not a pretty body that. Lots of missing pieces."

"I don't remember a backdoor," said Ames.

"He didn't have one."

Ames felt the floor fall out from under him, remembered Anderson's advice. Dead Anderson. But not, evidently, before someone had their way with him. Did that mean Barber knew where the girl was? No, he didn't think so. Hence, the insistent messages on his service. Did that mean he thought Ames knew where the girl was? Would he believe Ames if he said he didn't?

He looked to Haines.

"Wilson, I've never seen you so upset."

"I think I made a mistake."

"With Barber?"

"Yes. Can you help me?"

Haines pursed his lips, his eyes continuing to measure Ames with ironic undertones. *He knew it would come to this*, thought Ames. He knew when he heard about Anderson. *No*, he thought again, *before that. He knew when I walked out his door last time*.

"I'm not sure that's a good idea," said Haines slowly. "If you really want to be on your own, then you need to report to the one who hires you." He paused deliberately. "Or have you changed your mind, and want to work for me."

Ames looked to the ceiling, then back to Haines. It was time. He had been thinking about this scene, this conversation, ever since he left Anderson's. The one last desperate chance. The rules.

"I haven't changed my mind," he said slowly. "I want to be independent. But I'm learning that might be more difficult than I thought."

"I don't want to say I told you so…"

"But you could," agreed Ames. "Listen, Geoff. I've been thinking about this on the flight back, and most of the night. I get your point, but I can't live the…life. I can't do that. I won't be good at it. For you, or anyone. I have to have at least a semblance of autonomy. I can't have that if I work for you, and we both know it."

"So go report to Barber and collect your fee." Haines's expression was as flat as his voice.

Here's another man who knows the answers to the questions before they are asked, thought Ames. He brushed a hand across his knee. *Except, he's wrong this time. I know the questions, too, and the answers. All of them.*

"I'm not sure I'll make it back from my meeting with Barber," he said matter-of-factly. "In fact, I know I won't."

"Ah," said Haines, pursing his lips, but obviously not surprised. "I see." He tapped his finger on the desk. "That does complicate things." He frowned at Ames. "I warned you, Wilson."

"I know."

"This *is* the life, you know."

Ames hung his head. "I know."

"So, we're at that part of the movie," said Haines, again with that knowing smile. "Are you going to ask me like a man, or bitch like a funeral director?"

Ames was staring at the floor as if searching for answers, or courage, but he already knew what he was going to say. "Don't get mad, Geoff, but I'm not going to ask."

Haines did grow mad, a flicker of mounting frustration across that otherwise placid profile. When he spoke, it was with a slight edge now, a warning. "I like you, Wilson. I don't want to see something happen to you. But, I'm not going to act out of the goodness of my heart. This is business."

"That's just it," said Ames, smoothing out a wrinkle on his pants leg. "You run a business." His voice was calm, his eye contact deliberate but natural. "Are you sure someone like Barber should be a part of that?"

"You want me to get rid of Barber for you?" asked Haines with an incredulous chuckle.

"No," said Ames with an answering smile. "I would never say that. Don't even joke about that, Geoff."

Haines looked uncomfortable, his face marked now by lines of suspicion, even regret.

He's wondering if I'm a mistake, thought Ames. Maybe I am. But I'm an opportunity as well. I have to make him see that.

"No," repeated Ames, lifting his hand delicately off his knee in a gesture of gentle correction. "I'm just offering you, my original client—you'll recall you did ask me to report on the Anderson project as well—I'm just offering a full and comprehensive report. You mentioned earlier that Barber wanted to break into the business at your level. In my professional opinion, I do not believe that Barber would be an asset to you in that regard. In fact, I believe he would be a risk. A risk of the worse sort…for someone in your business."

Haines stared at Ames without saying a word. Slowly he leaned back in his chair, his eyes never leaving Ames. "In your professional opinion," he said, raising a wry eyebrow. "You and all your vast experience in *my* business. Barber's business, too, for that matter."

Ames folded his hands together, met Haines's eyes. "Let me tell you more about my meeting with Anderson."

"Not Barber?"

"No. You asked me to talk Anderson back into the fold. I didn't do that. I didn't even try." He watched the frown deepen on Haines's face. "That's not really what I do. I don't talk people into things…"

"You could have fooled me."

"What I do is present a case," continued Ames, ignoring the jibe. "An objective. The best case scenario. I lay things out for people in a way that lets them see things clearly, or maybe in a new light, or maybe for the first time. I don't come at things completely neutral of course—I'm not sure there is such a thing, anywhere. But I come damn close. I can, and do on occasion, represent an interest, maybe yours if you hire me, and I try to get the other side to see your point. But even then I'm open to the other side's position. I have to be, or it won't work. Negotiations break down if no one is truly open, listening."

"Wilson, you said this before. Or something like it."

"Please, Geoff. Let me finish."

The other waved him on, his mouth a tight line of impatience.

I have to reach him, thought Ames. *Haines, of all people, has to understand this.*

"I didn't try to talk Anderson back because I knew he wouldn't come. He had already made up his mind. He had already considered every angle I could present. He knew the risk, the likelihood that things might…end the way they did, but he was prepared to take that risk. There was no point in going on."

"You knew this," said Haines, his voice touched with sarcasm. "How did you know, Wilson?"

Ames blinked, looked to his hands. "That I don't know. Experience. Instinct. Talent. All of the above. I just know when I can push, when I have to pull, when something is open—even just a little—and when it doesn't matter what I say. You said once yourself I have a way of getting people to do what I want. That's not exactly true. I have a way of knowing when and how I can get results, and when I can't. There's a difference."

"And what kind of result do you think you're getting now?"

"You're still listening," answered Ames. "That's all I know."

The other frowned, then shrugged, "Go on."

"I knew Anderson was going to do things his way. Just like I know Barber is not a good fit for you, or the others."

"So, what you're telling me is you failed with Anderson, and now you want me to save your ass with Barber."

"No," countered Ames. "I didn't fail." He ignored Haines scowl. "I delivered the opportunity to Anderson. I assessed it would not be accepted. There was never going to be another context or condition with Anderson. He saw to that with the girl."

"The girl? What does she have to do with this?"

Ames shrugged. "Nothing, everything. She was a condition Anderson put on himself. She was his bottom line. I saw that. He knew I would see that. That's one of the reasons he told me the story."

"You know where the girl is?"

"I don't. But that's not important, Geoff. What's important, to you, is that Anderson would not come back. Ever. I am reporting to you that result. You can trust it is an accurate assessment, even if it isn't the answer you want."

"So?"

"So, that's what I can offer you. You can act now on that information."

Again Haines scowled. "Oh, come on, Wilson. I knew that before you walked in the door."

"No. You knew Anderson was dead. You didn't know he would never come back to the life. You didn't know Barber was the reason for that."

Haines leaned back in his chair. "All that may be true, but it doesn't change the fact your…" He searched for the right word. "Proposal won't work. You can't go it alone, Wilson. You have to report to someone. That's the lesson in Barber."

The lesson you wanted me to learn, thought Ames.

"My mistake was saying yes to Barber," said Ames. "My mistake was not insisting on the rules beforehand."

"Rules?"

"You said it yourself," said Ames. "The last time we met. There has to be rules."

"I said no such thing."

"No. But that's what I'm taking out of all this. I need guidelines, rules, or it won't work."

"Wilson, be realistic. You can't expect people to play by your rules."

"I can if it is in their best interest."

Haines stared a moment at Ames, his eyes crinkled in concentration and impatience.

"At least consider the opportunity," said Ames, shifting in his seat, leaning forward. "Geoff, I'm in a unique position to help you and your partners in a way no one else can. I know, without knowing. I'm safe, unattached, but not ignorant." He let his eyes carry the rest of the message. "I can be that set of ears, eyes, and mind that operates on multiple levels, yet remains safe enough to use without fear. By letting me represent positions, not details, by keeping me out of the details altogether, operating as an independent, I can be that person in the room that does not have to please anyone, or answer to anyone, but can truly arbitrate a situation fairly, or at least as productively as possible. It happens all the time in real world politics and business, why not yours?"

Haines blinked, the eyes losing some of their heat.

"I won't always get the results you want," continued Ames, "but no one ever does. Right now when that happens, you're left with acrimony. That leads to chaos, loss. Am I right?"

"We're not children, but yes, sometimes things get personal, and messy. Money, and other things, are lost."

"I can be an answer to that. I'll be the neutral ground, the demilitarized zone for you to talk through, negotiate with each other, knowing you're getting at least one impartial set of ears. If nothing else, I'll minimize the loss due to misunderstanding. Your friends will come to see I have that skill set. They'll come to see my value." He put his hands together on his lap. "And most importantly, I'll also know how, and where, and when to look the other way. When to stay out of the room, when to walk away. The rules will help in that way, as well. In fact, they become just as important to you as to me. By limiting my exposure, I enable my value. You won't fear an indiscretion, because I'll have nothing to be indiscrete about."

For a long time nobody spoke. The only sound was of Haines breathing slowly through his nose.

"Wait here," said Haines finally. And he left the room.

Ames took out his notepad and mechanical pencil. He held the pencil over the sketch for a long time, then made one quick mark near the base of the castle, a little vine along the stone—or was it a crack?

When Haines came back he sat in the chair without a word, stared at his desk for a full minute. "They'll meet you," he said, finally, looking up at Ames. "My partners. You lay it out for them. We'll see."

"Thank you, Geoff."

"Don't thank me. I don't think this will work. Go home, sit tight. It will be a few days getting this together."

"And Barber? Should I call him back?"

"No. Let him stew a bit."

Ames turned to leave.

"And, Wilson."

He turned back.

"Don't forget who your friends are."

Ames hailed a taxi outside the office. He didn't feel like going directly home, but he wanted to get away from downtown, too. He gave directions to a restaurant on the edge of town.

He pulled his notepad out as they traveled, made a few more tentative lines along the castle, deciding that they were vines after all. Looking at the work, it still wasn't clear to him what was wrong, or missing, or too much. But something was off. He put the pad away as they pulled up to the restaurant curb.

He paid the driver, and shut the door. Turning, he saw her. Cynthia.

She was sitting in the restaurant, at a table near the window, dressed in something white, shimmering, her auburn hair up in a loose but carefully contrived pile. She was with a man. She hadn't seen Ames. He watched her laugh at something the man said. The man was young, much younger than Ames. He was dressed like a model in a magazine. He looked like a model from a magazine. He was holding Cynthia's hand. She said something back, and something in the way she arched her brow, tilted her head, rubbed the hand that held hers, told him they were lovers.

He turned before she noticed him, walked down the street. He had no idea where he was going. He stopped eventually in front of a newsstand and bought a paper.

He looked down at the mast, knowing what he'd find even before his eyes fell across it.

Friday. Today was Friday. *She had plans for Friday.*

He hailed another taxi and went home. From there, he called her number, expecting and getting her answering machine. He apologized, but said he would have to beg off dinner tomorrow. Something had come up. He'd call her.

The group met in the morning. In the back of one of Haines's private restaurants. There were no introductions.

Haines simply called the room to order, and nodded to Ames.

Ames stood and made his pitch, similar to the one he'd given Haines, but tailored to this particular audience. He left out the bit on Anderson, though he did recommend they pass on future dealings with Barber. He finished by emphasizing the highlights of his proposal.

"You all have legitimate businesses. I'll simply be working with that assumption: I'm representing you on legitimate business. I'll be able to do that if you all agree to follow some simple rules. No names, if possible. Never discuss anything illegal in my presence. Anything. Never refer or infer to anything that is not completely legitimate. You must make your request in terms that can stand public scrutiny."

"We already have lawyers for that," said someone at the table.

"Too many lawyers," said another, drawing a laugh.

Ames smiled with the rest. "The difference here is that I will work for all of you—and you don't have to pay a retainer." A few chuckles. "I'm a case by case basis. And, as I think Mr. Haines will explain to you in a bit," he looked to Haines, who nodded, "I possess a unique knowledge set that will let me conduct your business without jeopardizing," he smiled again, "your business. In short, you're buying my unique talents, not a service."

"What the hell did he do before?" asked someone at the table of his neighbor.

"…a mule," came the answer from somewhere else. Somebody else swore.

"I will have to insist I be hired officially only on legitimate business errands," continued Ames, speaking over the growing impatience. "Things that can be documented, proven. Above suspicion. I will bill you for the services, in fact. I will file taxes on the work you employ me for." He paused. "The other things that might result from my work…that will be paid to a secure account elsewhere. I'll never bill you for that. I'll never mention it. If you are not happy with the service, don't pay. If you are, then leave an appropriate amount, whatever you think best."

Someone scoffed, and more mutters of disbelief and some disapproval sprouted around the table. Haines quieted them down with a placating gesture.

"I don't expect to be used often," continued Ames. "But I believe you'll come to appreciate what I can offer you."

"Like this assessment on Barber?" asked one of the older men at the table. He was dressed like the rest in an expensive suit, but he was one of the few not wearing dark glasses.

"Precisely."

"I met the guy. Bit of a hick, but he's all right," said one of the men near the back.

This brought up another round of muttered private conversations.

Until someone finally said above the others, "I still don't understand what exactly he does that we can't do ourselves. We have lawyers for the legit stuff, and a sit down for the rest."

Ames waited until the room grew quiet again. "There's a place where your lawyers can't go, for obvious reasons. And, you can't have a sit down every time a dispute or issue comes up. I'll be that person you can send in those situations. A professional consultant, answerable to none, but capable of working for all."

"I thought you worked for Haines?"

Ames looked to Haines.

"I've known Wilson since college," said Haines. "I did use him on occasion, including brokering a deal with Henry." The older man without the glasses nodded. "I would continue to hire Ames in the capacity he has laid out, but I do not expect him to answer to me."

Someone muttered bullshit.

"Try me, gentlemen," said Ames. "I won't make promises about happy endings. But I think I can promise satisfaction. As for Geoff—yes, I know him. And he knows me. He knows I won't compromise on this. The role won't work if I answer to anyone directly."

The frowns that greeted this announcement did not look promising.

At this point, Haines stood up. "Thank you, Wilson. We'll let you know."

Still flush with adrenaline and confusion, acting on pure impulse, Ames called Cynthia. He apologized again for begging off. She didn't seem to be terribly put off, but politely made a show of disappointment. He asked her if she were still free. She hesitated, said yes. Would she care for dinner at his place? He told her where he lived. A little longer hesitation, then, yes, why not? Fantastic. He'd send a cab. No, that wasn't necessary. She'd see him at eight.

He had five hours before dinner. He spent some of the time cleaning the apartment, getting the meal ready, selecting his wardrobe. That killed an hour.

He sat in his kitchen, in his nook, and looked through the bay window, found no inspiration. He got up and retrieved the notepad and pencils, began to work. Two hours later, he set the notepad aside, stood up, stretched. He walked to the counter and put the roast in the oven, and then went upstairs to shower, shave, and dress.

Back in the kitchen, waiting for Cynthia, he made a drink, a small one, something to settle the nerves. He opened the notepad to the sketch.

His original castle still sat in the open field, though now that field held bits of rock and pieces of abandoned machinery. The sky line was fuller, wisps of clouds starting to form around the castle turrets. There was the faintest hint of the sun just on the edge of the page. The castle itself had aged, becoming richer and more complicated with a patchwork of vines and shadows. It was no longer a one-dimensional drawing, but a real monument, a dwelling of history and possibility, fragility and strength. He nodded and closed the notepad.

At that moment the doorbell rang.

He hadn't heard her car approach. He checked his reflection in the kitchen bay window. Everything looked in place. He went to the door and let her in. She was taller than he remembered. Tonight she wore a green, off-the-shoulder gown—and her hair was down, for which he was grateful. He'd feared she would wear it up, like she had in the restaurant. He smelled the cigarette she must have had recently, and the perfume she used to try and mask it. She said she was charmed by his house, and envied the fact that he lived out of town. He said she looked lovely, which was true.

They had drinks in the living room.

She did most of the talking, with Ames stepping in with an appropriate comment or question when called upon. She chided him for letting her talk so much. He said that was impossible. He felt it was going poorly, but kept that to himself. He tried not to think of the man in the restaurant. It wasn't hard if he concentrated on Cynthia. He was mesmerized by her, the way she carried herself, even sitting down, every gesture calculated to draw attention or distract. She was the opposite of him in many ways. Maybe that's what drew him to her.

He asked if she was ready to eat. She said she was, and they retired to his little kitchen where she said she was charmed all over again. He said she lied nicely, which drew a laugh. After dinner, he cleared the plates.

She said she'd like to see the house. He gave her the grand tour.

"No, really, Wilson, everything is so nice," she said, standing in the bedroom doorway.

He smiled, enjoying the smooth, graceful length of her. He wondered if he should ask her to bed. *It was too soon*, he thought; though he suspected she was just as curious as he was.

They retreated again to the living room for more drinks.

"So tell me about you, Wilson. What's behind the man with the wardrobe?"

She slipped one long leg over another to reveal a calculated length of well-toned, tanned calf. There was a touch of something—disappointment? boredom?—in the question. Had he missed something upstairs? He couldn't say. He was used to sizing up people, reading their unconscious signals and languages. But she was something new. There was none of the carefully contrived identity of Haines, or the false bravado of a Barber. In some ways, in fact, she was like Ames: an enigma. But where he was a thousand layers of placid contradiction, she was a transparent piece of tangibility, a flame, visible but tenuous, nothing you could touch—except to get burned.

Then it came to him. The repeated compliments about his house, the hesitation to his invitation to come over. It wasn't for propriety sake. It was the neighborhood, a neighborhood outside the city proper. She'd been surprised. She thought he came from money.

He almost laughed aloud.

"I had an interesting week," he said, finally.

She nodded, still only half-listening.

"I'm going through a bit of transition in my career. Or maybe, I'm finding it."

"A move up, I hope."

"We'll see." He paused, a small smile on his face as he watched her struggle to pay attention.

"How do you know Geoff?" he asked.

There was a slight, surprised pause, which she covered as competently as anything he could manage. "Go to enough parties, and eventually you run into Geoff," she laughed.

He suffered a vision of Geoff holding her hand like the man in the restaurant, but smiled back at her. *Were they lovers at one time, too? Did it matter?*

"And how do you know Geoff?" she asked.

"We met in college."

"I can see Geoff in college," she said, her eyes dancing. "Hanging from chandeliers, sneaking out of the sororities, having the Deans over for coffee. But you...I can't see you with him."

"He wasn't like that. He was quiet, actually. Our friendship was casual. We kept in touch."

They chatted for a time about work, and school, and the past. She asked about his family, a last attempt to place Ames in a class or opportunity.

"Not much to tell. I'm the only child. He was a carpenter, she was a teacher. They're retired now, living in Florida."

The conversation, and interest, wound down like an old watch after that, and before long she made excuses and he was seeing her out the door.

He took a bus to town the next day and spent the morning in the museum. He preferred the Met, it comforted him with its cool marble floors and timeless spaces of human achievement. But an hour later, he walked out again. He stopped at a bistro nearby. He had the place to himself. The young girl at the counter took his order, brought it a few minutes later, and disappeared behind the counter with her IPad again. He sipped his coffee and sampled the pie, looking out the big front window, watching the people go by in tinted reflections. He pulled his notepad out, changed his mind, and put it back again.

A woman across the street caught his attention. She was sitting at a bus stop, her purse on her lap and her hands on the purse. She sat as still as a puddle of water, ignoring the people, the world. He watched her for fifteen minutes as the buses came and went and she stayed where she was. Was she homeless, he wondered? Surely, she couldn't be waiting for a bus. He finished his pie and ordered another cup of coffee. A half hour later, she was still at the bus stop,

Finally, he got up, paid his bill, and walked across the street. As he approached, he could see she was middle-aged, her chocolate colored skin freckled across her nose, her hair dark and pressed straight. She was wearing an outfit, something the modern world considered dressed up, but Ames thought cluttered and disjointed. He took a seat on the same bench as the woman, but not too close. He didn't look her way, but folded one knee over the other, arranged his coat. Buses came, and went. Neither moved.

"I don't think he's coming."

He turned slightly to her. She was still staring straight ahead.

"Pardon?" he asked.

"I don't think he's coming," she repeated. "He promised he'd meet me here."

"Oh."

He saw her blush slightly under the freckles. He stood up.

"Sometimes, they don't show up," he said. He waited until she turned to him. "And sometimes they do, and it doesn't matter."

"It's better when they come," she said, looking away again.

He thought about that. He turned, and left her there without answering. The world passed by, one bus at a time.

The doorbell woke him. He looked to the clock on the small table by his bed. It was one in the morning. He had come home from the bus stop, drank his dinner, and went to bed.

He sat up in bed, tasting the night and whiskey in his mouth. The doorbell didn't ring again. He climbed from bed, went to the bathroom. He rinsed his mouth, ran some water and splashed it on his face and hair. He was dressed only in loose cotton bottoms. He pulled a t-shirt on and went downstairs to see if anyone was still at the door.

She was.

She was dressed in an evening gown, though it had lost its luster and form somewhere in the night. Her face was flushed, her eyes drawing invisible lines from one side of his door to the other. There was a small bruise starting on her left upper arm, and a red mark along her cheek.

"I'm sorry," she said. "Can I come in?"

"Of course."

She did, with none of the grace or composure from the night before. She sat down in the living room like a fall blown leaf. Her hand was shaking when she pulled the cigarette from its holder.

She looked from the cigarette to him. "Sorry." She started to put it back.

"No. It's all right. Smoke if you like." He went to the kitchen, made two drinks, no ice, found an ashtray in a drawer, a heavy jade affair he picked up somewhere. He carried everything back to the living room, handed her the drink and put the ashtray on the coffee table beside her. She nodded gratefully and tossed the drink off, then stabbed the cigarette out in the ashtray. She took another one out automatically, holding it in two fingers like an extension of her will.

He took her empty glass and poured her another. This one he set beside her on the coffee table. He was careful to put it on the coaster. She lit the cigarette for something to do, her eyes refusing to meet his, her body language calculating, anxious.

He sat across from her in the chair, his drink in hand.

After a time she glanced at him, frowned at the cigarette in her hand, put it out. "I'm sorry," she said, her voice made listless with drink and smoke and tension. "I'm out of sorts."

"What happened?"

She grimaced, gave him a dark look from the corner of her eyes. "Men. Men happened."

He waited, let her come to it.

Cynthia took a sip from her glass, shuddered. Her chest rose briefly, the dress temporarily finding its form again. He noticed she had freckles along her breasts from the sun.

"But you're a man," she noted, ironically. "And I still came here."

He made a sympathetic gesture.

She stared at him, frowning again, as if his presence were confusing.

"Should I call someone?" he asked.

Her frown deepened, then fell apart. "No. It's not as bad as it looks." She glanced away. "A misunderstanding that got a little out of hand. I'll be all right. I just don't like scenes, or drama." She looked around the house, back to Ames. "I couldn't go to my friends. That would be… unbearable."

"I understand. Stay as long as you like."

"Can I?" she asked, her relief obvious but cautious.

"Of course." He stood up. "Wait here a moment."

He walked up the stairs and into his bedroom, found a clean t-shirt and a pair of sweats with a draw string. He brought them both back downstairs, set the folded clothes beside her.

"There's a shower upstairs. Why don't you take your drink up there? I'll make you something to eat."

She looked to the stairway. "Okay," she said quietly, reaching out to touch the clothes with her long finger tips.

He left her there and went to the kitchen. He put a pan on for eggs, and cut some bread from a loaf. Then he sat in the kitchen nook, staring at the black night in the window. When he heard her coming down the stairs some time later, he started the eggs and put the bread in the toaster.

Her hair was wet and hung in dark tangles of red and brown around her naked face. She was a woman who looked different without makeup, not better or worse, just different. His t-shirt hung loosely around her, and the sweat pants were two sizes too big. He felt a pleasant ache in his loins as she crossed the kitchen in her bare feet to take the seat across from his.

He poured her a cup of coffee. Her hands still shook slightly as she drank it.

He watched her eat.

"You're not joining me?" she asked. The green of her eyes were clearer, but missing the confident fire from the other night.

"I ate while you were upstairs," he lied. In truth, he couldn't see his way to hunger.

"I appreciate this, Wilson," she said.

He almost said he was glad she came here. But that was dangerous. That could be interpreted too many ways, some of them true, but not timely. He searched for the right words, couldn't find them. So he smiled instead.

She was starting to nod before she finished. Finally, he stood, took her hand and gently led her upstairs. He let her climb into bed and tucked her in.

"Help yourself to anything," he said softly.

She nodded sleepily, her eyes closed.

"I'll be down the hall in the second bedroom if you need anything. Sleep in tomorrow."

She reached out a hand from the bed, her eyes still closed. He took it, felt her squeeze his hand. She murmured something he couldn't understand, and rolled back into the bed.

He left her there, climbed into the fresh and cool sheets of the spare bed, wondering at the warmth in his chest, the sheer, silly joy that must be even now across his face in the dark of night.

***

Barber. The girl. Joel Anderson. The rules. Hello, asshole.

And Cynthia. There had been that night with Cynthia.

The memory of that night stayed with him as he slowly woke again to his reality now. He wondered if he was still grinning as he tasted the bitter, salty tang of his own blood, the pain starting again in his face even as his unconscious memories ebbed. He opened his one working eye, the other shut in its bruised and swollen flesh, and looked around.

Barber was lying on his couch, his dirty shoes perched on the couch arm, his hat covering his face. The room smelled of stale cigarettes. Ames saw a small cup of butts on the floor next to the couch.

The other—what was his name? His head ached with the effort to remember. Al. It was Al. Al was sitting in a chair across from him, watching. Al had taken his hat off, though he still wore his coat. He had a small, slightly concave head with fine white hairs lying in a comb-over from one side of the scalp to the other. He looked older this way, but the blue eyes remained timeless in their distance and smoldering hunger.

"He's up," said Al, his voice a wispy tremor of odium, a nail scratched along a board.

Barber started under his hat, pulled it off and rolled to his feet.

Ames was still bound to the chair at the wrists and ankles. The black bag was sitting in his lap, turned inside out, riddled with splotches of blood and spittle.

Barber stood and stretched, tossed his hat on the couch.

Ames looked to the clock on the wall. It was almost eight. Had he been out most of the day, or was it a day and a night?

Barber came to stand in front of Ames, bent down until his face was inches from Ames's.

"You don't look good, Ames," he said. Then he made a face. "And you stink, too."

"I think I could use a shower," agreed Ames, then suffered a fit of painful coughs, his head splitting with each reflex.

Barber backed away quickly, then started laughing.

A terrible dry itch, like a trickle of sand, started in the back of Ames's throat. His good eye watered. He needed a drink of water, but knew better than to ask. Eventually, the coughing subsided, though the dryness remained, a constant threat to a new round of coughing just on the edge of his control.

"Suppose you want something to drink?" said Barber, his hands on his hips. "Al, get our boy a glass of water."

Al retreated to the kitchen, came back with a glass of water. He held it for Ames, just below his mouth. Ames started to take a small sip, but Al lifted the glass away. Barber laughed again, a high whiny laugh, a schoolboy bully calling attention to himself.

Al did the trick two more times. Ames just stared back on the third attempt. Then Al forced the glass between Ames's lips, clicking the glass hard against his teeth. Ames struggled to swallow, and suffered another round of coughing as he choked on the rushing water, most of which was pouring down his chin.

Al pulled the empty glass away, and eventually Ames recovered enough to talk.

"Thank you," he said.

Barber laughed again, shrill and short. "He's a smooth talker, our Ames." He came close again, pushing Al out of the way. "Now, listen close," he said, sticking his foul mouth in front of Ames again. "I'm going to ask you some questions, and you're going to answer them...or not." He stood straight again. "It doesn't really matter to me or Al. We'll get what we want out of this either way. But if you answer, I might tell him to take it a little easy."

He nodded to Al. "Get what you need from the kitchen."

Al retreated again. Soon Ames heard the sound of drawers being opened, pots and pans being lifted.

"I guess you wonder why I'm here?" said Barber.

Ames returned his stare, his face empty of expression. He said nothing.

"This is payback time," sneered Barber. "That's what this is. I had to wait a very long time to get it, too, so it's going to be a lot of payback, friend."

"Payback?" asked Ames.

"Oh, don't be clever. Twenty five years ago you put the kibosh on my career. And your friends made sure I couldn't do anything about it." He cocked his head. "Until now."

"Why now?" asked Ames. It was difficult to voice even this much. His throat was raw, his lips swollen and broken.

"Because now I can," said Barber, perking up.

He wants me to talk, thought Ames. *This is part of the thrill for him.*

"I don't understand," he said, knowing that to not play would only infuriate Barber further.

"And you so smart?" mocked Barber. "It's simple. You're out. You've lost your favor. You're fair game."

Payback time. Things started to fall into place for Ames. He had wondered why Barber was acting after all these years. He thought it was safe; that Ames had lost his protection.

But Barber was wrong. He didn't know.

Ames licked his lips. "I'm not out," he said slowly.

"Yes you are!" insisted Barber with grin. "You fucked up with that policeman. That little tart wife of yours got you in trouble with the organization. You got the boot. I still got enough connections to hear that, Mr. Wilson Ames."

Ames started to shake his head, but stopped when the pain raced up the back of his skull like fire. "No," he said, again softly. "They gave you the wrong information. I'm still in. I just got back from a job. Call your contact. Call Haines."

The grin broadened on Barber's face. He leaned forward, whispered in Ames's ear. "I know. But I didn't get that memo, see?"

He stood back, laughing. "Go on, Mr. Consultant. Tell me how they'll be so upset. Make your clever, veiled threats." He laughed again, something just on the edge of control.

There were no sounds now coming from the kitchen.

Barber eventually settled down again. "You understand now?"

"Claiming ignorance won't protect you," said Ames.

This brought another sharp laugh from Barber. "So says the man who made a career of it." He reached out and patted Ames on the cheek, sending new waves of pain along Ames's face.

"I don't care," repeated Barber. "Don't you get that? I'll claim ignorance, sure, just to muddy the water enough to give them an excuse. But it don't matter. You think anyone will really worry over you now? After your fuck up with the police?" He shrugged. "And if they don't give me a pass, so what? What are they going to take away from me? You saw to it all those years ago that I'd never have anything."

"They'll take away your life," said Ames, meeting Barber's eye.

For a moment the other paused, his lips twitched, his eyes growing distant. "Don't care," he whispered.

At that moment, Al came back in. He was carrying a pot of water, the steam rolling out of it like a living cloud. Ames felt his heart constrict.

"And here's Al!" said Barber, turning from Ames to Al. Al stopped just in front of Ames, next to Barber.

"Al tells me the key to this is simple," said Barber. "Keep you alive and conscious—and in pain. Isn't that right, Al?"

Al didn't answer. He just looked at Ames with those hungry, empty eyes.

"What's on the menu first, Al? Looks like boiling water."

Ames looked to Al, tried to meet his eyes. There was no help in that direction. He turned instead to stare at Barber. "What do you want?"

Barber's grin was a broad, brown-toothed line of pure pleasure. "Where's the girl?"

"I don't know."

Barber closed his eyes in rapture. "Good. Al."

Al leaned forward. Ames saw the water wasn't boiling, but the steam still rose ominously from the top. *Does that mean something,* he thought, trying to find some small, desperate point of succor. *At what point does it leave a scar?*

Then Al poured a small stream across the back of Ames's hand, and he knew it didn't matter. He closed his eyes and cried out, a guttural thing ripped from his core.

A moment later, the pain still throbbing as if his hand were a giant nerve, Ames opened his eyes again. Only Barber was in front of him. Ames turned frantically, as much as his bonds would let him. Out of the corner of his eye he saw Al was standing behind him now, the pot held just above Ames's head.

"Where's the girl?" asked Barber.

"I don't know!" screamed Ames.

Barber nodded.

The pain erupted on the top of his head this time, and raced down his neck, face, and chest like liquid fire. This time he blacked out.

When he woke, both men were still standing in the same place. He couldn't have been out for long.

Barber leaned close. "Where's the girl?"

"I don't know! I don't know!"

Barber's lip twitched. He wasn't laughing now. The pleasure was gone from his eyes, replaced by hate and just a semblance of disgust. "You should see yourself, asshole. You look a red mess. You don't get that treated, that might leave a scar." He cocked his head to the side, considered Ames. "Scars," he added a moment later. "Where's the girl?"

"I'm telling you the truth," stammered Ames, all his collective calm gone. "Anderson never told me. He knew you might do something like this. I *would* tell you if I knew."

Barber looked to Al. Ames turned his aching head from side to side, trying to see where Al was going next, trying to brace himself for the next round of hell.

But Barber was chuckling again. Ames turned back to face him. Something was wrong. He'd missed something.

"Not that girl," said Barber. "The tart. Where's your wife, smart ass?" He leaned in again, his hot, fetid breath stinging Ames's burnt flesh. "I said this is payback. Twenty five years ago you took everything from me, including a girl. Now I'm going to show you how that feels."

An overwhelming dread, an impossible crush of fear, gripped Ames. His vision grew blurry, the pain temporarily retreating under a wave of panic. His world, already teetering, verged on collapse. *Cynthia! My god, he was going to do this to Cynthia!*

"Look at those eyes, Al," said Barber. "What's the matter, Mr. Consultant, nothing to say now?"

Ames swallowed the lump of pain and terror in his throat, trying to still his racing nerves. He looked from Al to Barber. He had to do something. He had to keep them away from her. But how?

Time, he thought. *Time is my enemy, and my hope.*

How long did he have? She had called Friday, said she was coming back on Monday, would drive straight from the airport. If this was still Saturday, he had a day and a half, maybe more. Cynthia would never take an early morning flight. She hated getting up early for anything. This last, desperate hope came to him like a drowning man slapping at the water for support. She won't be here until Monday, late.

A day and half, maybe more. A day and a half with Barber and Al—and the pain. Before Monday he had to convince them, convince them she wasn't coming back at all. A day and a half.

Please god, let it still be Saturday. Please god, Cynthia, don't come early.

"She left me," he said, sagging into the chair. "We fought. You're right. She was a whore. I had too much. I don't know where she went. I don't care." He didn't look at either man as he said this.

"So you won't mind if Al and I look her up after we're done with you," said Barber, lifting Ames's chin to see his face. Barber's expression was of pure malice.

He knew I would say something like this, thought Ames. *He's been living with this moment for years, playing it all out.*

Ames swallowed.

"Of course I care," he said. "Leave her out of it. I'll tell you anything you want to know. You can do anything to me. But she's got nothing to do with us. This is between you and me, Barber." He glared up at the man. "*I* took it away from you. Me."

Barber scoffed, his grin back in place. "I told you, Al. He's as slippery as an eel."

Al grunted.

Barber let Ames's face go. "Before Al and I came here, I told him all about you. Al don't talk much, but he's good at what he does. You know what he does?" He chuckled. "Well, you know a little about what he does now, and you'll learn a lot more before the end, but what Al really does is focus. He cuts through the bullshit. He's like the opposite of you. Aren't you, Al?"

"The waters getting too cold," said Al.

"Then get some more," said Barber with a frown.

Al left, carrying the pot.

"I told Al to watch you," continued Barber, leaning close again. "I told him you would try to weasel out of it. I told him not to let me grow soft." He reached up and grabbed Ames's chin hard, the pain erupting under his fingertips. "Where's your wife, Ames?"

Ames tried to put as much hate and anger as he could in his eyes. His answer was partially muffled by Barber's grip, but clear enough. "You don't listen very well. She left me."

Barber grunted, his eyes holding fire. He let go, turned slightly away, and then sent Ames's head rolling with a vicious slap. Ames felt the darkness approach again, like a monster from the depths. He almost welcomed it.

He woke, his arms and legs and head stiff with pain and fear. Al was back in his chair, Barber on the couch again. He glanced at the clock. Twelve. There was no sunlight behind the front room curtains. He assumed it was night, prayed that it was still Saturday.

"He's back," said Al. He stood and pulled a rolling tea cart over. It was Ames's. The tea set was gone, and in its place, laid out like a surgical tray, were tools and cutlery from the house.

Al made sure Ames had a good look. Then he slowly picked up the pliers, showed them to Ames, put them down again. He picked up the scissors, again showed Ames, and again put them down. He considered the other objects. Finally, he selected a butcher knife, the corner of his mouth twitching as if trying to smile.

All the while Barber was chuckling, watching Ames's reaction. "I told you," he said. "Al likes to cut through the bullshit. You're full of bullshit, Ames."

He came to stand in front of Ames, snorted and took a step back. "And you smell like shit! Good lord, man, did you shit your pants."

It was possible. Ames couldn't tell. His arms, legs, and most of his body were asleep but for a constant throb of pain. He looked down. The front of his pants was stained with blood, but there could be urine there as well.

"I'll be glad to take a shower," he said. "If you'll let me."

Barber's expression grew hard. "Fuck that. Now, I'm going to ask you one more time, and if you give the right answer, then Al waits a bit. If not—" He shrugged. "Where's...your...wife?"

Ames stared at Barber. He started to speak, looked to Al, swallowed. He let Barber see the fear in his eyes, which was genuine.

If it is Saturday night, I have to last another day, and a little more. He cringed at the thought of what that day would bring. But surviving wasn't enough. Wasn't an answer at all. *Monday she'll walk through the door and if they're still here it won't matter if I'm alive or not. So get them to act rashly, end it before they want to. They won't stay long in the apartment if I'm dead. The sooner the better. They'll get nervous...they'll leave.*

Won't they?

He turned to Barber, who was also watching Ames. His expression was hungry as well, but where Al's was constant, a hunger built on something twisted at its core, Barber was riding on emotion. His hunger was a bone he had gnawed through the years, but now that the moment was at hand he was living that moment to its fullest, giving his passions free reign.

Barber was his hope. Barber would never sit in the house, waiting, with Ames dead. There would be no point. Ames alive, tortured; Ames alive and watching Cynthia tormented; that's what he wanted. That would answer his hunger. But Ames dead…maybe it would end then.

So, make him do it. Drive him to that final mistake. He has no real control. He can barely hold himself back even now.

But the other has the knife.

He looked to Al. He was holding the knife like a child holds a bar of ice cream, watching Ames over the tip of the blade. What had Barber said about Al? He brought focus. Al would not let Barber act rashly. Al would never let it end that easily for Ames. Barber would rant and rave, strike without thought. But not Al. He had to get the knife in Barber's hands. But how?

He looked to Al again, the cold, empty eyes staring back in his. *That one would wait a week with my rotting body in the corner*, thought Ames.

And with that thought the reality came home and he knew utter despair. Even his death was no answer. If he did somehow manage to end it before Cynthia returned, there was still the problem of what happens after. Al would want to hurt Cynthia—he wanted to hurt everything. Barber might walk away once Ames was dead, but there would be no assurance with that one.

He felt his pain, imagined that and worse forced on Cynthia, and almost vomited.

Barber could stop him, he thought with rising desperation. *Barber owns Al.*

He had to find a reason for Barber to leave Cynthia alone, forever. A motivation that would force Barber to check Al. He took a deep, shaky breath, meeting Barber's glare.

And slowly an idea presented itself. He shuddered at what it would cost him, worried that he wouldn't have the will or strength to carry it out, but also recognized it was his best chance to insure Cynthia was safe.

"Where's your wife, asshole?" repeated Barber, glancing between Ames and Al.

Ames blinked, hung his head, saw the scene play out in his mind, knew what might happen once he started his plan, fixed an image of Cynthia in his mind and lifted his head again.

"She did leave me," he said slowly. Barber growled, shook his head, and looked to Al.

"NO! Stop!" cried Ames around his broken lips. "She did! She's staying at her sister's." This was true, for the most part, and he invested that truth in his voice, his body language. He focused on the truth of it, leaving out the details that undermined that truth. He willed Barber to hear the truth of it, knowing it wouldn't carry over completely. Knowing that Barber would hold doubt. But knowing, too, that it had to start this way. To make the rest plausible. To get the buy in.

He looked hopelessly to Barber. Then, he lied. "She's not coming back."

He deliberately glanced to the knife in Al's hand. The shudder that followed was not crafted or deliberate, but was necessary.

He knew the lie wouldn't stand. Not for Barber, not for Al. Not for Ames. He needed something more, something to immerse himself in, to finally, inevitably spill when Al began what was also inevitable, what those empty eyes were hungry to do. And under that merciless, knife-wielding hand, Ames would eventually break. To that there was no question. What was in question though, was what he said in that moment. He needed a lie that was truth, one that he couldn't avoid, one that Barber and Al would hear as truth even through his screams. A lie that would free Cynthia.

"I think you're lying, Ames," said Barber. "But Al will have the truth out of you soon enough."

Ames looked to the approaching Al. This time he did feel his bowels release.

A moment later, Barber realized it as well. "Good Christ! That's foul, Ames! Have a heart!" He laughed, looked to Al for a reaction.

But Al only had eyes for a point on Ames's chest, the knife slowly moving to it like a magnet drawn to north.

Ames felt his heart in his throat. Would he be able to hold to his half-truth?

Cynthia. Think of Cynthia. He tried to remember her that morning so long ago, the morning after she found shelter in his house. *What had she said over breakfast? Something about being safe. Yes, that was it. She said she felt safe with him. Asked him if she was being naïve—was he really that safe?* He had said something clever at the time. Something like, *in most things.* Then he took her to bed…

The knife touched his naked chest just above the V-neck angle. He felt its cool steel tip, like a fingernail gently caressing his skin. The image of Cynthia fell from his mind to be replaced by raw fear. He avoided looking at Al, searching instead for some sign of hope in Barber. But Barber was watching the knife now too, a simple smile on his face, his eyes glowing with expectation.

Ames felt the knife prick his skin, looked down to see the blood start around the tip. He watched, horrified as Al slowly drew it down, cutting the shirt, cutting his skin, opening him up like a piece of grape. Then he felt the cut. Somewhere he heard an animal bleating in pain and fright, realized a moment later it was him.

He tried to pull back, tried to pull away, but Al anticipated his reaction, grabbed him by the shoulder and leaned his body into his to brace him. The knife was still in his other hand, pulled now a fraction of the way from

Ames's chest while they struggled. Then, as Al gained the upper hand, it slowly returned.

"Haines!" screamed Ames, looking to Barber. "We fought over Haines! They're lovers!"

Barber frowned, nodded slightly to Al. The knife retreated again.

Ames hung his head, watching the blood drip from the long line of cut skin, felt the sweat pour from his head, hot then cold. He didn't meet Barber's eyes. He stifled a sob.

He heard someone chuckle, recognized it was Barber.

"So Haines is fucking your wife," said Barber above his head.

Ames didn't answer. It was the lie, or maybe it was true. He couldn't say. It didn't matter. This was his last, desperate chance. Haines was a force that Barber had to respect. Haines would, and could, scour the earth for Barber, could and would, do everything that Barber was having done to Ames and threatened to do to Cynthia, and worse. And if Haines liked Cynthia…

Ames didn't really believe Barber had nothing to lose. The real truth was Barber felt confident that he'd get a pass on Ames. The water *was* muddy. Ames had stepped, unintentionally, out of line by confronting the police. Yes, he returned. Yes, he once again proved his worth. But that didn't mean he was forgiven. That didn't mean his stock was sound. Maybe Barber was right. Maybe no one would care if Ames went away. *Michaels*, he thought suddenly. Had that been all it seemed? Was it a chance for him to assess Michaels, or was it the other way around? Was Michaels being groomed to take Ames's place? It was possible. Very possible. It would explain Barber's presence and actions now. Maybe Barber was right about everything: maybe Ames was out.

But even still, Barber couldn't afford to make Haines angry. It was a lie that might be true. It was a lie with teeth.

There was a long silence, broken only by the panting of Ames.

"He can have her," said Barber, trying to sound as if he didn't care. "She's been around so much, he'll probably catch a disease, eh, Al?"

Ames, his head still hung, felt a rush of relief so palatable he almost cried. But he was careful to show only defeat in his body language.

Barber, like a spoiled child denied a treat, misinterpreted the act.

"You're kidding me, Ames," he said derisively. "You really didn't know how big a whore your wife was?" He reached out, grabbed Ames by the hair, and pulled his head back until Ames was looking back at him. "She should get frequent flyer miles for her backside." He laughed, looked to Al again. But Al was as lifeless as ever, and Barber's glee retreated to a bitter frown.

"What do we do next?" asked Al.

Barber released Ames head. "We kill the asshole." He waited until Ames looked at him, then added, "Slowly."

Ames, his head rolling to one side, saw Al finally react. The smile was as cold as his eyes, but it was a smile just the same.

His fragile hold on consciousness was his sole ally now. Al started to work on him with the pliers. Barber held his foot as Al took ahold of his big toe nail. But before Al could remove it, Ames passed out again.

When he woke, he tried to feign unconsciousness. But Al was there, watching closely, waiting. He grabbed Ames's hand, and twisted it back against itself until Ames cried out.

"He's up," said Al unnecessarily.

Barber was back on the couch, his feet up. "Finally."

Ames looked to the clock. He had been out for about three hours. If his earlier calculations were right it was still Sunday.

Or Monday morning, he thought with sinking despair. What if Cynthia walked in the house in a few hours? It would change the dynamics completely. The lie about Haines might not be enough if she was there, in the room. Barber might not be able to resist. Worse, she would be a witness. They'd have to kill her. He was so distraught at the thought he almost asked what day it was. But he checked himself, the words on his tongue. Asking might give everything away. But not knowing was just as bad.

He couldn't think straight. His mind was an emotional mess, driven to distraction by his pain and discomfort. He looked down to hands. They were purple. He felt a pain in his groin. His bladder. Despite his previous release, he was in desperate need to go again.

"Time for the next act," said Barber.

He looked tired, his chin covered in five o'clock shadow. He had apparently raided Ames's liquor cabinet. A bottle of his best scotch sat by the couch.

"This is hungry work, waiting for you, Ames," said Barber. "And I'm getting bored with all this passing out. But good news!" He glanced cynically at Al. "Al says that's not going to happen anymore. He's going to be more careful. You'll appreciate that, I'm sure." He turned back to Ames. His laugh was slurred, hollow.

He's drunk, thought Ames. *He's losing interest.* Maybe he could use that, make the end quick. If he pushed the right buttons on Barber, Al might not be able to stop him.

Then he looked to Al. He looked exactly the same. He was still in his coat. His chin was free of shadow, as if he shaved, or couldn't grow a beard. His eyes were still, empty, but knowing.

No, it won't be quick, he thought. *No matter what I do to Barber, it won't be quick.*

He was filled with a sudden and pure hatred for these men. It was not just for the pain they were causing, but the threat they represented, to him, to Cynthia. They embodied a cruel and pointless end. The end to everything. He would never see another day out his kitchen window. Never walk through a museum again, or sip a cup of coffee, or make a sketch, or take a breath. He would never again see Cynthia in the morning, hold her, and feel her skin against his.

He wanted to scream at the empty man beside him. He wanted, for the first time in his life, to strike out, to hit—to kill. It was a new and terrifying experience for Ames, to hate this much, and he struggled to control it.

Al, watching him closely, smiled. "Yes," he whispered. That was all he said. But Ames understood. This was the world Al inhabited all the time. This was, in part, what he wanted Ames to experience, to understand, as he worked his will with knife and plier.

"What's that?" asked Barber, struggling to sit up on the couch.

"I need to use the bathroom," said Ames, looking straight ahead.

"What?" asked Barber. "Bathroom?" Then he fell back in the couch. "God, the room stinks too much already. Take him to the john, will you, Al."

Al blinked, looked in confusion to Barber.

"Go on," said Barber. "Let him shower down, too. I'm not going to sit here and suffer that foulness while you work. We'll have our fun when he's clean. Then will end it and get out of this place. God, I'm sick of it."

He laid out on the couch, closed his eyes.

Al turned back to Ames, considered his hands. "Okay," he said, with that oddly disconnected manner. "He's not going to feel anything in his hands the way they are now anyway."

"Whatever," said Barber, pulling his hat over his head again.

While Al worked at freeing his legs, Ames tried to collect himself, pull his racing mind into focus. Visions of Anderson—competent, powerful, gun rich Anderson— came to mind. Cameras and dogs and deep, ominous foreheads.

What do I do, Anderson? How do I protect myself? I have no guns, no dogs. Not even a camera. A camera would have let him see Barber and Al outside his door. He could have said go away. I have no cover-my-ass plan...Stop it! Concentrate.

He heard more than felt Al rip the duct tape from his wrist. He couldn't feel anything below his elbow, but he could see the raw white and red patch the tape left behind. *Like strawberry currant,* he thought. *Or a piece of bloodless flesh.*

Again he willed himself to concentrate.

This will be my one, my only chance. He took a deep, shallow breath as Al nodded to him to stand.

He knows I can't stand. He's playing with me.

But Ames tried just the same. He fell, as he knew he would. He used the time to think, even as Al kicked at him to get up again.

This is my house. I know this house. I can use that.

What will Al do? Eventually, he'll grow tired of kicking me. Eventually, my circulation will return. He knew his mind was still not working right. Something was broken. But he ignored this, and concentrated his efforts on formulating some kind of plan.

When I can stand, he'll take me to the bathroom. Which bathroom? Why does it matter? Because, the bathroom upstairs is a full bathroom. It has a shower and tub. Cynthia used it that night, that wonderful night, so long ago...

Stop! Stop! Stop! Think of now. Think of what you are going to do now.

Upstairs then. If Al listens to Barber. I'm to take a shower; Barber said so. Al will listen. To that much, at least, he'll listen. So, what does that mean? What does it mean that you are upstairs? Use it...

Al was lifting him up to his feet. The pain was starting in his legs, the circulation returning. Al began half-dragging, half-carrying him. They were heading to the steps. Something hot and salty ran down Ames's cheek.

Upstairs. I'm going upstairs. Upstairs meant he would be alone with Al. Barber would be downstairs.

Obviously.

Shut up, idiot! Concentrate!

Upstairs.

The bathroom upstairs was tight. Cynthia was always complaining about it. Why hadn't he moved them to a bigger house? Cynthia deserved that.

Cynthia was fucking Haines.

Shut up!

Al was going to have to make a decision. Did he carry Ames inside, hold him, watch him? Would he wash Ames?

He almost giggled at the thought, but it passed as his feet started to tingle with more awakening circulation. A slow electric fire was starting along his shins. They were at the bottom of the steps now. Seven simple steps. Seven pieces of agony, and then what?

"Just a minute," he said. "Let me get the circulation back enough to stand on my own."

That's clever, he thought. *Be helpful. Nobody wants to do all the work, not even psychopaths.* This time he did giggle.

Al removed Ames's arm from around his shoulder, looked at him, searching for more signs of Ames's crumbling sanity. Ames reached for the guardrail, couldn't grip it with his lifeless hands, and fell. Al pulled him back to his feet, which were now a constant stream of pulsing pain. He was still watching Ames curiously, like a child watching a dying ant.

Ames started to fall over again, but this time managed to prop himself against the stairwell wall. From this position, he slowly rubbed his wrists, ignoring the new levels of pain this caused. Then he did the same with his legs. He almost cried again to see the conditions of his feet. When he could stand, he started up the steps, slowly, painfully, but on his own. Al followed patiently.

Al has all the time in the world. You don't.

Upstairs. Up the stairs...And then? And then?

And then the tight space of the bathroom doorway. The decision. Al's decision. If he could get Al to stand outside—watch me, Al, don't wash me. There's something Al doesn't know about the bathroom. Al doesn't know about Cynthia's bad habits. He doesn't know about the hairdryer.

Now you're thinking boy.

Poor, sweet, beautiful, Cynthia. Why would Cynthia sleep with Haines?

Not now. Plan.

Al will turn on the light. He'll see the room is tight. He might stand close, hold Ames's hand while he tinkled.

He fought off another giggle.

Stop that!

Okay. Okay. Let's say he stands just behind you. He's there, maybe with his hand in his coat, maybe on his gun. He has a gun? You know he has a gun? Yes, I saw it while he was tying me up. Didn't I?

It doesn't matter. Assume he has a gun. There he is standing just behind you. You do your business. You find your chance. You put the hair dryer, which still sits on the sink, in the toilet. The lights go out.

You have to turn it on first.

Yes. I'll turn it on first. Then, in the toilet it goes.

And then what?

You use the distraction. Then you go down for Barber.

Barber will have a gun.

So say you.

He will have a gun.

I have...I have...

Then he saw he had it. The final part of the plan.

They were at the top of the stairs now. It was dark. Al flipped on the hall switch, bathing everything in soft white light, Cynthia's favorite kind of lighting. Ames felt his bladder constrict painfully at the sight of the bathroom door. As if from a distance, he considered his plan again. Now that he was in it, he had a sudden moment of clarity. The plan, such as it was, was risky, incomplete. He shuddered as he realized he'd been arguing with himself.

But it was all he had.

"Go on," said Al, reaching around Ames to turn the bathroom light on.

Ames stepped through the door. Al followed him, stood just behind him, inside the doorway.

He's not really a professional, he consoled himself. *A sick, twisted, heartless freak, yes. But Anderson would have him for dinner.*

You're not Anderson.

He looked to the sink. The hair dryer was there, in its wicker basket on the sink. The plug was resting just below the right outlet. He had taken it out (yesterday?)

when he was shaving. Because he was careful. *But thankfully not careful enough to put the hairdryer away.*

Ames slowly undid his pants. He didn't want to do it slowly, he just couldn't move any faster. He was painfully aware of Al, just behind him. He looked down in his pants, saw the mess. He took himself out, feeling his feces there as well.

Nothing happened. As desperately as he had to pee a moment ago, now he couldn't.

"I need a little space," he said.

"No."

They stood like that for a time. Al breathing softly right behind him, Ames holding his filth covered self, the room filling with his stench.

And then it started. A small trickle, followed by a spurt, then a heavy constant stream. His relief almost brought him to his knees again.

He felt Al take a step back.

He finished. He dropped his pants, stepped out of them. Casually he reached for the cold faucet by the sink, turned it on. He stepped closer to the sink. From the mirror he could see Al watching him.

"Can I wash my hands?" he asked.

Al shrugged. "Wash everything."

Ames reached for the soap, and, as if completing a natural ritual, casually put the hair dryer plug in the outlet. Then he reached for the soap. Only then did he look back in the mirror. Al was staring back at him, but the eyes were as empty as always.

Ames finished washing his hands. He reached for the hand towel. He dropped his hand on the way, flipped the little toggle of the hair dryer on, and pushed it into the open toilet.

There was a brief flash, a sharp electrical spark from the outlet, and everything went dark.

Ames spun as fast as he could, throwing his right elbow around and behind him. He had spun with the intention of driving his elbow into Al's head. Instead, he was falling off balance, his tortured feet failing him in this most crucial moment. He sensed Al's arms passing above his head, heard a grunt of surprise as his elbow landed against the other's midsection. Something banged against the tub. He heard the shower curtain rustle angrily, the rings snapping from the rod like metal popcorn. He guessed his off-balance strike had caught Al by surprise, sending him tripping over the tub, pulling the curtain down with him.

It was pitch dark. He had blown all the fuses. Ames crawled through the door, climbed to his knees and then his feet. He raced barefoot down the stairs. He heard Barber shouting below, Al scrambling in the tub behind him. He reached the bottom of the stairs, turned to right, and ran to the foyer hall closet. He quietly opened the closet door, reached for and found the bag, quickly felt the clubs, and grabbed the heaviest iron he could touch.

Barber was still hollering for Al.

"Be quiet," answered the wispy voice. Ames froze. He guessed the voice to be at the bottom of the steps.

"What the fuck happened?" asked Barber.

"Be quiet!" said Al. Barber stopped yelling.

"Is he free?" asked Barber more quietly.

"Yes. Did he go out the door, front or back?"

"No," said Barber. "Turn the lights on."

"Where's the fuse box?"

"How should I know?"

Ames heard a soft step to his left. He closed his eyes, visualizing the layout of his house. He's heading to the kitchen. He's about ten feet from me. He held the club tighter, twisting his hands deep into the grip. To his right was the front door. He could try to make it out. But the door was locked. It would take a moment to find the lock, turn it. It would make noise.

"You got your gun out?" This from Al, much closer now.

He's heading this way, thought Ames.

"Yeah," said Barber.

"Well, don't shoot. I'm going to the front door. I thought I heard something there. Keep still until I tell you it is clear. Keep an ear to the back."

"Just a minute," said Barber.

Ames heard the familiar thin snap of a lighter, saw a brief flicker in the living room.

Barber's a smoker.

Everything was still. He couldn't tell where Al was, if he was moving closer. He pictured the twisted man holding his gun, stepping silently closer. He felt the club begin to tremble in his hands.

He heard the metal snap again, saw the flame leap in Barber's hands from a distance. Closer still, he saw the shadowed outline of a man, his head turned back to look at Barber.

The flame went out again with a curse from Barber, even as Ames swung the club with all his strength at the memory of Al's location. He struck something, hard. The club fell from his hands to the floor. There was a low moan, then something heavy hit the carpet.

Ames retrieved the club as Barber struck another spark, then another. He raced across the darkness broken periodically by the flickering light. He raised the club high as Barber caught the flame again. He heard a gun go off. He swung the club down at the flame lit face of Barber, all his hatred and fear put behind the blow. The club smacked into Barber's head, making a sickening crunch. The flame went out as Barber dropped the lighter, but not before Ames saw Barber start to slump to the floor. He swung the club again in the direction of the shadowed lump. Heard a moan. Swung it again.

And again.

He didn't remember stopping. He was standing in the darkness, gasping for breath.

He dropped the club, shuffled in the darkness to the fuse box in the hallway. He found the switch by habit and flipped it.

His heart was in his throat when he walked back in the living room. The light, after the darkness, seemed harsh. The scene was surreal. He didn't recognize it as his living room. Barber lay in a bloody mess on the plastic tarp, his head crushed in on the left hand side, his arms and legs at awkward angles. Ames looked for the gun, didn't see it. He bent down, lifted Barber like an edge of carpet. The gun was under his body. Ames retrieved it and put the lifeless body down again.

He turned then to the other.

Al was still on the foyer carpet in a similar ragdoll display. He had a large, ugly bruise, like an overripe plum, along the side of his head. Ames found Al's gun near the door. As he bent to retrieve it, he heard a moan. He looked over to see Al watching him, his eyes distended and unfocused, but his tremoring hand reaching for Ames.

Ames stood up, watched him struggle for a while, and then went to the kitchen. He found his cell phone in the small drawer where he kept it. He picked it up. The number was in the memory under friend. He looked to the kitchen clock.

Five o'clock.

He dialed the number as he walked back to the living room, holding the gun in one hand and the phone in the other.

Haines arrived an hour later. Ames was sitting in his kitchen, watching the sun come up outside his bay window. He let Haines and his companion in through the front door. Both men were wearing hats and heavy coats with the collars up. They stepped quickly through the open door.

It's a day for hats, thought Ames distractedly. Maybe they were back in fashion and he had missed it.

Haines's companion was a big man. Bigger than Anderson, though not as tall. He wore dark shades. He took his hat off, revealing a shaved head with a series of small scar lines along the top. He left the glasses on. He gave Ames a quick once over, then moved into the living room. Haines stood a moment with Ames in the foyer.

Barber was still in the middle of the tarp. Al was now beside him, bound at the wrists and legs with duct tape, another piece of tape on his mouth. Haines put a hand on Ames's elbow and moved him closer to the living room. Haines looked to Barber, then turned to Al.

"Does he one mean anything to you?" asked Haines, addressing the big man.

The big man looked closely at Al, then back to Haines, shook his head.

Haines met his eyes, then nodded once, sharply. The big man pulled a knife as Al started to struggle.

Ames tried to turn away, but Haines stopped him.

"You will watch this, Wilson."

When it was over, the big man wrapped the two bodies up in the tarp like a burrito. The dead, featureless faces and hands were just visible under the heavy plastic. The big man used the duct tape to seal the ends.

"If someone asks," said Haines, turning to Ames. "You had visitors. Don't volunteer it was Barber. If the police call you in, don't say anything. Call this number." He handed Ames a card with a name of a lawyer on it. "I was never here."

The big man looked up from the rolled up tarp. "I need a bedspread or sheet."

"I'll get it," said Ames.

"Just tell him where it is," said Haines. "We have to talk."

"There's some linen in the upstairs hall closet," said Ames.

The big man turned to Haines. "We'll take them out the front and put them in the van. It's isolated, and the porch is blocked off from the street by the van."

Haines nodded. The big man moved up the stairs.

"In here," said Haines, taking Ames by the arm and leading him into his own kitchen.

"Drink?" he asked.

Ames shook his head, sitting down and staring out the bay window again. He heard the other man come down the steps, then the front door open.

Haines took a seat, studied him carefully. "They worked you over pretty good." He pulled his gloves off, put them in his lap. "Where's Cynthia?"

"Her sister's."

"When does she get back?"

"Monday." Ames turned with a frown. "What day is it?"

"Sunday."

Ames turned his head, as if surprised. He heard the front door open again, saw two shadows pass by the kitchen archway.

"You need a doctor," said Haines.

"I can't go to the hospital," said Ames.

"I didn't say hospital." Haines pulled out a cell phone, dialed a number, and told someone on the other line to come to Ames's address. "Be discreet. Bring your bag." A pause. "Pretty bad. Looks like some burn work, a few stiches, too." Another pause. "Yes." Then he hung up.

"It won't be too long," he said, putting the phone away and addressing Ames. "Just enough time to have our talk."

Ames looked back at Haines, hearing something in his voice, something different.

"You know why I came, Wilson?" asked Haines.

"You're my friend."

Haines shook his head regretfully. "No. That's not it. I am your friend, I guess. As close as you or I can get to a friend."

"You told me to remember my friends," said Ames. He heard the slur in his voice, wondered how long it had been there.

"I did," agreed Haines. "I remember the day I told you that. It was the day you started your…work. The day you started your rules."

Ames nodded. He was a step behind. Haines was telling him something, or was going to tell him something, important. He needed to concentrate. But even as he tried to listen, the image of Al's last frantic, desperate moments filled his mind, he saw again the terrible washed out faces pressed against the plastic.

"I knew I would get this call one day," said Haines, interrupting his thoughts. "Though, I didn't expect it to come quite this way." He looked in the direction of the living room where two men were dragging the heavy bundle, now covered in a bedsheet, to the front door. Haines turned back to Ames. "Nor did I think it would take this long." He shook his head. "Twenty-five years, Wilson. Remarkable."

Ames tried to blink himself into focus, but his concentration kept slipping away like a retreating tide.

"Do you know what I said to the others that day, to convince them to give your crazy plan a try?" Haines leaned back in the metal chair, frowned, and looked down at what he was sitting in. "What is this, lawn furniture?"

Ames didn't answer.

Haines looked at him with some concern. "Wilson, can you hear me?"

"Yes."

Haines continued, still watching Ames closely. "They were not going to have you, or your precious rules that day. Not because they didn't see the value of your proposal. But they all believed, deep in their seedy little hearts, that I owned you. They believed you were just some gambit on my part." Haines slapped his gloves lightly against his lap, met Ames's eye, and smirked. "They were right."

Something important, thought Ames, struggling. "What do you mean?"

"So you are there! Good. Now listen close."

"I think I want that drink now," said Ames.

"You sure? It might kill you. God! You are a mess. Okay, just the one. I'll join you." Haines put his gloves on the table, retreated to the living room where he found the bottle, and returned. He made them both a drink with what was left, and sat down again. He raised his glass in a toast to Ames. "To the life."

Ames blinked, knowing now what was so important, what was at stake. He sipped his drink. *What does it matter now, anyway?*

Haines took a long sip, looked appreciatively at Ames. "You have good whiskey, Wilson." He put the glass down. A flicker of something close to animosity crossed his face, settled into his eyes. "You understand? You are in the life now."

For a moment, the old instincts, the will for independence, cried out to respond, to stop the direction Haines was taking. But before he could formulate the words, he heard the front door open, watched two figures pass the kitchen archway, one with a brush and bucket. A moment later, he heard the sounds of deep, heavy scrubbing against the carpet.

"Yes," said Haines, pulling Ames's attention around again. "That's the price." They listened for a time to the continued scrubbing. "Are we in agreement?"

Ames winced around an answer, then nodded once.

"Good," said Haines. He looked to the bottle. He poured what was left in his glass. He left Ames's alone.

"That's a nice view," said Haines, looking out the window, his drink in hand. When he spoke, his voice was soft, reflective. "Twenty-five years ago I took a chance. I told the men at the table that day you were not mine. I didn't expect them to take my word for it. But I had faith in you, Wilson. I knew you could convince them, given a chance. Try it out, I suggested. Let Wilson Ames show you just how independent he can be. And of course, you did. It was clear, early on, that you were what you said you were. No strings, particularly not to me. Nothing illegal, nothing troubling. And the rules, your rules, worked, just as you said they would."

Haines turned from the window.

"And gradually," he said, "oh so gradually, Wilson Ames became what you wanted: an independent operator." He smiled with distant memory, took a sip of his whiskey. "I couldn't have asked for more. Except, of course, that this moment not take twenty five years to arrive. That, I didn't see. You were too good, Wilson. You didn't make a mistake. You didn't bend your rules, ever. But maybe it worked out for the better. Maybe it had to take all this time. It certainly makes what we have stronger."

"What we have?" asked Ames.

Haines leaned forward. Another part of the mask fell away and Ames saw, for the second time in his life, the raw, inimical power of the true Haines.

"You are in the life now, Wilson," said Haines. "The bodies in that bag make it so. And—pay attention to this bit, Wilson—you belong to me."

It was Ames's turn to look out the window. It looked to be a beautiful morning. He was thinking how he would like to get in some yard work today.

"But you knew that when you called me, didn't you?"

I did, thought Ames. *I knew the cost when I dialed the number of my friend, my friend Haines. I knew, too, somehow, that Haines had been expecting this call for some time. I've always known.*

"You'll continue to work, of course," said Haines, "as if nothing has changed."

The voice was a drone of sound in Ames's ear. Registering, not to be forgotten, but unwanted, like the hum of a blown out speaker.

"But," continued Haines, "with two important differences. First, I will, from time to time, call on you to tip things in my direction. Look at me, Ames."

Ames rolled his head back to face Haines.

"It will be unfair," admitted Haines wryly. "It will break hell out of your precious rules. But it *will* be my way. You will see to that. You understand?"

A deep instinct too ingrained to be dismissed, made Ames note the obvious. "For a time. Until they figure I've been compromised."

"It will be up to you to make sure that doesn't happen any time soon." Haines waved his gloves in dismissal. "Oh, I'm not a fool. I won't abuse the opportunity. And, they won't believe you're corrupted right away—not for a long time, in fact. They can't afford to; they have too much invested in your role now. That's the beauty of this."

Beauty, thought Ames. "And second? You said there were two important differences."

"You will also kill for me," said Haines.

I'm not surprised, thought Ames. *Why am I not surprised? Why am I not shocked?*

"Not like that, of course." Haines glanced again in the direction of the living room, where they could hear the sound of a vacuum cleaner. "But you will kill for me."

He paused, sipped his drink, watched Ames. "Powerful men," he continued. His words fell softly, effortlessly, one after the other, each syllable breaking against Ames like a relentless tide. "Unreachable men. Men like me. They will welcome you into their worlds, their homes, trusting in the safety of your reputation, trusting in the word of Wilson Ames. And you will drop something in their drink, or on their dinner rolls, and you will see to it that they die."

Ames stared at Haines, trying to fit this new reality into his fragile, bruised mind. *Haines said kill.* The very word was so far removed from the rules, it seemed impossible he said it aloud. But he had. The word had been spoken here, in of all places, Ames's kitchen.

"I'll use that particular difference," continued Haines, "even more carefully than the first. Maybe only once. Maybe a few times." He paused. "But I promise you, there will come a day you will kill for me, Wilson."

That word again. It was on Ames's lips to protest he hadn't heard Haines correctly. Or, if he had, that he couldn't possibly do that; he wasn't built that way. But he knew—better than anyone—this was no negotiation.

There was a soft knock on the door. Ames started, looked up.

"Sit," said Haines. "It's all right. It's just the doctor."

One of the big men passed the kitchen entrance again. They heard the front door open, a soft question and answer. A moment later, a middle-aged man stood in the kitchen doorway. He was dressed in a heavy wool coat and carried a metal bag.

"Just a moment," said Haines.

The doctor retreated to the living room.

"Well, Wilson," said Haines. "Do we have a full understanding?"

Ames couldn't bring himself to say yes, but knew there was no going back now, no points to contend. Again, he nodded slowly.

"Good." Haines stood up.

Only then did Ames find his tongue. "One thing, Geoff."

Haines stopped, frowning slightly, his body language tense and aggressive.

"Cynthia," said Ames.

Haines visibly relaxed. "She stays out of everything, of course."

"No," said Ames. "But thank you for that. No, I want to know…"

But again he couldn't say the words aloud, couldn't ask the question. '*So, Haines is fucking your wife.*'

Haines squinted down at Ames. When he spoke it was almost sympathetic. "What is it you want to ask me, Wilson?"

"Nothing. Never mind."

Haines stared a moment longer, then shrugged. "I'll be in touch."

"Thanks, Geoff. For everything."

Haines hesitated, looked at Ames as if to assess hidden damages. "Not a problem," he said distractedly. He turned to someone outside Ames's view. "You can go in now. Take good care of him. He's a friend."

The doctor entered the kitchen, started to look Ames over. Ames paid him no attention. He heard the front door open and close. Something closed in his mind as well, and he retreated back to his world now.

"Doctor," he said, trying to smile. "I'm expecting important company tomorrow. I would like to look my best. Can you manage it?"

The doctor, looked up from his work, snorted. "You'll be lucky to get out of bed in a week."

The doctor did his best, and Ames hid the rest under makeup and strategically placed clothing. There was little he could do about his face. Fortunately, most of the real burn was on the top of his head. The doctor gave him pills for the pain.

He tried to put the house back in order. It was not as clean as he would like, but the doctor had been right and it had taken all of his will just to pat himself clean and dress. As it was, he overslept and it was almost noon before he walked downstairs. Fortunately, Cynthia took a late flight, true to form.

He met her at the door. Her smile fell away as the afternoon light betrayed his efforts. "My god, Wilson! What happened?"

"Hello, dear. How was your trip?"

She looks fantastic, he thought. *A dark brown nut with freckles.* He reached out to touch the natural highlights in her hair, bent in, kissed her gently on the lips and ignored the pain this caused to his own.

"Fine, fine," she said distractedly. "I caught a break and got a seat in business. But Wilson, you look like you've been dragged on the street. *Are those burns?*"

He turned to pick up her bag. She pushed his hand away, and dragged it through herself. Then she took him by the hand and led him to the living room. "Sit," she ordered. She went back, closed the door, and then took a seat next to him. She studied his face with growing dismay.

"I'm afraid I was foolish," he said, taking her hands carefully in his own. "I got distracted, went down the wrong street, and got mugged."

"A mugger did that?"

"Well, a very disturbed person."

"Did they catch him?"

He shook his head sadly.

She ran her warm hands lightly down his cheeks. "Oh my poor, Wilson. Does it hurt as bad as it looks?"

"Not at all," he said, smiling. "The doctor says there shouldn't be any scarring. Not on the face anyway. I got lucky."

She looked relieved. He understood. A burned husband was not an accessory Cynthia relished. Then she did a double take.

"What do you mean, not on the face? There's more?" She searched the rest of him, seeing the conditions of his hands for the first time.

"Well, I'm afraid there was a little knife work."

She raised a horrified hand to her mouth. "Wilson!"

He touched his chest lightly. "It's just a little line down the middle. It will fade in time."

Cynthia reached out to put her finger tips on top of his. She started to cry softly.

"And to think, there I am, sitting by the pool in the sun and here you are...." She searched for the right words, shook her head in frustration, sending tear drops across her cheeks.

He reached up and gently brushed them aside. "I'm sorry, dear. I didn't want to put you through this."

She stared at him in disbelief. "Put me through this? Honestly, Wilson."

He smiled, kissed her fingertips. "I'm glad you're home."

She bent over and kissed him carefully on the cheek. "I am home, darling. And now it's time for me to take care of you. You must be exhausted. Put your feet up, never mind the couch." She looked around, stopped. "Jesus, Wilson, you must be hurt. It's not like you to let the house go."

"Sorry, dear. Planned on getting it shipshape before you arrived, but a bit stiff this morning."

"Never mind. I'll take care of it, as a penance for my sins." She winked at Ames and started off to the kitchen.

Ames, almost shaking with exhaustion, closed his eyes, wondering what sins she needed penance for. He heard Cynthia talking in the kitchen, though he wasn't sure it was to him.

"Wilson!" she called a moment later. "You drank all the booze."

"Sorry, dear," he said, but it came out a mutter.

"What?" She poked her head out the kitchen.

"Sorry."

She smirked. "I see you have some penance to do as well."

He grinned sheepishly. She retreated back into the kitchen. He heard the clatter of ice in a glass. Apparently she found some booze after all. Or maybe she brought it with her.

My penance, he thought idly, falling again toward sleep. *My penance, for sins past and present.*

And future.

He wondered if there was a house messy enough to answer.

IV

Ames sat on a stool in a corner table of the food court, sipping beer from a tall glass. He was looking over the balcony rail at the perpetual blue of the Singapore skyline, carefully avoiding eye contact with the elderly Asian across the way. Smells of western and eastern cuisine created an oddly subtle fusion in the late afternoon. An industrial fan, as large as a bank vault, was pushing the humid air around with mixed results. Ames was dressed for the heat. He wore a blue short-sleeve shirt, with light beige linen pants and (a first for Ames) sandals. They were handmade, genuine leather sandals, not your average crocks, but sandals just the same.

He took another sip of beer, feeling the perspiration between his shoulders despite the fan. This was the third afternoon in a row that the two men sat catty-corner of one another. As usual, the elderly man was having his cigarette and bucket of beers. Six beers on ice, no more, no less, and one cigarette, held like a lover's hand under the table to be raised occasionally for an illicit and lengthy kiss. Sometimes the old man ate a plate of wings, or maybe a crockpot of frog, but always the beer and the cigarette.

Ames came to appreciate the ritual of that beer on the balcony. He was by habit a scotch drinker. But after the first night, watching the old man slowly pull one frosted bottle after the other from the ice, he switched over. He didn't think he could handle a whole bucket, so he settled on a single tall pint. Sipping from an hour-glass shaped stein, watching the cotton-ball clouds roll over and over in the impossibly blue, impossibly humid afternoon sky, he started to see why the old man preferred cold beer. For a brief moment the afternoon food court ritual distracted him from the harsher reality. For that brief moment, he almost forgot that he was there to kill a man.

He had arrived in Singapore four days ago, exhausted and weary, having spent the long flight in a restless fever of anxiety. He settled into Singapore quickly, finding it oddly familiar in its carefully planned streets and living spaces, its conflicted need for discreet but purposeful conformity. Singapore worked for him on many levels, particularly that odd sense of propriety amid diversity, a paradoxical mix of multicultural commercialism and timeless tropical retreat. Everything, including the social norms, was carefully staged for maximum profit and enjoyment. But if paradise was for sale, at least it was still paradise, with brilliant blue skies, palm trees, and bright, clean smiles.

Yet for all the complex charms and distractions of Singapore, he might as well have been sitting at home, worrying the bones of his new truth.

Everything had gone wrong. In the end, the rules had failed him. Completely.

The days after his confrontation with Barber were a waking nightmare, his head filled with the afterimages of the body laden tarp. Particularly haunting were the pink, washed out faces vaguely recognizable as human through the plastic wrapping. Faces with names—*Barber. Al.*

He lost weight. He took to drinking more, and more often. He couldn't sleep.

Cynthia noticed of course. She blamed the cause on his recent "mugging." She was sympathetic, caring, worried, helpful. She woke him reluctantly, time and again, from screaming nightmares, comforted his sweat soaked body like a mother would a child. She tried to get him to eat. Occasionally, she stayed up with him when he couldn't sleep.

But it was hard on her. Ames knew she was frustrated. Frustrated with his pain, with him, with herself. He understood she was genuinely anxious for him, genuinely concerned, but he understood, too, the limits of his wife. Cynthia didn't do selfless very well.

He started staying in the second bedroom at night. That way, if he did manage to sleep a precious hour or two, he would spare her the drama of his nightmares. He asked her a few days later if he still kept her up. She waved the matter off, then confessed with a blush to wearing earplugs. He told her he was grateful.

They rarely talked now without both conscientiously stepping around his decline. They didn't go out—well, Ames didn't go out. They didn't make love. He couldn't. He tried once, to both their frustration and embarrassment. But the image of the plastic wrapped bodies was too constant a backdrop, and he crawled from the bed, mouthing apologies as impotent as his self-will. Their home became a site of muted and awkward self-recriminations.

This went on until he got the call from Haines.

They met in the office. By then, Ames had healed for the most part, at least physically. The meeting was been terse, one-sided, absent of their former (albeit, slightly guarded) camaraderie. Haines told him where he was going, when, who he was seeing, what was to be done, and how best to do it. Ames listened, looking at a space just above Haines's head, cringing inside at every spoken detail, name, and illegal obligation. The rules, clearly, were no longer in play.

He would be traveling to Singapore, ostensibly to broker a deal for Cal-Dale, one of Haines's legitimate operations. The deal was all above board, but complicated. It could take day, maybe weeks. During that time, Ames would kill a man.

"The negotiations can go on as long as you like," explained Haines. "That will give you time to find and arrange for a personal meeting with Mr. Yoto. He'll expect something of that order." Then he reached across the desk and put a small liquid phial in front of Ames.

"Don't lose that," said Haines, nodding to the phial. "Or get caught with it."

At which point, Ames finally broke his silence. "Please, Geoff, don't you have professionals for this?"

"Yes," said Haines. "And Yoto would know the minute one of them landed in Singapore, or the moment he laid eyes on them. That's why it has to be you. You are clearly not a professional, at least not that kind of professional. He'll know who you are, of course, and that you're there for the Cal-Dale negotiation. He'll know, too, your precious rules. And knowing all that, he'll know you are safe. And because of that, you'll be able to get close."

Haines glared at Ames, as if daring him to argue the point. Ames could only stare mutely in return.

"And just so you know, this is not personal, Wilson," continued Haines. "I'm not asking you to clean up my mess. Eliminating Yoto will simply help me establish credit with my friends in the East."

Ames stared at the carpet. *Simply credit.* He felt like getting sick.

"You will do this, Wilson," said Haines, his voice tight with suppressed tension.

"I don't know if I can," whispered Ames.

"But I do," returned Haines. "I saw the proof of that in your house, remember? This is far easier. You simply sprinkle what's in that little phial on Yoto's dinner, or in his drink, and walk away. No one will ever know what killed him. It will look like a heart attack." He paused, and then added, "Wilson, you don't have to feel any remorse for this piece of dirt. If you like, I can show you some of his work. Yoto had two cash crops: underage sex traffic and murder. Take your pick, you'll see enough to motivate you."

Ames shook his head. Disturbing pictures and rationalizations would not help. Logic and rational did not help with Al and Barber. How could they help with a stranger, one that had done him no personal harm?

It was Al that was most troubling to Ames. Barber, too, had died, and at Ames hands, no less; his head crushed in by repeated blows from a golf club. But Barber had been instinct, self-preservation, an act of defense. Barber had a gun. Ames had swung the club at the bitter, hate-filled face framed by Barber's lighter even as he heard the gun go off. And he kept swinging until he was certain he was safe. There was no time to think with Barber. But Al…Al had been alive. Hurt, concussed, yes. But alive. He saw again the tiny bubbles of blood and saliva seeping from the tape on Al's mouth, the way his concussed eyes grew frantic when he saw the knife coming down.

Al was a sociopath, he thought. *Al would never stop.*

What does that make you?

"Wilson!"

Ames snapped to attention. Haines was glaring at him. Ames wondered how much he'd missed.

"Get yourself together, man," said Haines.

Ames nodded slowly, met his eyes.

Haines measured him. "Good. Now remember, Yoto will know who you are. He will know that you are there for the Cal-Dale negotiation, which he is also part of. He will *expect* you to approach him separately at some time. You know how to arrange these things, but I will give you some of his personal haunts and habits to move things along. I think that should give you all the opportunity you need, correct?"

Ames nodded, because it seemed Haines expected him to.

"Now, listen to me carefully, Wilson. You will not be representing me in any capacity, Cal-Dale or otherwise. Yoto must not know I am involved. Do you understand?"

Again, Ames nodded.

"Say it," demanded Haines.

"Yes."

Again, Haines studied him for a time. "As long as we are clear on that."

"We are clear, Geoff."

And that had been the end of the meeting. Ames left with a plane ticket, hotel reservation, and the phial. He didn't remember the cab ride, or walking inside his home. He didn't remember sitting down in his kitchen, a glass of scotch in his hand. He only remembered the washed out flesh of Barber and Al behind the plastic.

He heard Cynthia coming down the steps, heard her say something about going out, and smelled her perfume as the door closed behind her. Belatedly, he wished her well.

He drank his scotch, finished it, and made another drink. He went to the living room, looked to the innocent carpet. Haines's man had been careful to remove any signs of the drama that had taken place that night, including the bullet in the wall where Barber had missed him. But the stains were still there, in his mind.

He saw his notepad and pencil on the coffee table where he had left them. He had tried to sketch once, afterward, failing as miserably as he did with Cynthia in bed. He picked the pad up again now, holding it like a summons. He took the pencil in his other hand, feeling its slick, cool surface under his fingertips. He studied the soft blue lead, trying to visualize a scene.

And suddenly it was all too much. With a strangled cry, he slammed the pencil tip on the metal cover of the pad, breaking it to the nub. Then he threw the pencil across the room, heard it smack against the floorboard. He held the pad up as if to do the same, but stopped. He took a deep, shaky breath, and set the pad carefully back on the table. He stood in his living room, staring at nothing, breathing heavily.

Eventually, he picked up his drink again, finished it, and then took the glass back to the kitchen to set it in the sink. He went to the spare bedroom without changing. Later, he heard Cynthia return late in the night. She went directly to her room.

In the morning, he climbed from the tiny bed, still in his clothes. For a time, he stood in their bedroom door and watched Cynthia sleep. She was sprawled across the bed, still in her slip, one long, tan leg poking from the silk sheets. He saw the tiny onset of varicose in her calf, noted the subtle red of her painted toenails. For a terrible, wonderful moment he wanted her. He wanted to cross the room, put his hands on the length of her calf, kiss her open mouth, and take her before she was completely awake.

But then the moment passed.

He turned from the doorway with one last long look at the naked calf, and went quietly downstairs. He wrote a note saying that he was called out of town on a business emergency. Not to worry. Would call her soon. Don't expect him back for some time. He put the note on the refrigerator. He left without saying goodbye.

He had called her, as promised, from his hotel room in Singapore. She had been out, which he took as fortunate. He left a more detailed message about contract disputes, lengthy negotiations, apologized again for leaving so suddenly. It was not the first sudden trip he made. He knew she wouldn't worry. He thought she might even understand.

Now, sitting in the humid Singapore air, across from a man he was ordered to kill, he remembered again that morning departure. He could still see the dark, carnal length of Cynthia's leg, could still feel the fickle stir of desire in his belly. Waking her would not have made a difference to his current state, but at least he would have the memory, something to balance the vision of faceless bodies and terrible, impossible burdens.

He looked up from his beer, glanced briefly at Yoto and then looked away again. He had acted along the lines Haines suggested. The negotiations with Cal-Dale were going slowly. He spent his days in the conference room, distracted and oddly muted. In truth, he was doing poorly. In the evenings, he sat in the food court, sampling different dishes, drinking his beer, watching the old man with his bucket of beer and precious cigarette.

He risked another glance in Yoto's direction, who was now concentrating on a paperback book. Ames guessed it was some kind of puzzle book, judging from the frequent marks Yoto left on the pages. Yoto was wearing his reading glasses today, a pair of half-moon lenses that sat precariously on his nose. A chain kept them around his neck when they weren't in use.

Ames turned to his left, to the line of stalls that ran in a block down the middle of the food court. The stall closest to Yoto was a Sake bar. Yoto sat just outside the bar section, at a private table in the back corner of the food court. Ames watched the now familiar frame of the Sake proprietor clean glasses and checking stock. He had no reason to believe that the proprietor worked for Yoto, but suspected he might. The deferential, protective manner with which the young Sake owner treated the old man held more than just good business sense or cultural tradition.

He turned his attention back to the old man. The book had been put aside. Yoto was now looking out over the balcony. The sun was going down, and the dinner crowd starting to arrive in small but steady trickles of singles, couple, and the occasional group.

Not long now, thought Ames. *He never stays long after the sun goes down.*

A moment later, Yoto rolled the book up and tucked it under his arm. He stood slowly, the glasses dangling along his chest, and walked carefully but steadily out the back steps of the balcony. In going this way, he avoided passing Ames.

Ames took his time finishing his beer. He stayed until the sun was completely set. All the tables around him now were full, and there were lines at many of the food stalls. He stood, freeing up his table.

Back at the hotel, he left another message on the answering machine, and then spent the night staring at the ceiling, thinking, *tomorrow?*

Thus his new reality.

He woke around noon, having finally fallen asleep in the early morning. It was Monday, a holiday. Cal-Dale had agreed to suspend negotiations until Tuesday. He had no plans for the day. He had no idea where Yoto would be, or if he would hold to his dinner routine at the food court on a holiday.

He took a long, hot shower, and dressed in his swimming suit and a bathrobe. On his way out, he picked up the empty bottles of scotch and wine. He tried to remember when he bought them. It wasn't that long ago. He stashed them in the hall garbage can and took an elevator to the outdoor pool.

The sun was painfully bright. He found a lounge recliner under an umbrella stand and near a small wading pool. The air was slightly cooler here. He spread the towel out on the chair and almost collapsed on top of it. He closed his eyes, but sat up again a moment later, taking deep, shallow breaths, trying to still his roiling stomach and spinning head.

It's not the booze, he thought. *Well, not just the booze*. There was also the lack of sleep. And Cynthia. And Haines. And a thousand other things that kept tripping through his mind like hot metal flashes. But most of all, it was dread. A crippling anticipation of what came next, what was unavoidable.

He had put it off as long as he could, taking Haines at his word that he had all the time he needed for Yoto. He had hoped with time he would grow used to the idea. Hoped, somehow, to find the will to go through with it. He hadn't. The longer he put it off, the worse his anxiety became. The drink only deadened the dread temporarily, made it possible for him to get the few hours of sleep he did manage. But it also made things worse. He could feel his blood circulating in spits and fizzles, like a spurting oil line, hot and dirty and losing pressure. His head was hot, his back cold, his stomach an alternating mix of both.

No more booze, he thought, sitting on the edge of lounge chair, shaking and sweating in the hot, humid air. The decision brought small comfort to his fevered body, but it planted a seed of hope somewhere in his mind. He stood up, shed his shirt, sandals, and glasses. He climbed slowly into the pool, sinking under the surface like a lost dream. The cool comfort of liquid space caressed his ravaged nerve endings, bringing, if not relief, then a temporary distance to his pain.

When he surfaced, he started treading water for a time, then floated on his back, closing his eyes against the bright sun. A short time later, he rolled over, and with more determination than energy, started doing laps. He took breaks at either end of the pool. His form was terrible. After the first lap, he fought for breath and struggled to ignore his protesting muscles. But he kept going. When he had visions of Al's face under the plastic, he kept going. When that face became Yoto's, he kept going.

Finally, exhausted and fearing his next lap might not see him rise from the water, he stopped. He climbed carefully from the pool, feeling the ground sway slightly beneath his trembling footsteps. He made his way back to the chair, and almost collapsed across it. He didn't bother to dry off. He felt sick. He felt weak. He felt like a water-soaked rag.

Five minutes later, the ground steady again, his heartbeat more or less back to the norm, he opened his eyes. *Not yet*, he thought. *I'm not done yet.*

He picked up the towel and found his way to the sauna. It was a small affair, with tiled benches and a glass door that wouldn't close all the way. It smelled like mildew and feet. He set the temperature to 51 degrees, Celsius. He didn't expect to last that long. He just wanted to feel it, and fast.

When the thermometer read 36 degrees, he started sweating profusely. He hung his head between his knees, his body shaking with physical exhaustion and fatigue. But like the pool, he pushed on. At 40 degrees, he stood up, swaying slightly. He opened the glass door and stepped out, the steam spilling out and around him. He stood for a time leaning on the cool porcelain of the bathroom sink, wondering if he was going to die, wondering if he wanted to. It was impossible to focus on either answer.

When he woke, the sun was going down over the hotel palm trees. He was in the lounge chair again, though he didn't remember leaving the sauna. He sat up, watching the sinking ember sun until the dark blue sky became black. He gathered his belongings and went back to his room and took a long, hot shower. Finished, he dressed for dinner. He was tired of the food courts. He wanted to sit down to a meal with four real walls around him and centralized air, a place where he could wear his jacket. But the thought of a taxi ride (or god forbid, a walk) was too much for his overheated, over worn state. He compromised by using the hotel's restaurant, a mere elevator ride to the bottom floor. He took a booth in the back, and ordered the biggest steak he could find on the menu.

He saw the girl after dinner, as he was having coffee. She was sitting by herself at the end of the bar, dressed in black, her dark hair hanging like a curtain to the middle of her back. Her legs were crossed and tucked under the stool. She was small, but held herself with careful deliberation, a stilled elegance, like a pool of moonlit water. She turned once, briefly, and he caught her profile. Full lips above a delicate chin; long dark lashes over oddly rich eyes. He suspected they were amber.

As opposite to Cynthia as could be, he thought, *but for the beauty.*

He finished his coffee and went to pay his bill at the register. He was conscious of the woman's glance, but when he turned in her direction she was looking down at her drink again. A moment later another woman walked in and sat next to her with a familiar greeting. They were soon lost in conversation. Ames paid his bill and walked out.

He tried to call Cynthia from his room, but got the answering machine. He didn't leave a message. He went to bed. It was just a little before ten.

The next day, he was up before dawn. He ate a small breakfast, and spent most of the morning getting ready for his noon meeting. Though Cal-Dale was a cover, he knew he was not performing anywhere near his ability. He was too lost in personal angst to pay attention to the negotiations and had been little more than an empty suit at the table. He'd correct that today. He acted from an intuitive sense of responsibility, and—like the exercise— a desperate need to instill some kind of normalcy, some foundation against the nightmare of his recent past and pressing future. He made some notes for himself as he had his second cup of coffee.

And in a sense, it worked. The meetings went well, and for a time the nightmare retreated. But then the meeting was over, another session scheduled for tomorrow, and he was on his own again. He took a cab home, debated skipping the food court again. But the nightmare worked in both directions, compelling him forward now, demanding some kind of resolution.

Yoto was in his usual place, with his usual bucket of beers. Ames took a seat a few tables across from him. He held to his resolution, ordering a juice with his salad. He tried to eat, but his stomach was too tied up in knots. He had better success with the juice, and finished it quickly, ordered another. Eventually, inevitably, he glanced in Yoto's direction. Yoto was looking back. He held Ames's eyes for a moment, nodded slightly, and then slowly, deliberately looked away.

Ames picked up his juice bottle, tried to still his racing nerves. There was nothing about Yoto's look that was accidental, casual. It was a knowing look, an expectant look.

"*He'll know who you are.*" Haines had said as much, or something to that effect.

Ames finished his drink in one long pull, left the half-eaten salad on the table and walked away. He was careful not to look in Yoto's direction again.

Back at the hotel, he spent the night staring at the ceiling, holding the phial in his hands. *He might ask me over tomorrow,* he thought. *I'll have my chance tomorrow.*
He didn't call Cynthia. He left no messages.
Tomorrow.

He left for work with the phial in his pants pocket. He felt it pressing against his thigh all through the Cal-Dale negotiations. The meeting was a disaster. He was distracted and made mistakes, losing most of the gain he'd made the day before. But it didn't matter, he consoled himself. It was all a farce. A façade for his real task. *Everything and everyone is a farce.* He suffered a fleeting image of Cynthia walking out the door, smelling of perfume.
The phial rubbed against his leg like a piece of cancer as he climbed the steps of the food court. He took the phial out, and put it in his hand, wondering how the late afternoon could be so bright, so disconcerting.
Yoto was there, in his usual place.
But something was different. Something in the tableau had shifted, changing the very atmosphere of the court, of Yoto, of Ames—if only in their limited circle of drama. Ames felt a rush of extra adrenaline as he realized the Sake bar was closed, the proprietor noticeably absent.
He walked straight to Yoto's table, the phial still in his hand. Yoto watched him approach, pointed with his cigarette to the stool across from him. "Beer, Mr. Ames?"
"No. Thank you."
"Try one. I insist."
Yoto took a beer from the bucket, held it briefly, decided it was not right for some reason, chose another one. This time he nodded. He twisted the cap off and placed it carefully in front of Ames.

"Onion ring?" Yoto gestured to the basket beside the beer.

Ames shook his head.

"Wise," said Yoto.

"You know my name," said Ames.

"I do," agreed Yoto.

Up close, Yoto looked older and somehow familiar. His skin tended to sag along his cheek like a spaniel, and tiny lines and spots of age formed brown constellations across his nose and forehead. His eyes were rheumy and dark, but still hard. He was not an overly large man, but his hands and head bore the marks of his street-fighting youth. His nose had been broken at least once, his fingers swollen and thick around the knuckles. He was tanned above the loose, open collar of his golf shirt. His baggy shorts revealed stumpy sailor legs and canvas shoes.

Ames raised his beer, took a long, slow drink, trying to identify what made the other man so familiar. Yoto folded his arms across his chest and watched him, a small amused smile playing on his lips.

My father, thought Ames. *Somehow Yoto reminds me of my father.*

It was not a physical resemblance. His father was a mix of Irish and German descent, a small man with thin black hair that tended to curl over his forehead. Nor was it personality. Unlike Yoto, his father was as slight in persona as he was in frame. But there was something in the way Yoto listened, the way he looked just to the right of the speaker. That, and the eyes; two shadowed doorways, open but somehow impossible to penetrate. His father had eyes like that.

"Do you know why I am here?" asked Ames.

The smile deepened. "It certainly isn't to broker a deal for Cal-Dale. You're doing an appallingly bad job of that—apart from yesterday."

Ames dropped his eyes. "You've been monitoring the sessions."

Yoto grunted noncommittally. "Who sent you?"

Ames said the name of the party Haines had given him, the one supposedly behind the Cal-Dale negotiations.

Yoto shook his head. "Who really sent you?"

Ames looked away. Rules and clever answers rushed to his defense. He dismissed them for the empty props he now knew them to be. He rolled the phial in his hand like temptation. An image of Cynthia pulled momentarily at his attention, replaced the next moment by a dark profile with long lashes over amber.

"Does it matter?" he asked.

"Haines sent you," said Yoto, his mouth now a tight line of resolve. "You don't have to confirm it."

Ames took a sip of beer.

"You don't look very well, Mr. Ames," continued Yoto. "If you don't mind me saying so."

"I don't feel well."

The two sat in silence, each looking away. For his part, Ames was unsure what to say. Without the rules, he was set adrift, only the troubling weight of the phial to ground him, a stone he carried in his hands as he stepped into deeper waters. Yoto, on the other hand, was apparently in no hurry. The food court was almost deserted, but it was his. It was Ames that was the stranger, who was out of place. Yoto sipped his beer, waiting.

When Ames finally spoke, it was to break the most fundamental of rules. As he said the words, he felt no guilt or fear or self-recrimination. There was no relief or surprise. He felt, instead, oddly disappointed. The world did not end.

"Yes. Haines sent me."

Yoto raised an eyebrow. Clearly he had not expected the open admission, not from Ames. He reached out for an onion ring, obviously buying time to think. He considered the fried circle objectively, then looked to Ames, marking options and possibilities. "He thinks he's clever," he said finally, his voice calm, friendly, as if they were discussing the merits of the food. He took a bite of the ring, chewed, and frowned. He put the rest of it on a napkin. "They're not bad," he explained. "I just have no appetite." He looked again to Ames. "What is the offer?" he asked. "What does Mr. Haines want?"

Ames felt his stomach turn in on itself, looked to the skyline for inspiration. *What do I say? I've already admitted to Haines's involvement. How far do I go with this?* He squeezed the phial in his hand under the table.

The silence stretched beyond comfort. Yoto waited, watching.

"I have to say, Mr. Ames, you are a bit of a disappointment."

Ames struggled to make sense of the words, frowned.

"I was not at that famous meeting so long ago," continued Yoto, folding his arms across his chest. "But I heard all the details." He leaned back in his chair. "The wonderful Mr. Wilson Ames. The guiding light, the calm voice in the storm, the arbitrator of arbitrators...the man with the rules." He smiled. "I was actually looking forward to this meeting. I figured you would eventually come to me—you were here, after all, and eating across from me every night. Surely, I thought, Ames is really here to see me. The Cal-Dale negotiations are just one of his clever covers. But imagine my disappointment night after night as you sat there like some wallflower hoping to be asked for a dance. But then I thought, perhaps this is another ploy? One of your famous tactics." He shrugged. "I even began to worry that I'd somehow broken one of the rules. I was surprised by how much that bothered me."

He leaned in, caught Ames's attention. "But now, I worry about something else. You are making too many mistakes in the negotiations for it to be a ploy. You are distracted. You don't appear to want to close. You don't seem to have a direction, at all. In fact, there doesn't appear to be any rules anymore. We're using names. *You* are using names. I feel I can say anything I want, and that you just might. Not to mention, you look like hell." He leaned back again. "All of which leads me to say, again, you are quite a disappointment, Mr. Ames."

The rules are over, thought Ames, *their purpose, extinct. Everything is upside down.*

"I'm not myself," admitted Ames.

"Clearly."

Yoto took a long pull from his beer, looked around. "Did he tell you it wasn't personal?"

Ames started, saw the confident, ironic knowledge in Yoto's face. *My god, he knows. He knows why I'm really here.*

"So clever," snorted Yoto, looking down at the table. "Haines. Like his father. He thought he was clever, too. I showed the elder Haines to be otherwise." He looked up again with a smile. "It *is* personal, Mr. Ames. It is always personal in our line of work."

"How long have you known?" asked Ames, thinking of Barber and Al wrapped in plastic. *It is always personal...*

Yoto squinted. "Known?" He shrugged. "I suspected since that long ago meeting, your introduction to our little world. I suspected even then that you would be a tool for Haines. I watched and waited for the truth to show itself." He shook a thick finger at Ames. "But you gave me doubt, Mr. Ames. Year after year you went on, performing just as advertised, strengthening your reputation, and with no signs of Haines's control. I began to think I was wrong. That you were, in fact, on your own." He shrugged his arms. "But now you walk around like a drowning man. Now you make mistakes—not calculated mistakes, but genuine errors. Now you break your rules. Now you are here. When did I know? I have always known. I've been waiting for this for a long time. An old man eventually meets all his fears."

He finished his beer, opened another. Did the same for Ames. Ames let it sit there.

"But why you?" continued Yoto, his face wrinkled in confusion. "Now that I see you here, I don't understand. You are not made for this kind of thing, Mr. Ames."

"He thought you wouldn't see it coming," answered Ames. *There are no rules!*

Yoto waved this away. "No, I didn't mean Haines. I understand why the clever Mr. Haines would use you like this. No, my question was to you. Why are you doing this?"

Ames rubbed the top of the beer bottle with his thumb, but couldn't find an answer. He shrugged, not meeting Yoto's eyes.

"He's ruining you," said Yoto. "After this, you'll be no good for anything. You'll lose all your value. Your neutrality. That's why people use you, Mr. Ames. Your reputation for detachment. Without that, you are nothing. You are dispensable."

Ames glanced once at Yoto, then returned to his bottle.

"I am not trying to talk you out of anything," said Yoto quickly, as if answering an unspoken question from Ames. "I am simply trying to understand something that makes no sense to me."

Ames turned from the bottle to the skyline.

"He threatened you," suggested Yoto. "He has something on you? You have no choice in the matter..." Yoto reached out and touched the tip of his finger on the back of Ames's hand, forced his eyes around. "That's it? Am I right? Ah, yes. So, what does clever Haines have on the inscrutable Ames that would bring this fall from grace?"

"I..." Ames swallowed around a suddenly dry throat. He picked up the beer, drank half the bottle. Yoto waited.

Finished, Ames put down the bottle, and looked to Yoto. *Why not? There are no rules, and Yoto was as good as anyone, maybe better. He was there to kill Yoto. Did that make him special?*

Maybe. It didn't matter. He told Yoto about Barber, and Al. He told Yoto how they came to his door, and spilled his blood, and threatened his wife. He told Yoto how he escaped long enough to kill Barber with his own hands—and how he watched Al die at Haines's insistence. He told Yoto everything.

"Haines made me watch," said Ames. "But I called him there. I knew that's what would happen. I knew that's what I wanted to happen." He looked up into the flat face of Yoto, saw the dark eyes blink once, twice. "That's what Haines has on me," he said. "He cleaned up my mess, and now he owns me."

There was a long silence, then Yoto got up and went to the side of the Sake bar. He unlocked a door there and went inside. When he returned he had a bottle of chilled Sake and two small clay cups.

"Ginjo," he said, setting down the bottle. He opened the bottle and poured. He set Ames's cup carefully in front of him. He lifted his own cup in a silent toast.

Ames picked up his cup, returned the toast. The Sake was a delicate, chilled trickle that bloomed somewhere in his chest, raced to face and arms. He nodded gratefully to Yoto.

"I've been avoiding or keeping secrets for so long," he said softly. He shuddered as the Sake found its final home somewhere in the center of is chest.

Yoto poured two more. "Such secrets are difficult to carry," he said. "Even for men such as ourselves."

Ames stared at Yoto. "You remind me of someone. Someone who used to listen, who I could talk to." He looked down at the table. "It helps, of course, that you're in the business. I can talk to you about this, and you understand. I could never imagine sharing this with that other person. But you have...similar qualities."

Yoto sipped his Sake, watching Ames over the cup. "Perhaps it also helps that today I am the business."

Ames grimaced, looked away. "Maybe."

"Well," said Yoto, putting his cup down. "How were you to manage it? I don't see you pulling a gun or knife here, and Singapore is a small island. There's nowhere to run or hide. I can say that," he added with a smile, "because I am hiding here."

Ames rubbed the sweat from the back of his neck. Like a variation on a theme, he suddenly remembered his father making a similar gesture in the fading sun. His father lived alone now, in a small house in the Florida panhandles. Thinking of his father, he wondered where he had gone wrong.

With rules, he thought. *Rules that led to compromise. Rules that led to Haines.*

He opened his hand and put the phial on the table. Yoto looked to the tiny brown ampoule, then to Ames.

"I was to sprinkle that on your food, or in your drink," explained Ames. "It would look like a heart attack."

Yoto's eyes met Ames, glanced at the phial, then back to Ames. "You look like you're ready to drink that yourself."

Ames drew a breath, held it. He shrugged. "I might as well. Haines is not a forgiving man."

"You don't mean to do this thing?" asked Yoto.

Ames shook his head. "Which is why I might as well take it myself."

"You fear Haines?"

"I *know* Haines."

"Clever, clever Haines," said Yoto quietly, looking away. "But you're right to fear him." He lifted his cup. "To clever men."

After a moment, Ames joined him.

"Why don't you try?" asked Yoto, his face wrinkled in curiosity.

"The truth is," said Ames, looking into his empty cup, "I just don't have it in me. Even if you were seven Barbers rolled into one, I can't do it. I split a man's skull with a golf club, and watched another die in my living room, but I can't do this."

"The difference being?"

Ames shrugged. "I don't know. I just know I can't."

It was a long time before either man spoke.

"Haines is an idiot," said Yoto finally, and poured more Sake.

When they had finished, Yoto put his hands on the table, as if to conclude. "Now listen to me, Mr. Ames, it so happens that I hate clever idiots like Haines. They create waste where there need be no waste. Waste is a great crime." He shrugged. "Understand, I too, am one of those clever men, and in the end, no less wasteful. But we hate the things that remind of us of our own faults most of all." He looked to Ames with a grim smile. "Sending you out here, to do this, is a senseless waste. Succeed or fail, you will be nothing when you return. Waste." He leaned forward. "But, perhaps clever-idiot Haines knows this. Perhaps, he does not see this as a waste."

Ames frowned, but met the old man's eyes.

Yoto nodded once, then leaned back again. "So this has occurred to you, as well. Good. You are not a stupid man." He paused. "Perhaps, too, it explains your current appearance and state. You don't strike me as a man that falls apart easily, Mr. Ames. But learning just how clever an idiot, how wasteful, Mr. Haines can be—ah! That would be most disturbing to anyone."

Ames remained silent.

"Take heart, Mr. Ames," said Yoto. "There is fate. This," he waved a hand between them, "is fate. I will tell you a secret, a secret that will serve both of us." He sighed, turned again to the skyline. "I'm dying anyway. Cancer. Inoperable. Maybe three weeks, maybe three months. Very painful." He looked back to Ames and slowly smiled. "Yes. Waste."

Ames stared back, blinking at the implications.

"You see?" said Yoto, nodding at what he saw in Ames's expression. "It would do my heart good to cheat clever-Haines in his revenge. He thinks he is directing the knife, but I will make him merely the instrument of my release." He chuckled. "That pleases me on many levels, Mr. Ames. Levels too complicated to express." He tapped his finger on the table. "So, I tell you truthfully, you'll be doing me a favor."

Ames felt the floor fall from under him. But even as he clutched at the straw, even as he imagined the desperate escape, he saw it slip through his hands again. *'Do what Haines asks of you.'* But he couldn't do it. He'd said as much just a moment ago. It had been true then, and was just as true now.

"In my experience," said Yoto, as if reading his mind, "people are capable of almost anything, when properly motivated."

Is that what happened with Barber? Al? He looked to Yoto. This was not the same.

"There will be no returning empty-handed to the clever-idiot-who-wastes," added Yoto, pointing out one of the differences.

"It's not that easy."

"Ah, but it is."

Yoto stood up. "Tomorrow, I will come here at my usual time, and I will order a big dinner. I will get up to use the restroom at some point."

Ames reflexively looked to the Sake bar.

Yoto smiled. "He will not bother you. You will sprinkle your little philter of death, and that will be that."

Ames searched for words, failed.

"With my blessings," said Yoto. "Guilt free." He reached out and pressed the back of Ames's hand again with his finger. "It will be our secret. Though, if you tell Haines one day, I won't be hurt."

Then Yoto poured one last round of sake for both of them.

"To an end to waste," said Yoto, his cup raised. He waited for some response, then shrugged as Ames did not move or speak. Yoto tossed his drink off with a relish.

"Well, you think about it, Mr. Ames," he said. "If you do decide to accept my gift, then put your little poison in my beer, if you don't mind. I don't want it to ruin the taste of my dinner." He stopped suddenly, looked to the floor. "And you better make it two days from now. I need to say goodbye to some people first." He waved goodbye and left.

Ames sat at the table for a long time, looking to the darkening night.

His first reaction on returning to the hotel was muted disbelief. He sat in the room chair, struggling with a growing sense of relief. He had a schedule, a plan. Yoto was giving him a gift. Cancer. He couldn't believe his luck. Yoto said it was fate, a fortuitous fate. He would be doing Yoto a *favor*.

And best of all, Haines would be none the wiser. He had no intention of telling Haines any of this, any time. And Yoto wouldn't care; he would be dead. Ames could meet the conditions of his task, and avoid the inevitable repercussions of failing. He would have a tenuous sense of his autonomy, keeping the secret of Yoto's gift from Haines. And all of it, as Yoto claimed, guilt free. It would work.

But for how long? Success would only encourage Haines to use him again. Eventually, inevitably there would come another day, another task. And then what? He knew there would be no fortuitous cancer victims next time, no death wishes, no passes on guilt. He could not rely on another twist of fate.

He felt the Sake dissipating like his brief respite. Desperation gripped him again and he jumped for any possible answer to the future. Could he manage to find, orchestrate—in both reality, and his own conscience— justifications, rationalizations, paradoxes of ethical hierarchy? Could he paint the act as a necessary evil, even a greater good; to act without guilt, or at least, with a livable guilt? In short, could he find a way to kill and not feel it?

He had done something similar with his double-life, his rules. Even with Cynthia. Could he build on that, take it to another level, a different direction? The idea both compelled and repulsed him. Like all rationalizations, there was a semblance of logic to it, even hope. But it came at a cost.

For the first time since the events with Barber and Al, he had a sudden urge to sketch. He looked around for paper, some kind of pen and pencil. He tried the hotel stationary and desk pen. It didn't serve. He looked to the clock. It was eight o'clock. He put on his shoes, grabbed his wallet and went looking for the nearest supply or art store.

It took some time, but he finally found a crafts shop that carried a Pentalic, 3.5" x 5.5", black espresso, pocket sketchbook. He bought two. He then considered his stylus. He looked first to the mechanical pencils, high end and budget, making small marks in his new sketchbook with each version, looking for the right fit.

Nothing suited. The dark shadow lines all looked flat and uninspiring. He asked the clerk—a middle aged woman wearing a burka—to switch the lead. The clerk showed him a high end Clutch, asked him what color he would like to try.

Ames hesitated. The word "blue" was on his lips without thinking, but he couldn't bring himself to say it. Somehow that color left him disconcerted.

"Red. Your darkest red," he said, finally.

The clerk suggested a soft lead crimson.

Ames drew a few tentative lines on a new page, using the tip of the pencil for a thin line and the edge for a wider mark. He stared at the results, forgetting the pencil in his hand, the clerk waiting patiently by his side. Finally, he heard a delicate cough and recalled himself.

"I'll take it," he said. "The pencil, and the crimson leads. And a pack of refills."

The next day he woke to the alarm, and pulled himself from a deep, dark hole of unconsciousness. It was not the lengthy healing sleep his mind and body required, but it was a start. He sat in the bed for a moment, returning slowly to his new reality. Twinges of guilt and anxiety, like a persistent cough, again tickled the back of his mind, but there was a new element to his angst now, diluted in part by Yoto's permission and time—"*And you better make it two days from now, Mr. Ames.*"

Two days. He had two days. Two days of freedom. Two long days of empty, decision-free prologue.

After a quick shower, he dressed in his best suit. He went downstairs, enjoyed a bagel and coffee in the hotel restaurant. For lack of anything better to do, and to maintain his distance from the impending moment of truth, he considered his notes from the previous Cal-Dale sessions. He cringed at the mess he'd made of the negotiations. There was a lot of work to be done if he had any hope of correcting the situation.

Two days.

Suddenly the thought of spending his precious remaining time in the boardroom made him ill. He resolved to end that particular façade today. He made his plans over a second cup of coffee.

He was lost in his notes and plans for a time, only vaguely aware of someone approaching, taking a seat across from his. When he eventually looked up, he saw the girl from the other night in the next booth. She was looking down at her phone, running a delicate finger up and down the screen. Today she was dressed in a simple blouse and skirt, her long black hair pulled in a ponytail behind her. Seen in the daylight, she was maybe half his age.

She looked up from her phone. Their eyes met briefly. They were amber, naturally or from a lens, he couldn't say. She smiled, then returned to her tablet.

He finished his coffee and left, thinking he must call Cynthia tonight.

The Cal-Dale meeting took most of the morning, but raced to a finish once the room recognized Ames was serious.

True to his plan, Ames gave the store away. They took it.

There were tentative smiles and handshakes all around when it was over. A few of his opponents still expected Ames to pull a last minute rabbit from his hat. He heard the room erupt with disbelief as the door closed behind him. Haines and the other invested partners would not be pleased. He didn't care.

He shed his work clothes and donned his swimming suit back in his hotel room, filled a tote bag with supplies and headed down to the pool. He took a long steam in the sauna, did a dozen intense laps, and then lay out on a lounge chair, soaking in the intense tropical sun. He lasted about twenty minutes before he felt he was starting to burn. He found another chair under the shade of the mushroom umbrella, and pulled out his new pad and pencil.

He stared at the clean empty paper for a time, then turned to the horizon, searching for inspiration. He returned to the pad, made a tentative start on a castle. He was distracted briefly by a woman with two small children climbing into the far end of the pool. Looking down again, he considered his red castle foundation, frowned, and turned to a fresh page. He tried a crimson flower, then a mountain, the excited screams of the children occasionally breaking into his internal world of lines, shading, and angles. He considered each piece carefully. They were not bad, but they weren't right somehow. Something was missing. Some part of the creative process and product had not brought its usual release this time. Maybe it was the color. Maybe it had been a mistake to buy the red.

He put the pad and pencil back in the bag, lay back along the chair. The heat, even under the umbrella, created a comfortable lethargy. He was getting hungry again. He should eat soon. Perhaps in the hotel, maybe out—but definitely not in the food court. Not tonight.

Two days.

Well, he corrected himself, *a day and half now*.
He would have to arrange for his ticket home tonight. And call Cynthia. He must remember to call Cynthia.

He decided to eat at the hotel again. The restaurant was never crowded, and he didn't feel like being in public. He brought his new pad and pencil, and took a booth near the back. After dinner, he ordered a drink and some coffee. He had the waiter clear the table. There was no waiting line of patrons, and plenty of empty tables, so he had no qualms of taking up a space.

He made a tentative red dash on a clean fresh page, held the pencil over it...and searched again for inspiration. Nothing came. Frustrated, he put the pencil down and took a sip of his drink, then coffee. He looked around the room.

The girl was back, sitting in the same seat at the bar. Tonight she was dressed in a dark brown skirt slit high along the thigh and a sleeveless matching blouse. Her hair was done in an elaborate weave that hung loosely around her shoulders. She was staring down at her cell phone again.

Ames admired her for a time, the way her thin brown arms moved in harmony with her head and shoulders. She seemed perfectly content, perfectly at one with herself. Occasionally, her little foot would bob in her open sandal, keeping time to hidden music or impressions. Ames sensed an answer to all his worries and frustrations in that simple gesture, if only he knew what it signified.

He turned back to the sketch pad, picked up the pencil. He didn't like working with profiles normally, but he made a tentative attempt to capture the girl. After he had the general frame and lines, he worked from memory and a vague sense of that relaxed, secret answer in her dancing foot. He took an occasional sip from his drink or coffee, sometimes one after the other, and found, finally, his muse.

His attention was caught by a shadow falling across the nearly finished sketch. He looked up. It was the girl.

"Hi," she said. "I am so sorry to bother you."

He was lost for a moment in those eyes, that rare shade of gold with tiny flecks of brown. Somehow he knew hers were real.

"I saw you sitting here alone," she continued. Her words, like most Singaporeans, came fast, with unfamiliar pauses and inflections. She smiled. "My friend has stood me up, and I wondered if you would like some company."

He smiled in return. "Of course."

Her smile grew broader, the eyes becoming almost luminescent. She sat across from him, putting a small bag down beside her on the bench. She looked down at his sketch pad, started.

"Oh, I'm disturbing your work."

"Not work," he said. "Just a sketch."

"You're an artist?"

"Hardly. It's just a hobby. A distraction."

She leaned in a little curiously. He hesitated, then passed the pad over. She picked it up with another smile.

He watched her as she considered the drawing. Up close he could see she was slightly older than he'd guessed the other day, but not much. She had a small beauty mark just to the right of her lip. Her skin was smooth and lightly brown, and everything was in place, everything was perfectly proportioned. But it was the eyes that set her apart. Those eyes, half-hidden now by the decline of her head, seemed to glow with a life of their own.

She turned her head to the side, a small, wondering frown on her face. She looked up. "Is this…"

"Not very good, I'm afraid. But yes, it's you."

"It's lovely."

"I had a good subject to work with."

She smiled. "I'm Alice."

"Wilson."

"Have you eaten, Wilson?"

"I'm afraid I have," he said. "But please order something if you like. I will get a little something, too, if it makes you more comfortable."

"I'm starving," she said, her eyes opening up like a sun flower. She called the waiter over.

They talked while she ate. She was charming, careful with her food and her words. When she was finished they had more coffee. They talked of Singapore, the food, the weather, the sights. Nothing was personal, nothing was too real; nothing that couldn't be shared by any two people sitting beside each other on a long bus ride. When the casual conversation ran out, they sat in comfortable silence. The coffee finished, he suggested another drink. She agreed.

"I saw you the other day," she said. "Sitting alone."

There was nothing in the words or tone to indicate anything more than curiosity. But he sensed a change, a heightening of awareness. There followed the briefest of pauses, a chance for him to advance or retreat.

There were many answers to the unspoken question, of course.

He gave her one. "I'm here for work."

"Home is?"

"The States. A small place just outside of New York City."

"I love the States."

"And you?" he asked.

"I'm from here. But I like to travel when I can."

He thought of Cynthia.

"When are you heading out?" she asked.

"In a few days." He hesitated. "Maybe a little later."

She smiled again, and didn't look away.

She was quiet as she climbed back into her clothes. She made a quick stop in the bathroom, but was careful to hide the light behind the door. He could have feigned sleep as she walked to the hotel door, her shoes in hand. She clearly didn't need him to say goodbye.

As he heard her turn the handle, something fell into place. A question, and a possible answer. The question didn't have to be asked, the answer didn't have to be confirmed. He was content. His mind, for once, at peace, or at least distracted to the point of comfort.

It was curiosity then, and a perverse need to know, that made him say, "Alice."

She turned, now half way out the open door, a smile on her face.

"Yoto?" he asked, raising his head from the pillow.

She considered him from the doorway. She blinked once, twice, her wonderful eyes taking on a bemused worldliness that belied her youth. When she spoke, it was with that same sense of generous professionalism. "He sends his best."

He nodded slowly, then smiled. "It was lovely."

"It was."

He watched her walk out the door.

She didn't say goodbye, but then he didn't either.

It wasn't necessary.

He spent his last morning in Singapore trying to arrange a flight back, and debating whether to call Cynthia before he left. He got lucky with the flight. He couldn't bring himself to make the call.

It had nothing to do with the night before. Well, almost nothing. Guilt? Yes, there was certainly a little of that. But not as much as he would have imagined. Revenge? Spite? God knew Cynthia had given him enough reason for both. But their marriage was never built on fidelity. Yes, he had remained faithful over the years, but this was more a personal penchant, not a requirement. He lived with Cynthia's infidelity for the same reasons—it was part of who she was. To hide behind retaliation now would be hypocritical.

And yet...and yet....

Haines. There was the matter of Haines now. Barber's insinuation bothered him on a level that was deeper and more intrinsic than simple betrayal. The thought of Haines and Cynthia together undermined the core of him. But what proof did he have? The opinion of Barber, a man obsessed with hurting Ames on every level? His own deep-seated suspicion? Even if it was true, what made Haines so special? He couldn't say, but it did.

But that's not why he didn't call.

He didn't want to think about Cynthia. He didn't trust himself to talk with her. For the first time in their relationship, he worried that he would confront her. Last night had somehow tipped the scales, made the confrontation a possibility. He did not want a confrontation. He had enough of those.

He had Yoto.

He climbed the steps to the food court, a part of him hoping Yoto would not be there.

He was.

Ames nodded, and Yoto waved an invitation to the seat across from him. As he approached, Ames saw the usual bucket of beer, one already open in front of Yoto. There was also a plate of sashimi, and something he thought might be Tofu.

Yoto waited until he was close, then he stood. He studied Ames, glanced at Ames's closed hand. The old man sighed, reached out a hand and gently squeezed

Ames's arm. "Don't worry, Mr. Ames. One way or the other, it will all work out."
Then he walked away.

***

Ames returned from the airport, took to the kitchen and made a drink. Cynthia was not home. He had an early dinner alone, and put his luggage away. It was now late in the afternoon. Tomorrow he would see Haines, but that was tomorrow.

He stood in his living room, deciding what to do. The silent emptiness of his home fell around him, making the familiar strange, and the strange familiar. The living room floor was bare, clean of all the recent past, but memory imposed a shadow of Al and Barber wrapped in plastic. Jerking away from the image, he turned to the kitchen, only to relive his capitulation to Haines, feel again his crushing loss of control.

Then he thought of Yoto.

He stood that way until the cold press of his drink recalled him to the present. He knew there would be no relief or comfort here. To stay home tonight, most likely alone, meant to sleep with the dead.

Alone. *Where was Cynthia?* A sudden image of Haines's knowing smile left his stomach as empty and cold as the house.

Rising anger and revulsion sent him packing an overnight back. He couldn't stay here.

Before he left he wrote a note. A brief, impulsive reaction against the ghosts and suspicions of his new reality.

Gone to see Haines, Wilson.

He folded the note and put it on the refrigerator door.

They met in the afternoon. Haines was waiting for him behind the familiar desk. There was a newspaper beside him.

"Wilson," said Haines, standing up and walking over to shake Ames's hand.

Ames took a seat without being asked.

"Drink?" asked Haines. "I know it's early, but I feel like celebrating." He made two drinks at the wet bar against the office wall. He walked back, handed a drink to Ames, and sat on the corner of the desk.

"I'm very pleased, Wilson." Haines looked to the paper on the desk. "Mr. Yoto's official obituary appeared today in the Singapore news. Heart attack at home."

Ames looked for a time to the floor, then took a long pull at his drink.

"Easy, man," said Haines with a chuckle. He took a small sip of his own, his eyes crinkled above the glass. "You look surprised."

"It's just..." Ames searched for words. "Hearing it like that." He winced around a memory. "He was alive when I left."

"Of course he was. I told you, it takes a little time."

"Yes," said Ames. "I remember now."

"Anyway, you did it, Wilson. Well done."

"Let's not talk about it anymore, Geoff."

Haines nodded slowly. "I see. Still with the little games of denial." He shrugged. "I suppose as long as the job gets done, I don't care how you deal with it." He swirled his glass around, then gave Ames a wry look. "Of course, you'll still want to be paid every time."

Every time, thought Ames. *There will be more.*

"Wilson?"

Ames looked up, nodded.

Haines measured him for a time. "Good." He finished his drink, looked to the empty glass. "I won't, of course, ask you to do it again any time soon."

There was a heavy silence as the men considered each other. Finally, Ames stood up, took Haines's glass, and walked to the wet bar. He refilled both glasses, and brought them back. "I understand, Geoff," he said, handing Haines his drink.

Haines smiled, and raised his glass.

"But," continued Ames, "I need a few concessions."

Haines stopped with the drink halfway to his mouth. "Such as?"

"I can't be used this way again, without my full participation. The whole Cal-Dale/Yoto affair was sloppy. I need to be more involved with the planning and timing. I'm good at planning. But more importantly, it gives me the necessary piece of mind I need to...act."

Haines seemed to consider this. "Okay. You may have a point. I agree. You will be more involved in the planning in the future."

"Thank you," said Ames, sipping his drink. "Now, the one you won't like."

Haines stiffened, again the glass never making it to his mouth.

"I need to be able to walk away if I feel it's too risky," said Ames. "I need to know I could do that, Geoff—without repercussion. Otherwise, I'm just a tool, something that can be lost, replaced, thrown away. I can't live that way, Geoff. I won't."

Haines finally took a slow sip of his own drink. When he spoke, it was almost apologetic. "I thought you might say something along those lines, Wilson. I understand this is hard for you. I really do. But we're not returning to that."

"Or what, Geoff?"

"What do you mean?"

"What will you do to me if I insist on this?"

"Wilson, you are in no position to insist on anything." Haines lowered his glass. "Don't push me."

"In negotiation," said Ames, sitting up straighter, "no one ever gets everything they want. There's always a push."

Haines snorted, shook his head, looked down at his drink. "That's what you think we're doing? Negotiating?"

"I know we are."

Haines rubbed the side of his head with two fingers. "Wilson, you are exasperating." He finished his drink in one long, angry pull, stood and went around the desk, sat in his chair. He put the empty glass down. "All right, go on," he said, "explain to me how this walking away works."

After that, it was just a matter of details. They sat across from one another, and they negotiated. And almost, it was like before. Almost.

"Admit it, Wilson," said Haines, when it was all over. "You just love to argue." He looked to Ames with a smile. "So, did I win or lose?"

Ames looked to his nearly empty drink, thought of Yoto. *It doesn't matter now.*

The meeting concluded. Haines promised to contact him again soon.

Ames stood, turned to leave, and then turned back again. He walked to the desk and put the empty phial in front of Haines. "I almost forgot."

Haines stared at the phial with a frown. "You should have disposed of that in Singapore."

"I thought you might want to use it again—or need proof."

Haines tapped the newspaper with a distracted finger. "I have all the proof I need, Wilson." He took a tissue from his designer box and carefully wrapped the phial in it. He then tossed the tissue into his bin.

The note remained on the refrigerator when he got home, apparently unread. There were no signs that

Cynthia had returned. He collapsed on the couch, watched the afternoon sun through the living room window, and fell asleep.

When he woke it was twilight. He grabbed the pad and pencils and walked to the kitchen, put everything on the table. He made a sandwich, and drank two glasses of orange juice in quick succession. He looked out the kitchen window at the setting sun, remembered, forgot, and remembered again.

The first few tentative sketch marks were an exercise in will. After a time, he had a vague outline. Then a shape. Slowly, tentatively he felt the familiar immersion, the calming, regressive release. But the shape remained just that, an odd impression, with no final form or purpose. A dream image, an incomplete thought. He was still searching for something. His success in Singapore had been a one-time event, a temporary fix. It stilled his troubled mind for a time, but it was not enough. Not now, not here.

He pushed the pad aside, stood and stretched. Night stood dark and lonely outside the kitchen window now. He turned his back on it, poured himself a drink at the sink. He looked to the clock. It was six in the evening. Cynthia was still out. He carried the drink, pad and pencil to the living room, sat on the couch near the lamp, trying to ignore the dark echoes of the room's recent past.

But the past, all of his past, would not be so easily disregarded. The pencil remained forgotten in his hand as he saw again the bodies wrapped in plastic. Saw again Yoto at his table. And Haines…Haines with his drink and his smile.

One way or another, Yoto, he thought.

The images became impressions, the impressions emotion, and everything mixed together in an overwhelming, silent cry of frustration.

And in that cry, he understood. He saw the purpose and the form and the function.

He started to sketch.

First a ragged red circle, a warning sign, a symbol. The circle took on small spots of shading across the face, a sense of the subject taking root deep in his mind. He was careful to stay at the top of the page. Why he couldn't say. When it was finished, he had a harvest moon, large and dark with purpose, ethereal clouds, like bits of the river Styx, running across the face. He ran a light finger across the crimson lines and dark, red shadows, sensing their significance.

But it was still incomplete. It still lacked that final essence that brought release, that final expression that silenced the darkness. The color, the moon, were right, but they weren't enough. He thought again of Haines, saw again the small, knowing smile before he sipped his drink. No, they were not enough. It was missing something, something essential.

He stood suddenly, crossed to the side of the living room, looked along the edge of the wall. He found the pencil under the couch. It must have bounced there from the wall. He clicked new blue lead into the end, and felt something deep inside settle, release. He returned to the couch, now with both pencils, and started again.

When he was done, the red moonscape now overlooked a small windowless blue tower. The tower was perched precariously on the edge of a darker blue cliff. It was hardly his best work. But it was right. It worked.

He looked to the clock. It was two in the morning. He should shave and a take a shower. Cynthia might return in the night.

When he was finished, he went to bed. He fell asleep almost immediately.

"Wilson!"

Cynthia was standing in the bedroom door. She was wearing her coat and a pair of dark sunglasses.

Ames blinked, sat up in bed. He glanced at the clock. It was eleven in the morning. "Cynthia." His voice was full of sleep. He reached a hand out for her.

She stood fixed in the doorway. "Wilson, you're home."

"I wanted to surprise you." He pulled his hand back. Now he could see the tension in her, a rigidity that ran the entire length of her body. "Cynthia, what's wrong?"

She looked down at her coat, pulled distractedly at the belt. "Wilson." Her voice was mere reflex, disconnected from the turmoil clearly playing out inside her.

"What's wrong, darling?" he repeated, standing up now, going to her.

She remained in the doorway, shook her head. He took off her glasses. He could see she'd been crying.

"He's dead, Wilson. Geoffrey is dead."

It was his turn to mumble distractedly. "My God."

They stood staring at each other. She started to reach out to him, stopped.

It was on his tongue to ask her how she knew of Haines's death, where she had been. Instead, he took her in his arms, buried his face in her hair, unsure what expression he should be wearing. He felt her stiffen, then relax. He made comforting noises as she cried.

After a time, she pulled away, found a tissue in her purse and wiped her eyes. "I'm sorry, Wilson," she said. "I'm so sorry."

For what? What are you sorry about, Cynthia?

He brushed the hair back from her face. "What happened?"

"I don't know." Her eyes retreated again into distraction. "Some kind of heart attack."

He comforted her again as fresh tears fell.

"I have to make some calls," he said eventually, gently disengaging. "Why don't you take a hot bath and lay down. I'll bring you a drink." He started to turn, but she reached out and grabbed his arm.

"Wilson. He was your friend."

He brushed another stray hair from her head, kissed her forehead. "I'll get that drink." He left her there, clutching at her coat and confusion.

Downstairs, he found his note still folded up on the refrigerator. He took it down, and threw it in the garbage. It didn't matter. He made two drinks, deciding to join her.

He stood for a time looking down at the glasses, hearing the ice crack in the brown-gold. Did she wake to find him dead beside her, or was she on her way to see him and discovered the police line? Maybe she heard it from one of her friends?

He heard the distant sound of running water above.

It didn't matter. It was done. Cynthia was home again. He picked up the drinks and headed for the stairwell.

And with each step his world revolved once more into blue.

But now that world was touched with red. Always, now, to be touched with red.

Meet our author
Timothy Vincent

Timothy splits his time between his home in Kentucky and his work in Nanjing, China. A published writer and scholar, he teaches for an American Overseas program. His previous creative writing publications include: "Awareness" (Xchyler Anthology, Jan 2015); "Prince of the Blue Castle" (The Bacon Review 2013); "Star-Crossed" (Winner, Terri Ann Armstrong Short Story Contest, Suspense Magazine, 2012); "The Blanket" and "Standing on the Doorstep with Borges" (The WriteRoom Literary Magazine). He was a top 25 finalist in Glimmer Train's new writer contest in 2010.

Also by Timothy Vincent

The Red House on the Hill

Chapter One

Later, after she was in the ground and the pain was finally, mercifully over, he remembered the red house on the hill. He pointed it out to her once on a trip through the Appalachians. She pronounced it too small, too lonely, and too out of the way. She didn't care for the looks of Torview either, for that matter.

In those days her every whim or mood was law to him: a glorious, benevolent, and wanted necessity. Now that necessity was gone, taken by a terrible and unforgiving reality found in her breast on a cold Wednesday morning. Three months later she was finally free of the pain, even if his still persisted and took on new and deeper realities.

It was not hard to absent himself from the day to day process of being. He simply cut all the inane and un-important ties he once believed so significant. In truth they were significant to her, and so by consequence important to him as well. Now she was gone, and they held no more meaning than useless bric-a-brac.

There were no close friends to say goodbye to, just acquaintances, and most of those were hers. No children to watch over or comfort, or be comforted by. He declared it a blessing. They were enough for each other, he insisted, and she smiled.

Over the course of their marriage he would see that smile again and again. He wondered at times if he ever really understood that slight ironic curve of her lip, the dolphin-like profile that hinted at other levels, levels playful and knowing, and yes, maybe even sad.

Now it didn't matter. Now she was gone. And everything else was just useless bric-a-brac.

The house was the easiest thing to let go. Their home for twenty-five years was not just suddenly empty, it was full: full of ghosts and memories and countless echoes of familiar events never to be heard or felt again. It became almost physically painful to crawl beneath the cold sheets of their bed, to reach out for the warm leg that should be beside him, to wait for the whispered goodnight that never came. He took to sleeping on the couch for a time, but still the unfilled expectations remained.

* * *

He took a temporary room in a local hotel while the real estate agent showed the house. His possessions were reduced to the contents of two boxes and a carrier bag (everything else went to Goodwill or the trash). It was while he was waiting for a buyer that he remembered the red house and asked the real estate agent to check on its availability.

The agent called him back the same day. "I had to do a little digging, but if I have the right house it's still there and I think we can get it. Your timing is good. It was tied up in some crazy town proprietorship for the longest time but the bank owns it now—an out of town bank—and wants to sell. The listing's not cheap, but it's a fair price. You want me to make an offer?"

"Just give them what they're asking for."

"Are you sure? I think we can come in a little under..."

"Just get the house."

Frank couldn't say why it was so important for him to have the house. He was certain there was no rational or financial motivation behind it.

Two days later the house was his, the paperwork signed and witnessed, the funds transferred, and the deed passed. It was all of a moment for Frank, with no intrinsic pleasure or sense of accomplishment. Like paying his last utility bill or registering at the hotel, or putting her in the ground, it had to be done.

His reaction, or lack of one, must have bothered the agent. It didn't stop him from making the sale, but he did appear to suffer a moment of conscience outside the lawyer's office on the day of closing.

"Well, congratulations," he said, offering a hand and his best smile. Frank shook the hand mechanically. The agent searched Frank for signs of pleasure, shock, or even regret.

"You should know," he continued, his smile firmly in place, "I heard some grumblings from the town about the sale. The bank doesn't care of course, as long as they get their money and everything is in order. And it is. I assure you. You own the deed, free and clear. Don't let anyone tell you different."

He looked to Frank again for some reaction, appeared slightly puzzled but relieved to see none. He handed Frank two keys.

"This one is to the gate at the end of the drive," explained the agent, pointing to a common lock key. "And that old man is to the front door. You can probably change it later if you want."

The 'old man' was a heavy piece of iron work from a different age. Frank rolled the key over in his fingers, feeling the weight and admiring the odd teeth and ornate bow.

"As you know there's no electricity," said the agent, "so you don't have to worry about that."

Frank didn't rise to this, or the ironic wink that accompanied it.

The agent nodded as if this was all perfectly normal. He padded Frank on the shoulder, glanced briefly at his watch, and pushed the selling points one last time.

"Running water and ten acres of land. Great outdoors, huh?"

Frank put the keys in his pocket and walked away.

He packed his car the next morning, checked out of the hotel, and left without a word to anyone.

* * *

The road was a twisting, ever rising blacktop that lay like a discarded ribbon amid the heavy pines. It was a lonely stretch. He had the roadway to himself most of the time with only the occasional farm houses or rest stop to break up the running line of trees and hills. He remembered to fill up in a gas station about an hour out of Torview.

He knew he was close when the road started to dip and rise like a coaster. The woods to either side grew heavier, and the shadows longer and somehow more permanent. It was almost four when he passed the small bent white sign, *Torview 15*. He assumed it was fifteen miles and not the population.

The exit was little more than the size of a driveway and nearly hidden behind a copse of overgrown pines. He drove up the tarmac and out of the trees, stopping at a crossroad to overlook the valley of Torview and the hills that surrounded it. He was the only car on the road and he took a moment to look around.

It was still there: a flash of red, visible in the late afternoon like some secret doorway to another time, another place. For a fleeting moment the lonely ache in his chest was replaced by bittersweet excitement.

And then the moment passed.

Now what? Crossing the intersection and going straight would take him back out to the small highway. The road to his right led down to the town. He assumed the way to the house was to the left.

He rolled his window down, letting the cool night air brace him, in no hurry to make a decision. He caught his reflection in the rearview mirror. At fifty two, he had always looked ten years younger, a gift of genetics and regular exercise. Now it was closer to the truth to say the opposite.

He turned around, glanced at the boxes in the back seat of his car: his worldly possessions. He ran through their contents in his mind: a few books, his overnight bag, fresh linen, and some winter clothes. With no electricity there would be no need for his computer or entertainment devices so these had gone the way of the bric-a-brac. What was in the house? Certainly no food. He was hungry, and would be hungry again. He should buy some things for the night and morning.

He looked to the right and the shallow skyline of block buildings that was Torview, a scar of humanity sitting among the tree-lined hills like an abandoned car on the side of the road. *My new home,* thought Frank.

He turned right.